CW00742006

Tales of a Durham Village

Robert Harrison

Durham City Publishing Company
Tel No: 0191 373 1484

© Robert Harrison

Published by Durham City Publishing Company, Esh, Durham
Tel No: 0191 3731484

Printed by Trade Union Printing Services Ltd., 30 Lime
Street, Newcastle upon Tyne, NE1 2PQ.

Cover photograph by courtesy of George Nairn, Chester le
Street. Co. Durham.

ISBN 0 9534655 0 0

This book is a work of fiction and any resemblance to any
fact, place or person is purely coincidental.

Contents

To Dennis, Christine and James

1

The Village

High on a hill, overlooking a small valley, it stood alone. The stone built houses, some of them whitewashed, huddled closely together, each seeming to gain some comfort from the proximity of its neighbour. The village was a small oasis amidst a sea of verdant pasture, woods and copses, with the fell, heather crowned, rising sombrely in the background. A tiny stream, a tributary of the Wear, meandered its seemingly aimless way along the valley floor bordered by deep, dark woods that extended along either bank as though to fence it in. The valley was known locally as the Gladda and it had been the playground to each generation of village children for centuries. Thus the tiny hamlet of High Cornhill survived, unmoved and unchanging, the passage of the years. Only the folk themselves ebbed and flowed with the ebb and flow of life's tides, the place itself remained unaffected and impassive.

Its nearest neighbour, Low Cornhill, nestled snugly, safe and warm, near the foot of the prominence occupied by its older counterpart. If rivalry existed between the two it was rarely evident, except for one day each summer, the day of the Cornhill Test Match. Both communities lived their separate lives in peaceful harmony without any familiarity or particular closeness, as is the way in country villages; self contained and sufficient unto themselves.

The focal point of each village was its pub, the one being the Oak Tree whilst in High Cornhill it rejoiced in the name of the Swan With Two Necks, or, as it was irreverently known by the regulars, 'Th' Double Duck'. Each satisfied in its own way those of both communities who had a fondness for a pint of good English ale and a 'bit o' crack'.

The Swan stood in splendid, monochromatic isolation at the North end of the rectangular village green. This was a feature that was unknown to its neighbour until, that is, the local authority demolished the defunct brickworks and grassed over the site. That they made an excellent job of it was indisputable but there was really no comparison to High Cornhill's few green acres that had been common grazing land for nigh on a thousand years.

About fifteen solidly constructed houses with walls over two feet thick clustered companionably around the green, standing four square against a sometimes bitter North wind. Their roofs were mainly slate or stone, no thatch here but something a great deal more substantial. Thatching was for those who lived in balmier climes. Here one had to be certain that one's roof was going to remain where it had been placed when a Siberian gale came screaming down the valley refrigerating everything in its path.

It is perhaps, a common misconception amongst those unfamiliar with the more Northerly regions of these islands that freezing winds, driving rain, snow, frost, cloth caps, mufflers, pigeons and whippets are the normal ingredients of everyday life. However, it is fair to point out that many things, including the climate, have changed as the mines in the Durham coalfield have closed. Industrial smog, along with the heavy industry that created it, has disappeared to be replaced by a greener, fresher environment.

High Cornhill was never subjected to even the vaguest kind of industrialisation; unlike its neighbour which once boasted a small pit, complete with pit heap, as well as the aforementioned brickworks. Down the centuries it existed purely as an agricultural community and the land was the key to the village's entire existence. Land that had been passed on from father to son, from generation to generation in families such as the Stobbarts or Cousins.

Other families had either died out altogether or left, never to return. Those cottages that had been abandoned by their original owners, for whatever reason, and had fallen into ruin, had gradually been bought up and rebuilt by people from the towns who fancied a more rural way of life. These were the incomers, who, by and large, were made welcome, the indigenous inhabitants recognising that new blood was vital to a tiny community such as theirs.

The publican himself was, in fact, a newcomer having being the incumbent of the 'Double Duck' for only about twelve years. He had originally been a car salesman in York but chance and an intrinsic sense of adventure had urged upon him this new life. He had been accepted almost immediately by the villagers, mainly at first, it must be said, because of what he was rather than who he was. Slowly he had impressed them with his wry Yorkshire personality and before long his hostelry became the most popular night time haunt for many a country mile. He only ever opened the doors at night, seeing very little reason to succour the occasional daytime traveller, no matter how thirsty. A myriad of tales and opinions passed across his bar, as many as pints of ale that were passed in the opposite direction but Davy Dobson, canny Yorkshireman that he was, mainly listened and kept his own counsel. Unless an occasion arose which allowed him to exercise his own brand of sardonic humour.

His pub was probably one of the oldest buildings in the village. Every year its walls were whitewashed and the woodwork painted black so that, standing alone as it did, there was no mistaking its purpose; particularly as the inn sign was displayed prominently over the door. It squeaked constantly as it swung in the wind. He was ably assisted by his good wife Glennis, a forthright, no-nonsense Yorkshirewoman of ample proportions who was also gifted with a ready wit, a sharp tongue and a highly developed sense of humour. She it was who ran the ship.

Davy may have been the skipper but there was no doubt about who was chief engineer and as such she kept the whole place absolutely spotless. Their one and only son, Andrew, looked after the cellar and his mother's high standards in the kitchen were equalled in the consistent quality of the ale.

It was, therefore, an entirely family affair. They cared greatly for the village and its people and in turn were cared for by them. To see the welcoming yellow glow of their lights reflected brightly across the green on a frosty winter's night and to know that within those sturdy walls burned a cosy fire, a warm welcome and a tot to keep out the cold meant a great deal to their neighbours. And not only to them but also to the folk who climbed the hill from the valley and its surrounds, drawn by 'th' ale an' th' crack'. It was the focal point of their community, the pivot around which much of their life revolved.

Significantly, there was neither church nor chapel in either High or Low Cornhill.

2

The Blue Pig

Tom Dandridge was a frequent visitor to the 'Double Duck'; in fact he had been a patron for over forty years. He often boasted that he was 'as well known as a bad ha' penny aroond these parts,' a statement no one had cause to dispute. For Tom was the local cattle dealer and travelled the North country buying beasts from the many scattered farmsteads and smallholdings and then selling them on at the various marts and auctions, after a suitable period of fattening on his land. He wasn't a tall man, about five foot six, but what he lacked in height was more than compensated in girth and he could often be seen, his belly pressed hard up against the bar, whilst at first glance he appeared to be standing some distance from it.

"It's just as well your arms are as long, Tom," Davy would gently chide him, "else y'wouldn't be able t'pick y'r glass up."

He always gave back as good as he got and his blue eyes would twinkle merrily in his round, florid face as he laughed. But he hadn't always been a cattle dealer. He first started by keeping a few pigs. That was shortly after the war, when meat for human consumption wasn't as strictly regulated as it is today and he was able to feed his animals on scraps collected from the locals. He was a common sight, driving around in his large pre-war Ford shooting brake, three or four dustbins in the back, overflowing with everyone's leftovers. If he was upwind he could be smelled for about two miles, particularly on a hot day, which was as good a warning as any for the local populace to deposit potato peelings, carrot tops, mouldy loaves, rotten meat, or anything else that was remotely edible at their back doors.

This nauseous mess was systematically emptied into a large boiler back at the piggery by Tom's younger brother, Lennie, who, being slightly 'touched in't heid,' was unable to find any other employment.

However, it had to be said that, when it came to boiling up other peoples' leftovers, he was almost cordon bleu standard. The pigs always seemed to enjoy whatever it was that, mixed with a little corn, was emptied into their troughs on a daily basis.

"Th' finest pork in th' whole o' Durham," was Tom's proud boast to anyone who would listen, Lennie nodding eagerly in agreement. And it must have been for he never had any difficulty in selling the animals on when ready for slaughter.

Late one evening he called at the 'Double Duck' on his way home. The landlord in those days was a long, thin, rather mournful individual called Jack Snowden. 'Smiler,' to his regulars, but strictly behind his back. He had been invalided out of the army after the war and with his savings and gratuity had bought the pub from the previous owner upon his retirement.

"Y're lookin' pleased aboot summat th' neet," he commented, his sad expression unaltered as though in accusation as Tom stood at the bar exuding bonhomie.

He grinned broadly, "Aye, y'could say that. P'raps Ah've summat t'be pleased aboot."

The landlord raised heavy black eyebrows, feigning interest. The gesture made his expression even more lugubrious, like a bloodhound's. "Oh, aye, an' what might that be, then?" The question was posed merely in the hope of selling another pint rather from any real concern in what lay behind his client's obvious good humour.

"T'day Ah've done summat as Ah've allus wanted," Tom said proudly, "Ah've bowt mesel a prize sow, an' a reet bonny 'un an' all." His grin became broader as he thrust out his chest, which was quite a feat if one considered just how far his stomach preceded it.

The landlord was as interested in prize pigs as he was in flying to the moon. "Oh, aye. A prize sow, eh?" was all he could think of to say.

"Aye," Tom nodded confirmation, "an' be her pedigree she should produce mebbe three, four good litters a year, mebbe eight or ten to a litter. Aye sh's a fine big pig," and he held out his glass for a refill, which was of infinitely more interest to Jack Snowden.

And indeed she was, as Tom had said, ' a fine, big pig,' and she did prove to be everything that he hoped, regularly producing numerous progeny which earned her the grateful accolade of 'Gloria'.

About a twelvemonth after his prize acquisition, Tom was driving though the village on his rounds late one morning when he had to slow down for a herd of black and white Friesian cows which, heavily laden udders swinging with each laborious step, were slowly entering the Stobbarts' farmyard. Old Herbert Stobbart was at their back driving them on, ably assisted as usual by his wall-eyed Welsh collie, Jess. On recognising the old shooting brake he stopped to have 'a bit crack'. After five minutes spent exchanging pleasantries the old man was about to go when he was struck by a sudden thought. "Be th' way, Tom," he said, a note of caution creeping into his tone, "Ah've heard th' Ministry man's aboot. Y'd better get rid o' that owld boiler o' yours for a while, just t'be on't safe side, eh?"

Tom grimaced his thanks. The Ministry of Agriculture inspector was, in his candid opinion, 'nowt but a bloody nuisance, allus pokin' his damn' nose where it wasn't wanted.' They also frowned upon the use of feeding pigs on household refuse these days, even though the practice was quite widespread, for it was becoming increasingly apparent that pigs could pick up human diseases and pass them on in the food chain. Although no outright ban had yet been implemented the day was fast approaching when boilers such as his would become ancient history.

He stopped outside the Duck and went in for a consoling pint, it being lunchtime. As it happened there were a couple of his cronies already installed at one end of the bar and, as one thing led to another, he consumed rather more than he had intended. Not that he was drunk exactly; he simply found it difficult to get his words past his teeth.

He was just about to down another pint when the door burst open and there stood his brother, Lennie, eyes wild, his hair looking like a cornstack that the wind had grabbed by the scruff of the neck, sweat pouring down his plum-coloured face. He also looked like he had just run a four minute mile for his chest was heaving mightily beneath his greasy dungarees. He staggered up to the bar and grabbed at Tom's arm, causing most of his beer to spill down his chin.

"Ha'way man, wha'th'hellsamarra?" Tom slurred trying, not without some difficulty, to get his eyes to focus.

"Tom, man, Tom, h'way," Lennie urged desperately, pulling at his arm. He seemed almost in tears.

"Ge'roff, y'stupit bast'd," Tom growled in response, trying to pull his arm free and in the process spilling more of his pint.

Lennie, his simple mind unable to comprehend anything but his own particular plight became even more agitated at his brother's supposed intransigence. "It's Gloria," he wailed, "sh's lyin' doon an' Ah canna ger'a up."

The mention of his beloved Gloria's predicament was like a slap across the face and had a somewhat sobering effect. He staggered back from the bar and stared unbelievingly at his sibling, "Aw, pissoff, man, Lennie. Sh's prob'ly just havin' a kip."

But Lennie was not to be mollified, "No, y'll have t'come noo, our Tom, sh's mekkin' some funny noises an', an'........"

"Ah knaw, Ah knaw," Tom sighed, "y'canna ger'a up. H'way then, let's gan doon an' see what all th' bloody fuss is aboot."

Up until he actually clapped his own eyes upon Gloria he wasn't too perturbed, the drink having something of a tranquillising effect. The truth was, until he looked over the wall of her sty, he felt distinctly euphoric. But things changed dramatically when his inebriated eye fell upon her heaving flank. Not only was she lying on her side, a position not usual for this time of day, she was, as Lennie had said, making some very peculiar noises; rather like a cross between a snore and a snort every time she breathed. But worse than all of this, if anything could actually be worse, she had turned a very peculiar but delicate shade of pale blue.

Tom's sobering was quicker than instantaneous, "Jesus bloody Christ," he howled, in extremis, "what th' bloody hell ha' y'bin feedin' her, y'stupit.......?"

This time the tears really did flow down Lennie's cheeks. His plain, simple face contorted as he cried, "Nowt, nowt, honest, but what we boiled up f'r her two days since."

Suddenly his brother froze rigid, staring at him, "Shit," he exploded, "the boiler, the bloody boiler." (He was sober enough now,) and he began to run up the yard towards the shed as fast as his fat little legs would carry him, Lennie, uncomprehendingly but ever faithful, hard on his heels, his nose an inch or two from his brother's back. Before the shed was reached Tom stopped suddenly and turned. The result was that Lennie cannoned into him nearly bringing them both down onto the concrete.

"Gerroota me way, f'r Chris' sake," Tom snarled, hurling the unfortunate Lennie to one side. "Th' pig, we gotta get rid o' th' pig." He was becoming more and more panic-stricken whilst Lennie, who by now was utterly and totally confused, tearful and bewildered, began to run around in circles howling, "Why, why?" the tension just too much for his enfeebled mind to cope with.

"Why, bloody why?" roared his brother, the spittle flying from his lips in his fury, "cos th' bloody Ministry man's in the area, that's why."

As they entered the sty once again poor, unfortunate Gloria uttered her last breath and closed her eyes for good. Tom simply stared, open-mouthed. "Shit," he swore vehemently, "me best pig."

Now this pig weighed four hundredweight and more and four hundredweight of dead animal is not easy to shift, particularly when all that was available to shift her in was an old wooden wheelbarrow that they used for mucking out. Notwithstanding the obvious Herculean effort required but realising that they had very little choice in the matter, they set to. Tom brought up the wheelbarrow and parked it next to Gloria's inert body. A low groan escaped his lips as he contemplated her demise and considered how best to deposit her massive bulk into their one and only means of conveyance.

"Reet, Lennie," he commanded, mentally girding his loins and sallying forth, "let's see if we can get her heid an' forequarters at least into this auld barrer. We'll see about th' rest o' her later."

That was the easy bit for her front end was nowhere near as heavy as her huge hindquarters. They constituted an altogether different problem. After a great deal of heaving, straining, struggling and cursing they were getting nowhere and Tom, who feared he was in very grave danger of instigating a heart attack, vociferously cursed the day he had ever clapped eyes on her.

"Damn y'to hell an' back, Gloria," he swore, his chest heaving and the perspiration running in rivers down his plump cheeks, which by now were about the same colour as Gloria's hide, "why me, why t'day of all days?" He ran agitated fingers through his thinning hair as he cudgelled his desperate mind for a solution to the most pressing problem he had ever been faced with, considering the proximity of the Ministry inspector.

As he gazed about him his forlorn gaze alighted upon the old mounting block that stood near the gate. It wasn't very high, having only two steps and its platform was just about wide enough to hold a pig. A germ of an idea began to form. "Lennie," he snapped, "go an' get th' rope an' a couple o' scaffoldin' planks, quick now."

His brother did as he was asked and returned in a very few moments with the required items. As he was doing this Tom backed his old car close to the side of the mounting block, the side opposite to where his pig lay. Leaving the engine running he quickly laid the planks on the steps thus forming a shallow ramp after which he tied the rope to Gloria's back legs, the other end he fastened to the tow bar on the back of the car after running it over the top of the mounting block.

"Reet, Lennie," he called for his brother who had been watching these antics with his mouth open, "Ah'm goin' t'pull Gloria onto th' block here wi' th' car. You just make sure sh' goes up th' ramp nice an' steady, got that?"

Lennie grinned, showing the gaps in his teeth, as comprehension slowly dawned.

As the shooting brake inched forward, Gloria began to move. It was their first piece of real luck that day for she slid onto the top of the block as smoothly as if she had been smeared in butter.

"Now what d'we dae, Tom?" Lennie enquired, as he admired their handiwork.

"Well, we don't just stan' around gawpin', that's f'sure," his brother snarled. "Just bring that barrer up here." He indicated the side of the mounting block with a quick nod of his head. The barrow in place, they gently eased Gloria into it, Tom trying manfully to prevent her falling too heavily by supporting her weight from underneath. Fortunately the old wheelbarrow didn't collapse under the strain, not just at that moment anyway, and they successfully achieved their objective.

Having finally got this far they then collapsed against the yard wall, chests heaving in unison and with sweat trickling freely into their eyes. They remained in this position for some minutes, quite unable to speak. Eventually, Lennie's heart ceased its mad pounding, slowing down sufficiently to allow him to ask, "What d'we dae noo, Tom?"

Tom raised a weak arm and pointed, "Get y'sel inter th' shed and ger'a sack or summat t'cover her wi'," he gasped.

Slowly his brother hauled himself to his feet and went to do his bidding. Behind the piggery, about five or six hundred yards away over some rough ground, was an old abandoned quarry. It was here that Tom had decided to store Gloria until he could give her a decent burial, or until the Ministry man was safely out of the way. But, 'the best laid plans of mice and men', caused a major rethink in his strategy for the weight of the pig, the rough terrain, the age of the wheelbarrow and their own failing strength proved to be insurmountable and well before the quarry was reached the wheel on the barrow had collapsed leaving Gloria in an undignified heap.

All that was left to do was to cover her with bracken and branches and hope that no one would notice her, for they still had the boiler to attend to.

Utterly weary and despondent they traipsed back to the piggery only to find a small man in a brown suit and trilby hat standing near the shed door.

"Oh, bugger me," Tom groaned quietly to his brother as he espied the stranger, "too late, he'll already've seen the bloody boiler." But, putting as brave a face as he could muster upon the situation, he walked purposefully up the yard. "Aye, now then," he greeted the visitor, "you'll be from the Ministry, no doubt?"

The stranger appeared slightly taken aback, a frown appearing between his eyes, "What ministry?" he asked pointedly.

"Th' Ministry o' Agriculture, what else?"

The man in the brown suit shook his head, "Naw, not me mate. Ah'm just a butcher an' Ah'm here t'buy a pig. Ah was told y'breed th' best pork in Durham."

3
Our Winnie

In times gone by the bus service from High Cornhill to Durham and its outlying districts was a deal more frequent than it is today; which was just as well considering that not a single shop existed in the village, nor ever had done. There was, however, a substantial Co-op in Low Cornhill which had been purpose built at the end of the last century to serve the surrounding communities. It was a store of many departments, the epitome, the very epicentre of retailing, or so the pompous little manager, Mr. Sykes, was always proudly telling himself.

Here, behind the row of large plate glass windows that fronted onto the main street, the white coated staff beavered away in the grocery department. (Hardware was next door.) Beneath the dozen or so twin gas lights they packed orders into boxes prior to delivery, weighed tea, that had been transported from India and Ceylon in plywood tea chests, into quarter pound bags, ground dark, shining coffee beans scooped from aromatic sacks, cut cheese with cheese wire, patted butter straight from small wooden barrels and sliced bacon on the large red bacon slicer that stood in splendid isolation at the end of the long counter. Only the chosen few were allowed to operate this machine as the large circular steel blade was quite capable of slicing the fingers off the unwary.

It had an aromatic ambience all of its own, fondly remembered by a generation unused to the soulless atmosphere of the modern supermarket. At the very end of groceries and provisions, directly opposite the main entrance, was the butchery department, its marble counter top hazily reflecting the large sign which hung suspended on chains above it, and which proudly proclaimed its status. The manager and his two assistants, when they weren't attending to their variety of customers, kept the place spotless, the white tiling gleamed from constant washing and cleaning, fresh sawdust was scattered on the floor every day and the large butcher's block which stood in the middle of the floor, was scraped and cleaned every night after closing time.

From his office on the second floor Mr. Sykes kept his well-experienced eye on all aspects of his operation and stalked about his empire, his slicked back hair glistening like patent leather, a gold watch chain, which he wore like a badge of office, decorating a paunch that threatened to fire the buttons off his pin-striped waistcoat. A martinet undoubtedly, but he did have a soft spot for one or two of his employees, one of whom was Winnie Thompson.

Winnie was seventeen years old and had worked in the millinery department of the store, situated on the second floor, since she had left school at fourteen. A natural hard-worker, she had quickly proven her worth and was now the manageress's, Mrs. Bruce's, right-hand girl and very highly thought of.

Those that aspired to the rarified atmosphere of the upper floors generally considered themselves a race apart from the mere mortals that worked in grocery or butchery or hardware; not so Winnie. She lived in a small terrace of cottages that, like others in the village, ran from the pit to the edge of the surrounding fields. Her mother, a large, proud and solid Northerner and a staunch Methodist (chapel twice on Sundays and once during the week) had raised her girls (Winni6e had a younger sister) in the best traditions of her church.

That she loved them both dearly was never in doubt but she was definitely not accustomed to having her opinion contradicted or her will thwarted. She was also aware that her elder daughter was turning out to be quite a beauty for she had a ready smile, sparkling green eyes and a shock of luxuriant golden hair that hung halfway down her back. She knew, did Winnie's mother, that she would have to keep a careful eye on her daughter's extra curricular activities for, as she was always saying to her neighbour, Mrs. Page, 'Y'just never know what the young'un's are up to these days, an' that's a fact.'

If she had known what went on in Jimmy Goldsmith's agile mind her worst fears might have been confirmed. Jimmy worked in the butchery department of the Co-op and was recently out of his apprenticeship. He had had his eye on Winnie for quite some time but, being a noted lothario around the villages, he knew how to bide his time. 'Th' sweetest fruit takes th' longest to ripen,' he would often tell his younger colleague with a knowing wink.

He was an extremely handsome young man and his looks and his sense of sartorial elegance he used to his utmost advantage. He spent a lot of time and money on his appearance; he had been known to splash out as much as five pounds on a three piece suit and he could often be seen on a Saturday night in Durham, a girl on his arm, sometimes two, doing the rounds of the public houses. He was definitely the type that women such as Winnie's mother warned their daughters about. It was rumoured that he had fathered more than one child 'on the wrong side of the blanket', but nothing had ever been proved.

"Eeh, Winnie, y've never said that y'would, surely?" Alice asked her friend, wide eyed.

The two girls, their work done for the day, were walking home arm in arm, as they did every evening. Winnie clung to her friend's arm and giggled conspiratorially, their heads close as she nodded. "Aye, Ah have, next Saturday night. He wants t'go t'th pictures in Durham."

"That's not all he wants, Ah'll be bound," Alice sniffed suspiciously.

"Well, he won't get anythin' here, no matter what he wants. A quick kiss an' a cuddle mebbe, but that's all." Winnie smiled cheekily, obviously pleased and not a little flattered to be asked out on her first date.

Alice, who was about a year older than her friend and therefore considered herself much more worldly wise said, shaking her head sorrowfully, unable to understand Winnie's foolishness, "But Jimmy Goldsmith, lass. Ah just can't fathom it. Why, wi' your looks y'coulda had Rudolph Valentino....."

Again her friend giggled, "Aw, don't be so daft Alice, an' don't worry so much, Ah'll be alright, you'll see. But," she went on, gripping her friend's arm earnestly, "y'will cover for us, won't yer, if me mam asks, Ah mean?"

Suddenly Alice smiled, "Aye, y'know Ah will," she said softly. "Y'r out wi' me on Saturday, don't fash. Just enjoy y'self an'," she emphasised the last two words, "be careful."

For all of his infamous reputation the young Mister Goldsmith knew all there was to know about giving a girl a good time. He was polite attentiveness personified, wouldn't allow Winnie to pay for anything, ushered her into the best seats in the house and provided a gift wrapped box of chocolates to go with them. It was enough to turn a girl's head and Winnie was no exception. She enjoyed being seen on the arm of this good looking, exquisitely dressed young man; who wouldn't?

They caught the last bus home and as they alighted in the village Jimmy suggested a drink in The Oak Tree before he saw her safely home.

"Well, Ah'm not too sure about that, mind, Ah've never been in there before," Winnie was very hesitant. "Ah don't know what me mam would say."

"It's not y'mam Ah'm askin'," grinned Jimmy, "it's you. H'way, man, one little drink won't hurt," and he smiled his most persuasive smile.

"Alright, then, but just th' one mind, an' then Ah'm off," Winnie relented.

But she enjoyed her first port and lemon so much that she readily agreed to a second and by the time they left the pub she was walking on air, for her feet never seemed to make contact with the pavement. At her front door she stopped and they lingered, talking for a while, their voices low, their heads together. Jimmy bent his face close to hers and kissed her softly. It was the first time she had been kissed in this way and, like the port and lemon, she enjoyed it. Sensing this he took her in his arms and pulled her even closer.

"No, Jimmy, not here," she whispered, pushing him away, "it's too public."

"Where then?" His whispered reply sounded disappointed.

"Come with me," Winnie said, taking him by the hand. She led him round the corner of the little terrace to the back of the houses where a dark lane ran along the edge of the fields. She stopped when she got to her own house and leant her back against the rough wall of the outhouse or 'nettie'.

She turned her face up to his and was rewarded by the soft pressure of his lips eagerly seeking hers. He moaned softly as again he pulled her to him gathering her in his arms. Needless to say, he was well practiced in the art of retaining a young lady's interest and soon Winnie was beginning to feel rather flushed and weak at the knees. She put it down to the port and lemon. Just as they came up for air for a third time, the heavens, without warning, opened, and within a matter of seconds they were in grave danger of drowning.

"Aw, shit," groaned Jimmy, his evening ruined, turning up the collar of his jacket, "what a time f'r this t'happen."

"Never mind, lover," Winnie couldn't help but laugh at his hang-dog expression, "we'll just dodge in here."

"What, in there?" said her ruined Romeo, wrinkling his nose as Winnie opened the door to the outhouse.

"Ah know it's not the best place in th' world f'r what you had in mind, but at least it's dry. Are y'comin' in or not?"

Considering the alternative, he followed her eagerly enough, his anticipation at what he thought might, after all, be a perfect end to the evening, electrically charged.

As he stepped inside, and Winnie had slipped the bolt into position, his nose was suddenly assaulted by the all-too-familiar smell, a smell he was well accustomed to, coming as he did from a very similar environment to Winnie; for every house in every village of the time had its outside nettie. It was the smell of old newspapers, cut into squares and hung on a nail by a piece of string. It was the smell of whitewash, which covered the rough hewn walls, the smell of lime, used to sterilise the contents of the ashbox which stood like a throne against the far wall, the smell of ashes which, along with the said contents, were removed once a week by, what were euphemistically termed by the fastidious, 'the night soil men.' But overlaying all of this was the faint but distinct smell of human excrement.

"Dear God," he thought to himself, "Ah've been in some funny places t'get me oats but this definitely takes th' biscuit," and he tried to console himself with Winnie's soft and eager mouth.

It seemed that they hadn't been inside more than ten seconds when they were shocked apart by a violent rattling at the sneck.

"What's goin' on here, who's in there?" demanded a querulous voice.

"Oh, God, no," Winnie breathed, her mouth close to Jimmy's ear, "it's me mam. Sh'll murder us if sh' finds us in here." Aloud she said, "It's only me, Mam."

"Well, c'mon hurry up, young lady," her mother insisted, "it's rainin' cats an' dogs out here and it's high time you were in y'bed an' all."

15

Desperately Jimmy looked about him, searching for a way out but as outhouses are built with privacy in mind, with only one door, he was singularly unsuccessful.

Winnie, however, was quicker on her feet. "In here," she mouthed, as she raised the lid of the ashbox.

Aghast and horrified young Goldsmith shook his head, preferring to take his chances with the dreaded Mrs. Thompson. He quickly changed his mind when the sneck rattled violently again and, closing his eyes and resigning himself to his fate, rather like a Catholic martyr about to be burned at the stake, he climbed inside. Crouching down on all fours, trepidation and disgust vying with each other in his mind, his hand came into contact with something, in the darkness he couldn't tell what it was, but it was soft and unspeakable. That wasn't the full extent of his tribulations; not by a long chalk.

Winnie finally stepped demurely outside, "G'night, Mam," she said, as she fled up the path to the house, her heart beating wildly and thanking her Maker that she had been allowed to leave the scene of her impending nemesis virtually unscathed. Unfortunately for her erstwhile lover, his nemesis was about to descend upon his unsuspecting head as Winnie's mother settled her very large bottom upon the seat.

Some time later, in the early hours of that same morning, Jimmy Goldsmith was observed taking a bath, fully clothed in his best suit, in a convenient horse trough. And it was a very long time indeed before he cast a roving eye in Winnie's direction again. Neither did he boast, in Winnie's hearing at least, of his latest conquest.

4

Not So Friendly Rivalry

The big new Fordson tractor roared its imperious way through the village and past the Double Duck, its huge tyres causing it to bounce and nod as it made for the entrance to Bill Stobbart's farmyard. Turning into the gateway it stood on the concrete apron with a distinctly superior air whilst the driver, obviously extremely pleased with himself, revved the engine, the sound reverberating off the walls of the surrounding buildings.

Inside the milking parlour, the owner of the farm grinned wryly at his head stockman, "No prizes f'r guessin' just who this might be, eh?" he enquired.

The stockman merely shook his head, returning his employer's smile. Bill stepped out into the sunshine and raised his hand. He was a tall, wiry individual with a calm manner. A luxuriant moustache adorned his upper lip and he was very rarely seen, outdoors at least, without his flat cap sitting firmly upon his head. Quietly spoken and always slow to anger, he maintained a certain dignity whilst at the same time exuding an air of friendly warmth. Since the death of his father, Herbert, some fifteen years ago he had managed the farm with a degree of professionalism that was the envy of most of his neighbours. His unerring success meant that he was one of the biggest landowners in the district as well as one of the wealthiest. He could afford to, and often did, buy what he wanted but only when he felt it necessary and then he only bought the best. He was stickler for quality in everything. Second best was just not good enough.

His initial suspicions confirmed, he greeted the driver as he descended to the ground, his back towards him, "Mornin', John," he offered cheerily.

"Ah," said the driver, turning, "morning, Bill."

"Care f'r some breakfast?" The invitation was spontaneous.

"Well, that's very good o' yer," his visitor replied, "Ah don't mind if Ah do."

They walked across the yard together and into the large rear hall of

17

the farmhouse. It had stood at the outskirts of the village for more than four hundred years and was imposing without being pretentious. Built of stone, with walls more than two feet thick, its mullioned windows had looked out over the valley for generation after generation. The Stobbart family had occupied it now for more than a century. Who would occupy it when Bill and his wife Sarah, who had had only daughters, had no further use for it was a matter of conjecture.

He sat down on a window seat in the entrance hall and pulled off his boots, advising his guest to do the same. "No need t' get our Sarah's back up this early on, is there?" he laughed softly.

"Ah should say not," grinned his visitor, "and Ah could do wi' some breakfast, so......" and he grunted as he removed his footwear.

Bill led the way down the wide, flagged passage to the kitchen, calling, "Hello," as he did so.

From behind a door at the end a woman's voice replied, "Hello yourself," and they entered a large and airy room fitted out with the latest in kitchen furniture, cupboard doors of dark oak matching the overhead beams. Sarah stood at a big, modern Aga frying ham and eggs. A striking woman with large dark eyes and a shock of dark brown hair, she turned to smile at her husband, not noticing the visitor in the shadows of the hall behind him. "Nearly ready," she said, and then. "Oh, hello, John, I didn't know...." her smile, although welcoming, betrayed a hint of caution.

"John's just called to look over those beast he's thinkin' of buying. Ah invited him t' stay an' have some breakfast with us, if that's alright?" Bill walked across to the sink to wash up as he spoke.

"Yes, yes, of course it is. Sit down at the table there, John and I'll put some more bacon on." Her reply was quick, a shade too quick as she bustled about busily setting another place.

Halfway through their meal Bill threw a question casually into the conversation, "New tractor then, John?"

Their visitor beamed, obviously delighted to talk about his shiny new toy. "Aye, aye," he said proudly, "just took delivery o' it yesterday. Beauty, ain't she? Cost ower fifteen grand cash, but worth it Ah reckon."

Their visitor, engrossed as he was in manoeuvring his last egg onto a piece of toast, failed to observe the wry look that Bill cast his wife, a look which said everything and which very nearly caused her to choke on her coffee.

"Well, I must say," Sarah said as she cleared away the breakfast things, "I think I've just about heard everything."

Her husband, who was just finishing a final cup of coffee before returning to his duties, raised questioning eyebrows, although he was fully aware of what was coming next. Their visitor had departed some ten minutes previously.

Without waiting for a reply she continued, in the same matter-of-fact manner, "It doesn't matter what we do, he, John Sanderson, has to go that one better, doesn't he?"

"Umm, what d'you mean exactly?" Bill goaded her gently.

She rose to the bait magnificently, as he knew she would. "So it's a new tractor now, is it? And how long ago is it since you bought our new tractor, six, eight weeks? It was the same when you changed the car which, God knows, needed to be changed. Within five minutes he had rolled up in one of those enormous four wheel drive things." She quickly warmed to her theme as Bill continued to smile quietly. "Where did they go on holiday last year? Australia and the Far East," she answered her own question as she angrily threw cutlery into the dishwasher. "And why?" she slammed the door shut. "Because we went to America. I'll bet if you said you were going to take a hang gliding course on Mount Fuji he would have to fly the Atlantic in a hot air balloon."

This time her husband could contain his mirth no longer, "So what, my love?" he laughed as he rose to his feet. "They have a perfect right to spend their money in whichever way they choose. Just because they happen to constantly follow our lead only proves one thing: that they haven't an original thought between them." He kissed her fondly as he made his way to the door.

The Sandersons, although having lived at Snipe Brook Farm for some five years or so, were incomers to the village. Not only that, the village hadn't particularly warmed to them, making them fairly unique. John Sanderson was a big, bluff, ebullient sort of character, loud and overbearing, who had retired early from his position as a director of a multinational company to indulge his dream of playing at farming. His wife was a mouse, but a mouse who obviously got her own way for it was she who was essentially the social climber, the organiser, the puller of strings. What she lacked in personal charm she more than made up for in cupidity and tenacity. If she wanted something, and there was always something she wanted, either for herself or their only daughter, she usually got it.

Bill watched her machinations with quiet amusement and kept his own counsel. There was a time when he had had a swimming pool built at the rear of the farmhouse. He took the decision, quite deliberately, that it would be open to the elements as it was in actual fact on his tax return as a fire precaution.

That he had every intention of using it as such, should the need arose, was, to anyone who knew him, self-evident, which was why he needed instant access to it. He had seen too many ricks and barns burnt to the ground before the fire brigade could arrive at such remote locations. Needless to say, the Sanderson's swimming pool, although equally identified as a tax concession, was nevertheless enclosed by a hardwood timber frame with walls and roof of smoked glass.

The Stobbarts, along with their daughters and the rest of the village, were invited to the inaugural 'swim-in'. It was because of his daughters' relationship with the Sanderson's girl that Bill finally decided to end, once and for all, the ridiculous rivalry that had been forced upon him. Both his girls were accomplished riders and were well known on the summer circuit of three day events and country shows. Fortunately, they confined their equestrian ambitions to a purely amateur status and were popular competitors.

Not so Amanda Sanderson, for she was seen as one whose ambitions far outstripped her natural ability, although this meant little to her parents, particularly her mother, who was determined that her daughter should one day, even at this tender age, compete with the English equestrian team.

When she began entering for one or two of the more prestigious shows Bill began to get an awful lot of earache from his daughters about better and more expensive mounts and he knew that it had to stop somewhere, if only for their sake. He wasn't having his girls indulging in the type of social climbing that so epitomised the Sandersons.

"Let's have a party, shall we?" he suddenly announced to Sarah over dinner one evening.

"That sounds like a good idea," she agreed with enthusiasm. "When?"

He shrugged, "Oh, in about three weeks or so. We'll send out the invitations at the weekend."

Having obtained his wife's agreement he went the following day into Durham and spoke to a friend who owned a photographic studio.

The day of the party dawned bright and clear with high, lazily drifting clouds casting their shadows on the fell that rose, purple hued in the distance. A large striped marquee arrived and was quickly erected upon the lawn at the front of the house. Under its canvas protection a wooden floor was laid and a bar set up at one end. The new landlord of the 'Double Duck', Davy, and his wife, Glennis, had been prevailed upon to provide a catering and bar service and soon everything was ready for the kickoff at four o' clock. By seven the party was going with a swing with everyone dancing to the hired disco as if their very lives depended upon it. Everyone, that is, except the Sandersons. For John Sanderson was behaving in his usual loud, brash manner and had already consumed more alcohol than was good for him whilst his wife and daughter, overcome with embarrassment at his uncouth behaviour, sat huddled together in a corner pretending he wasn't with them and wishing that the floor would swallow them up. Eventually Bill took pity on them and quietly suggested to his neighbour that they go across to the house for a 'proper drink,' his enticement being a twenty year old Glen Morange.

They entered the oak panelled room which Bill used as a study and an office and as they did so John's inebriated eye fell upon a large framed photograph that hung over the fireplace. "By, but that's a crackin' photo, Bill," he said, tottering slightly, "Ah've not seen that afore." As it was the first time he had ever set foot in the room it was hardly surprising. He screwed up his eyes as he leant forward, his whisky-laden breath fogging the glass. "It's a crackin' nag, an' all, or Ah'm nae judge o' hoss flesh. An' is that one o' your lasses wi' 'im? Fust prize, eh?" he said, indicating the red rosette attached to the horse's bridle. "What show's this, then?" he threw over his shoulder at his host who was preparing whiskies and soda at the drinks trolley.

Without turning his head Bill replied, "Have a look at the background, John, y'll just be able t'make out the name o' th' show there, just behind Clare."

His guest did as suggested, then his jaw dropped in surprise, "Good God!" he exclaimed, "Ah had nae idea that y'r girls competed at this

21

level, man. Ah thought it was just y'usual little country show....."
His Northern accent became much more prominent when drunk, the
flat vowels, which normally only lay in occasional ambush, swarming
over the barricades of his more refined enunciation..

Bill handed him a heavy whisky tumbler with studied casualness,
"Only 'cos their old man supports them every inch o' the way." he
said. "B'lieve me, it's not for the faint hearted if y'want to afford
that quality o' hoss and enter that level o' competition. Why d'you
think so many o' them need sponsors?"

Sanderson's face had turned a sickly white, and not simply from
the drink he had taken. He tried to raise a smile, but failed. "So, so
what kind o' money are y'talkin' about f'r a season competin' at this
kind o' show?" he whispered weakly.

Bill scratched his head, "Oh, Ah don't know," he said vaguely, "It
depends if y'have a hoss o' the quality needed or y'have to buy one.
That one, Supreme Glory, cost twenty five."

"Oh, twenty five hundred doesn't seem so bad," Sanderson replied,
breathing a sigh of relief.

"Thousand," Bill tossed the figure casually into the air, "an' then
there's transport, feed, tack, entry fees, vet, farrier, y'can go on an'
on. A first season can set y'back at least fifty."

"Thousand?" echoed his neighbour, looking as though he had been
punched hard in the stomach.

Bill decided it was time to play his final card, "That's not the half
of it," he said quietly. "He's in constant training at one o' the top
yards in the county, an' that's not cheap either. No, bonny lad, at this
level it costs an arm an' a bloody leg. An' when there's two o' them
at it, well, y'can imagine, y'r talkin' really serious money."

A little later the same evening Bill went to relieve Davy at the bar.
"Ah've just seen a very strange thing, Bill," he said as they changed
places. And at Bill's questioning glance he went on to describe how
John Sanderson had just left with his wife and daughter in tow, looking
as though he had swallowed something nasty. "Ah heard him say
summat about them bein' satisfied wi' what they had got an' not
t'pester him about money ever again. Now what th' hell d'you think
that was all about, eh?"

Before Bill could make suitable reply a flash bulb went off behind him. "Ah Davy," he said, turning, "I'd like you t'meet a friend o' mine. He's the official photographer for tonight an' between you an' me," and here he winked knowingly, "he's an artist supreme when it comes to putting together a photo montage."

"A what?" Davy was mystified.

"You know," replied Bill, "a big photograph made up o' lots o' bits an' pieces from others".

5

The Cornhill Test

Although it has been pointed out that rivalry, per se, did not exist between the villages of High and Low Cornhill this was not strictly true. There was one area where the competitive spirit became almost primitive. Mind you, it only occurred but once a year but at that time it predominated all discussions; both pubs seeing many a heated argument during an evening's drinking.

Every summer a cricket match was organised between the teams of both villages, the previous year's victors having the match played upon their particular green. This was obviously known as the Cornhill Test Match and it was viewed, in particular by the male population, with as much enthusiasm as its professional counterpart. It would be true to say however that the enthusiasm generated in Low Cornhill, particularly over the last five years, had been much greater than that of its sister village. The reason being of course that they had emerged the victor on all five consecutive occasions.

High Cornhill had been unable, in those five seasons, to come up with anything like a competitive team ever since their star player and captain had emigrated to Darlington. In fact, each year the scoreboard had read like a typical England first team score against the Windies or Australia. The last summer had been their worst when they had lost by five wickets and one hundred and thirty two runs, but, in the true tradition of their forefathers, they were prepared to battle on.

Even with the advent of Davy Dobson, true Yorkshireman and rabid cricket fan that he was, they seemed powerless against the big hitting of Low Cornhill's Charlie Gibson and the demon bowling of young Chris Kelly. 'Gi' it some wellie Kelly,' they called him for the speed at which the ball left his hand was awesome.

July the twenty-third was the chosen date for this year's match and, as it crept ever closer, like the sword of Damocles, gloom and despondency began to creep into those team members who were of less heart than either Davy or Bill Stobbart. The main problem was, apart from their rivals being a better side, Low Cornhill was a bigger village by far and could always be relied upon to field a different side each year, having more enthusiasts to choose from. As a consequence High Cornhill never quite knew what they were up against until they actually walked onto the pitch. They had sent their spies out on numerous occasions to watch the other side practice but they had nearly always been spotted and asked politely to 'piss off.'

Davy stood at the end of the bar leaning against the cool shelf, one foot resting on the low sink he used to wash the glasses, arms folded, and from behind his rimless specs he surveyed the gloomy faces arrayed in front of him.. The main members of the team, for that is who they were, gazed despondently back.

"Ah've never seen such a bunch o' no hopers in me life," he said, grinning, attempting to generate some cheer into his forlorn team mates. "Y'look like we've already lost an' we've still another three weeks t'go yet."

Gerry Dixon, a small man with a haircut like an inmate of Durham prison, stared mournfully into his half empty glass, "It's not so bad f'r you, Davy," he said, "y're at tailend. You don't have t'face Welly Kelly when he's just bin cranked up an' he's spoilin' f'r a fight." Gerald was opening bat along with his cousin Bob, who also looked like he'd rather take his chances with a swamp full of alligators.

"An' as f'r me," Joe Freeman chimed in from the far end, "if Charlie Gibson hammers me all ower th' bloody pitch like he did last year an' th' year afore Ah'm hangin' up me box an' y'can count me oot next year." Joe was getting past the athletic stage of his life anyway, as the belly he was cultivating indicated, and was looking for an excuse to take things a bit easier.

Just then the door opened and Bill Stobbart entered. Davy greeted him with some relief. "Thank God you've turned up, Bill," he said. "This lot are about t'pack in afore we've even begun," and he picked up a glass and filled a pint.

Bill looked around him and laughed quietly, "H'way, lads, it's not that bad, man. It's only a bloody game after all. An' let's face it," he went on, "they do put on a damn' good spread an' as much free beer as y'can drink as consolation."

The truth of this had a cheering effect on everyone and somebody said it was worth losing just to get legless on their beer. So they all agreed, their spirits lightening, that all in all, win or lose, it was a good day out anyway.

"That's fine, no problem, we'll look forward to seeing you then, g'bye." Glennis put down the phone and picked up the reservations book.

"What was that, my love?" her husband enquired casually from behind his morning paper.

"Oh, just a reservation from tomorrow until Sunday. A gentleman who's doing research work at the university," she returned, finishing off the entry. "A Mr. Montgomery."

Davy made a face, "From th' university, eh? There's posh, we're certainly gettin' a better class o' custom these days. When's he arrivin'?"

"Tea-time tomorrow. He said that we had been recommended by Tourist Information in Durham."

"See," he grinned up at her, "Ah told you that bribin' that lass behind the counter wi' one o' y'mother's apple pies would dae th' trick."

"It wasn't a bribe, you cheeky so an' so," she smiled at him, "she bought it."

"An' she's still recommendin' us, well Ah never?" he shook his head in mock bewilderment.

"Now then sir, what can I get you?" Davy, in his best landlord's manner, addressed the somewhat nervous-looking individual who stood at his bar. This was his house guest from the university and Davy wasn't impressed, to say the least, although he naturally did his best to hide the fact. He appeared to be a typical member of the world of academe, as viewed by the rest of the population, hesitant, uncertain, his mind constantly drifting off to another, ethereal plane. To add to the illusion he wore a pair of heavy framed glasses perched upon a hawk-like beak of a nose, the whole being surmounted by an unwieldy shock of hair, greying at the sides, that had all the appearance of a rat's nest after a hurricane. His tweed jacket had been in his possession since he graduated or he had bought it from a passing vagrant, Davy was unsure which.

"Er, er, now let me see," the house guest murmured, gazing hopelessly along the row of pumps whilst Davy bit back the urge to yell at him to get a move on as he had a bar full of thirsty customers. "What exactly would you recommend?" Mr. Montgomery gave a nervous smile.

"Ah would recommend that y'make y'bloody mind up, an quick," Davy thought to himself. Smiling, at least he thought he was smiling although the overall effect was more of a grimace, he said aloud, "Well, th' guest ale is very good t'night..."

"Good, good," the academic nodded, suddenly arriving at a decision, "I'll try a pint of that, if you don't mind."

There was a moment's pause as Davy pulled the pint and then he asked, "Did you enjoy your meal?"

"Umm, yes indeed," Mr. Montgomery replied, reaching for the brimming glass. "Your wife cooks a truly wondrous fish pie..., oh, dear me..."

How it happened Davy had really no idea; one moment he was certain that his guest had taken hold of the glass, the next its contents were spilled all over the bar, the beer running freely over the edge and dripping onto his feet.

Again he bit back the expletive that rose so readily to his lips, saying, "Don't worry about it, Mr. Montgomery, Ah'll soon have that cleared up," and grabbing a couple of bar towels he hastily cleared away the mess. As he was doing so, Bill Stobbart walked in. "Ah, Bill," Davy greeted him hopefully, "let me just finish pulling another pint for Mr. Montgomery here then you an' he can go over there an' get acquainted, can't you?" He inclined his head towards a corner table.

"Oh," replied Bill surprised, looking as though he had suddenly fallen out of bed, "can we?"

Davy nodded vigorously, "Yes, please," he whispered, as he pulled Bill's pint, "f'r God's sake, get him away from my bar afore he does any more damage."

So it was that Bill found himself lumbered with an academic for the evening, an academic, it has to be said, who, once his initial shyness had evaporated, proved to be an erudite and amusing companion. Their conversation ranged from the research into microbiology that Mr. Montgomery was carrying out at the university, to politics, farming and the CAP through to literature and the theatre, of which Bill was particularly fond. It was almost closing time when Joe Freeman appeared, looking distinctly woebegone. His eye settled upon Bill and he wandered over to the corner where he sat. What was discussed exactly Davy couldn't hear but from the expression on Bill's face he knew it was not good news.

It was a fabulous day. The sort of day that should never be allowed to fade, with scarcely a cloud to stain an azure sky and just the occasional careless eddy that set the trees whispering amongst themselves. Down in the hollow of the valley the sound of leather on willow could be heard punctuated by cries of 'well played' whilst gentile applause drifted upwards on the breeze.

The visiting team had arrived in good time and most were surprised to find a new player included in their ranks. He had come with Davy and Bill in spite of Davy's protestations that he had grave doubts about his inclusion in the team.

"Look, man, Bill," he had said, out of earshot of the new player, "th' lad can hardly hold a pint, let alone play a straight bat, y'saw him y'self last night in th' pub." He was, of course referring to Mr. Montgomery.

But Bill had merely smiled in his slow, quiet way saying softly, "Just trust me, Davy lad, just trust me. We had t'have a replacement f'r Joe an' he's just th' lad, in my opinion."

Low Cornhill had won the toss and had decided to bat. Already they were into double figures although they hadn't had it all of their own way. Bill, as captain, had decided to open the bowling and had some luck in taking two quick wickets for twelve runs. However, Charlie Gibson had arrived at the crease some fifteen minutes earlier and from the way he had grinned at Bill the latter knew he was in for a bad time.

And so it turned out. In the short time he was at the crease Charlie played his usual game and smashed the bowling all over the place. He played with great abandon, thoroughly enjoying himself, and it wasn't long before the score had climbed to thirty eight, with Charlie barely out of breath.

Clarence Ford, a steady medium pacer with a good head on his shoulders kept his partner pinned down for the most part but Bill became increasingly frustrated as by the end of his third over he had seen the opposing team's score increase to a level that suggested that, if something weren't done soon, it would end up somewhere in the stratosphere.

Disgusted with his own performance he brought Davy on, who rather fancied himself as an off spinner. He rearranged the field and introduced a pair of slips and, on Bill's advice and much against his better judgement, he placed Mr. Montgomery at second slip. Whether or not it was, as many claimed, a worn patch or, as Davy was adamant about, his impeccable spin bowling, the result was that Charlie Gibson, who had obviously decided he was going to treat Davy in the same cavalier fashion that he had his predecessor, only got the slightest edge to the ball and was caught out to a beautiful one handed diving catch by second slip, Mr. Montgomery's reactions being akin to a streak of lightning, so quick was he.

"Owzat", the whole team screamed in unison, leaping into the air and hugging each other as they saw the fielder rise from the ground, the ball firmly clutched in his right hand, and a disgruntled Charlie Gibson walked as the umpire raised his finger in agreement. That was just the start, for the combination of spin bowling and slip catching proved to be devastating; all in all they removed six of Low Cornhill's players for just twenty seven runs and began to breathe easily again.

At tea, which was taken after the final player had been dismissed, the opposition scoring a grand total of eighty nine, the lowest score they had ever achieved in this competition, Davy could hardly contain himself, proclaiming to any member of his team who cared to listen that, he'd never seen owt like it. "What a combination," he chortled, as the rest of the team crowded around to offer their congratulations. "Ah must say, Mr. Montgomery, f'r someone who has some problem holding a pint y'can't half keep howld o' a cricket ball."

Mr. Montgomery ran his fingers through his wild, unruly locks, adjusted his heavy specs and exchanged a quiet smile with Bill.

Then of course it was the turn of the visiting side to bat and, as their competitors were smarting from the ignominy of being dismissed in such fashion, they were thirsting for revenge. Bob and Gerry Dixon managed to put on a tentative eleven between them before Bob went down to a beautiful inswinger from Chris Kelly, his middle and leg stump flying out of the ground behind him. Bill was next to go, and then after only putting on a further three before he was caught behind. Gerry stuck it out gamely and raised the score to twenty two before he saw his own stumps disappear in similar fashion to his cousin's as he became yet another victim of the indomitable Chris Kelly. Davy came in next and was partnered with a hefty young farm-hand by the name of Dick Langley who made up in enthusiasm what he lacked in finesse. Unfortunately, he lumbered rather than ran and was run out fairly quickly for five. Bill looked at the scoreboard as Davy, who was not the fittest amongst them, was finally run out also after vainly flinging himself and his bat bodily at the crease, saying disgustedly, "If they keep this up we'll all be out f'r about forty five this year, an' nae mistake. Right Donald," he addressed his academic acquaintance, "you'd better go an' see if you can stem th' tide an' the best o' luck."

He took his place at the crease and smiled slightly as 'Gi' it some welly Kelly,' stared down the pitch at him, tossing the ball from one hand to the other. He settled in, bat behind his right foot, left shoulder pointing down the pitch, and waited. The first ball was venomous but he let it go as it whistled past him at chest height, raising his bat in acknowledgement of a good delivery. The next ball, as he expected, was a bouncer, and meant to intimidate, but he ducked it easily and it sailed over his head into the gloves of the wicket keeper. The third ball he timed to perfection, his footwork superb as he got behind it and smashed it back over the bowler's head like a rocket. It finally came down off the edge of the green for six runs. There was a roar of approval from the crowd and Davy, his grin threatening to split his face in half, said, "Did y'see that, did y'bloody see that? Naebody's done that t'Welly Kelly afore, Ian Botham eat y'heart out," and he thumped his captain on the back.

And so it began. Bill's instructions to the rest of his team were simple; support their new batsman as much as possible and try to keep him on strike, "Leave him t'make th' running," was his advice and make it he did. He was sheer poetry to watch and no matter what the opposing bowlers threw down at him he dealt with it all in a most professional manner. He scored four superb sixes, three off Chris Kelly, and eight fours, his final score being eighty five not out, for whoever came and went, and come and go they did, he remained, like a rock against which the opposition hurled themselves in impotent rage. The final score read Low Cornhill eighty nine, High Cornhill one hundred and thirty six.

The host team took it with sportsman-like spirit and at the thrash afterwards their captain was effusive in his praise of their skill and tenacity. As the evening wore on and greater and greater quantities of ale were consumed in the bar of the Oak Tree, Charlie Gibson put a friendly arm around Bill Stobbart's shoulder and slurred, "H'way noo, Bill, come clean, bonny lad. Where'd y'get that new lad from, eh? Bloody secret weapon him, wasn' he'?"

Bill, his eyes red and his speech only slightly impaired, squinted back at him through a haze of cigarette smoke, "Ah honestly haven't got a clue, man, Charlie. Y'll need t'ask Davy, it was him as found 'im." So they called Davy over and asked him to explain his secret.

"No secret," replied Davy in all innocence. "He's stayin' at the Duck. All Ah know is that he's doin' summat at t'university this weekend."

"Aye, lucky f'r you lads, eh?" Charlie grinned ruefully, and he shrugged his large shoulders.

"Ah'll get him over an' y'can have a word," said Davy and raising his voice above the hubbub he called out, "Donald, come over here a minute, will you?"

Mr. Montgomery, in answer to the summons, thrust his way through the throng to his side. "Now then, Charlie," declared Davy with consummate pride, "this is th' lad that gave you a reet trouncing the day," he said proudly.

"Didn't he just," grimaced Charlie, sticking forth a huge paw. "Ah just wish it had been us y'were playin' for an' not this bunch. Y'certainly showed us how t'play cricket, an' nae mistake. Y've obviously played a bit, eh?"

"A little, a long time ago," Mr. Montgomery agreed modestly. It was a reply with which Charlie had to remain satisfied for his guest would in no way be drawn further.

About two weeks later Bill and Davy were enjoying a quiet pint together at one end of the bar of the 'Double Duck', the night being rather slow. It was here that Charlie Gibson found them. "Oh, be th' way," he said conversationally as Davy pulled him a pint, "Ah dug him out eventually. It took some doin' but Ah did it."

The friends looked completely blank, their facial expressions reflecting their obvious incomprehension.

"Found him, found who?" Davy ventured, frowning.

"Your academic friend, that's who," returned Charlie, wiping the foam from his upper lip with the back of his hand, "Mr. Donald Stewart Montgomery."

"Ah had no idea he was lost, Charlie, honest." Davy grinned benignly, wondering what the big man was driving at.

Charlie smiled slyly, his dark eyes alight, "Naw, but Ah bet y'knew that he was in Wisden though, eh?"

"Wisden?" Davy's jaw dropped.

"Aw, c'mon, man," the look Charlie threw him was evident of the fact that he thought he was having his leg pulled. All the while Bill kept his peace, leaving Davy to bear the brunt of a wave of scepticism which washed over his bar and threatened to drown him.

"Accordin' t'Wisden," Charlie growled, in an 'as if you didn't know' voice, "he played for Hampshire in th' early sixties from th' age of nineteen until he was invalided out o' the game wi' a knee injury at thirty two. He then resumed his academic career an' is now a professor o' some sort, er, microbiology Ah think..."

"Is that a fact," Bill said quietly, shaking his head in mock disbelief, a beatific smile spreading slowly across his features.

6

A Night in the Swan

"By, but it's busier than usual in here th' neet, Davy." Bill Stobbart had to shout to make himself heard above the din.

Davy grinned as he hurriedly pulled another pint. He wasn't averse to the decibel level; the more the merrier as far as he was concerned. He nodded to the other end of the bar. "It's mainly that noisy bunch, i'nt it," he replied, indicating the cricket team from which emanated roars of laughter and much ribaldry.

Picking up his pint Bill made to join them. Just as he sat down Bob Dixon began to relate a story about a parrot which went something like this:

A chap went into a pet shop to buy a parrot and was told that he could have this particular bird for about ten quid.

"Why so cheap?" he asked.

"Because," replied the pet shop man, "it has no legs."

"No legs?" said the prospective purchaser, "then how does it stay on its perch?"

"Well," said the pet shop man, conspiratorially, "it has an enormous organ which it wraps around the perch, like this, see."

"Ah," said the chap, enlightenment beginning to dawn, "and does it talk?"

"Loquaciously," confirmed its owner.

So the parrot was taken home and comfortably installed. The following day the chap returned from work and asked the parrot what sort of day it had had.

"Interesting," replied the parrot.

"How d'you mean?" the man asked.

"Well," the bird began, "after you had left for work this morning the milkman came in and started to remove all of your wife's clothes, piece by piece until she was completely naked."

"Really," said the man, "and what happened after he had done that?"

"Dunno," replied the parrot, "I fell off this bloody perch."

This induced further loud guffaws and when they had subsided Tom Dandridge, of blue pig fame, who had joined the party earlier in the evening, said, "Ah'll tell you a true story aboot a parrot," and, as Joe Freeman thrust another pint into his hand, he needed little further encouragement. "Do any o' you lads knaw the Blenkinsop's out at Grange Flatt farm?" he asked, by way of an introduction.

"You mean old Arthur Blenkinsop an' his missus, Jenny?" Bill said. "Aye, Ah know them. Not the cleanest people in the whole world."

"That's true mind." Tom, whose own background wasn't that pristine, agreed, nodding over his glass. "D'you knaw, Ah went in there one day an' they was burnin' a railway sleeper on the fire."

"Why, what's wrong wi' that?" someone asked.

"Man, they hadn't bothered to saw it up," Tom grinned. "They just stuck one end in th' grate an' the other on an owld pram an' as it burned doon they just shoved it further in."

It transpired that he had been given, in part payment of a debt, a handsome, white cockatoo with a large crest, cage and all. He hadn't the heart to refuse but what on earth he was going to do with a parrot he really had no idea.

His next call that same afternoon was at the Blenkinsop's which, because of its deplorable condition, wasn't exactly his favourite haunt. The yard was unpaved and a flock of scrawny chickens ran in and out of the farmhouse, scratching a living as best they could. He noted again that a cart, which had collapsed with a broken axle in Arthur Blenkinsops father's day was still in exactly the same position as it had always been.

"An' that must be more than forty year since, Ah'll bet," he mused. He looked around as he stopped his car and observed that the buildings were in the same state of disrepair as they were on his last visit, some six months previously. He cut the engine and stepped out, unwittingly placing his foot into a warm, wet cow pat which lay in wait for such a visitor as him.

"Aw, shit," he swore, which indeed is exactly what it was.

Scraping the odure from his boot he made his way to the front door of the dilapidated farmhouse, standing outside of which was a large, old fashioned and rusting refrigerator, about the same height as himself. He knew that it didn't work as the house hadn't the benefit of mains electricity but Jenny kept her few groceries in it anyway. She wouldn't have it in the house, though; it took up far too much room.

The door was eventually opened to his knock but not until after he had seen the yellowing net curtain at the window twitch in its usual manner. Mrs. Blenkinsop was a formidable woman; she would undoubtedly have been a formidable woman clean but, dressed as she was in tattered, filthy, cast off male clothing, only partly concealed by the ex-army greatcoat she wore tied at the waist with a large piece of baling twine, she was positively gargantuan.

"Afternoon, Jenny," Tom, being quite accustomed to the spectacle, was unmoved, "is Arthur aboot?"

"Oh, hello Thomas, it's y'sel," she always used his full Christian name. "Naw, he's not, he's away up yonder efter some beast. H'way in, man, an' Ah'll mek y'a brew."

The last thing he wanted was 'a brew' from Jenny's kitchen but he wasn't going to take the chance of offending her. So he followed her into a stone-flagged living room which was quite unique in terms of indescribable squalour. He had been in many a rough place, particularly in the army, but this, this was something else. His hostess grabbed two mugs from a table littered with dirty dishes, old pans with God knew what irridescing and mutating in the bottom of them, stacks of newspapers, empty tins, half eaten sandwiches and ancient loaves of bread which he swore could glow in the dark.

"Gerroff there!" Jenny screamed, taking a mighty back handed swipe at a chicken pecking away diligently at something interesting on the table top. Tom was fully aware that this was done merely in order to impress him and to engender a superficial air of civilisation; normally she wouldn't have bothered.

Over tea, sipped delicately from mugs that appeared not to have seen soap from the day they arrived, they chatted. "Be th' way, Jenny," said Tom, a sudden brainwave taking him by surprise, "would y'like a parrot?"

Slightly taken aback at the question, Jenny looked puzzled. Then she said brightly, "Naw, Ah don't think so, son. If we want a bird for oor dinner we just usually wring one o' them chickens'necks."

Tom shook his head in despair, laughing as he did so, "Naw, not t'eat," he said, "f'r a pet."

She frowned, her face settling into dirt encrusted creases, her simple mind struggling to cope with the thought of a pet and what that would entail, "Well," she began, "we've never had a pet afore, not as such, Ah mean, but, gan on then, let's have a look at it."

And so the deed was done and Tom off-loaded his parrot.

He never had occasion to call upon the Blenkinsops again until some eighteen months had passed, during which time the existence of his erstwhile feathered companion had been completely erased from his memory. However, one fine morning did find him once again in the familiar, dilapidated surroundings where he found the unsavoury couple together in the farmyard.

They were roping the kitchen table, upside down, onto the back of their old flatbed truck. Tom chatted to Jenny whilst Arthur, normally uncommunicative, carried on with his task. Although not wishing to display any undue curiosity, which might have given offence, Tom kept a careful eye upon the proceedings as Arthur nailed pig netting to all four legs, forming a secure enclosure, however temporary.

When he had done this he went into the nearest shed and returned, after much squealing and grunting, with two struggling, half grown piglets which he promptly threw over the netting and into his newly constructed pen. As he went to get a further pair of pigs his wife observed casually, as though using her kitchen table in this manner was the most commonplace occurrence, "He's off t'th' mart in a minnit."

As Arthur's old truck roared out of the yard in a haze of blue diesel fumes Tom was prompted to ask, "Be th' way, Jenny, how's th' parrot?"

"Aw, he's fine, man," she replied, "even though he's shrunk a bit. Come an' see."

Puzzled, Tom followed her into the living room which, as far as he could tell, hadn't changed at all, apart from the fact that everything that was once on the table now littered the floor.

In the dim half-light he could just make out the parrot's cage at the back of the room, but something seemed to him to be not quite right. As he moved closer he saw that the bird was standing on a pile of its own droppings which were so deep that its head was pressed against the top of the cage. In fact, it appeared to Tom that it was in grave danger of developing a hump on its back so great was the heap becoming. "H'way, Jenny," he protested, "gi' th' poor bloody thing a chance. Y'r s'posed t'clean th' cage out once in a while y'knaw......"

His hostess was unmoved, "Aye, aye. Ah was just gettin' aroond tae it," she said, "but there's that much hooswork t'dae aroond here, man, Ah've just nivvor had time."

"A humpy-backed parrot, eh," Bill laughed, as did they all at Tom's wry rendition of his tale, "well Ah've never heard the like."

During the general hubbub of more pints being ordered and new arrivals to the crowd being greeted, Gerry Dixon quietly left his seat and made his way to the kitchen. This was situated at the rear of the main building at the end of a narrow corridor. A door on the right, at the entrance to the passage, gave access to the gents toilets. He carefully opened the kitchen door and peered in. All was as usual in this kind of commercial establishment; that is to say that to the unpractised eye it looked complete chaos.

Glennis, a stray lock of blonde hair escaping from beneath her cap and falling over one eye, her complexion a delicate puce, masterminded the culinary activity at the griddle, where she was at pains to ensure that the five large steaks she was cooking were done to perfection.

In the meantime her small kitchen staff busied themselves frantically preparing salads, puddings or coffee whilst at the same time overseeing the deep fat fryer and the microwave ovens, of which there were three.

All of this young Gerald took in at a glance; no one had even bothered to look up from their allotted tasks so they completely failed to notice the small camera he slid surreptitiously from inside his jacket. Peering through the viewfinder he suddenly announced his presence with a "smile, please," and as Glennis looked up, startled, she screamed as the flash went off. "Gerry Dixon, I'll murder you, you,

you...." but she was too late as Mr. Dixon, grinning widely, had already vanished back to the bar.

"What's up wi' you, then?" his cousin, Bob, ventured as he resumed his seat, a wide smile still exercising his features

"Ah've just tekken Glennis's pitcher wi' this," he laughed out loud as he placed the small camera on the table.

"Oh, you'll be reet popular, you will," Davy chimed in, overhearing the remark from behind the bar. "Sh' doesn't like her photo took at the best o' times, Ah know, so you, Gerry Dixon, had better watch out, 'cos sh'll be out t'get her own back, you mark my words."

"Knaw," Glennis's tormentor replied with a grin, "sh'll just f'get aboot it now, until Ah show her th' pitcher Ah took, that is," he concluded, his cronies joining in his laughter.

His assumption couldn't have been further from the truth for even as he spoke Glennis was plotting her revenge.

Davy knew his wife very well. She had already despatched Lilian, her right hand girl, upstairs to fetch her own camera. She then issued instructions to her loyal followers to keep their eyes on the corridor whilst carrying out their normal duties and the instant they spied Mr. Dixon heading for the gents, they were to inform her.

About an hour later they were still on watch, "Goodness, how much can he consume and still sit there," Lilian, a certain admiration creeping into her voice, whispered to herself, and then, more loudly, as she continued to peer around the door, "Glennis, Glennis, he's comin', he's just goin' into th' gents now."

"Good," replied her employer, her lips set in a straight line. No sooner had the subject of their careful observation disappeared into the toilet than she quickly stepped through the door leading from the kitchen into the back yard. A large, rectangular window, appropriately glazed with modesty in mind, overlooked this area from the toilet and this she used to her advantage.

It was quite dark by this time and as she crept out into the night she could see her adversary's silhouette outlined against the glass. Creeping up to the windowsill she cried, "Gerry, smile please." At the same time she pressed the button on the top of the camera. In the darkness the resulting coruscation was brilliant in the extreme, illuminating the entire area for the briefest of seconds. There came a very satisfying roar from the interior of the gents as she ran back into the kitchen. She had only just returned to the safety of her own domain when the door leading to the bar burst open.

Framed within it stood Gerry, his face suffused with both embarrassment and fury, the twin emotions rendering his features a hot, dark crimson whilst a large, compromising stain spread down the front of his trousers. "Look what y've done woman," he yelled, wild-eyed, "Ah've pissed mesel'."

Glennis, shrieking with laughter, collapsed helplessly against the wall as she pointed a shaking finger in the general direction of his fly. Her staff, following her example, staggered about or clung to one another whilst the tears rolled uncontrollably down their cheeks.

Eventually, when a semblance of order had been restored and he thought that he had endured enough, he said plaintively, "Okay, okay, y've had y'r fun. Now can Ah get oot th' back way so Ah can nip home an' get changed."

"Not on your life, Gerry Dixon," Glennis said firmly, placing her significant frame between him and sanctuary, "you can go out th' front like everybody else."

"How can Ah go out there lookin' like this, have a heart," he squeaked, his voice rising to a falsetto in his exasperation.

"Oh, alright then," she appeared to relent as she stepped away from the door. He had taken but one step towards it before he was brought up short by her restraining hand upon his chest. The other she held out to him, palm upwards. "Ah, ah, th' camera, if y'please." She couldn't help but allow a note of triumphant glee to creep into her voice.

He ran his fingers through his hair in agitation, "Ah haven't got it, Ah left it in the bar," he groaned.

Glennis nodded to Lilian who quickly retrieved the offending article. "Right, now hop it and don't play tricks like that on a defenceless Yorkshirewoman again."

Gerry shot through the door and into the haven of the night as Glennis stood aside. "Defenceless, my arse," he thought as their laughter followed him out of the yard.

The only person who seemed to notice that it had taken Gerry an inordinately long time to pass water was Davy, who spied him coming back into the pub through the front door. "Bin out f'r some fresh air?" he enquired in all innocence.

Gerry's grin was sheepish, "Nope, Ah've had t'go home," and he related the tale of how Glennis had got one over on him.

"Aye, well, y'can't say as y'weren't warned," Davy replied with a sympathetic smile as he pulled yet another pint, "sh's a terrible woman t'mess wi' an' Ah sh'ld knaw, we've bin married f'r thirty-two year.

Aye," he continued philosophically as he handed Gerry the foaming glass, "th' only other love in me life were motorbikes an' Ah've had some good 'uns in me time, Nortons, Triumphs, AJS, you name 'em an' Ah've owned 'em. But y'knaw," he went on, warming to his theme, "th' best bike Ah ever rode was an old 250 BSA."

"Oh," Gerry said, only mildly interested.

"Aye," Davy nodded, smiling happily as he recalled the long lost days of his youth.

"Reet, Ah'll tek it," said the young man, holding out his hand.

They shook on the deal and Davy, extremely pleased with his first sale said, "If y'come back this afternoon wi' th' cash Ah'll make sure that she's all ready for you." With that he returned to the office which he shared with his manager and two other salesmen. "Well that's th' fust one, then Ted," he exclaimed delightedly.

The manager, a large man with a florid face and white hair, looked up from where he was poring over paperwork at his desk, "Good," he replied encouragingly, "let's hope it's the first o' many, eh? Incidentally," he enquired conversationally, returning to his books so that Davy was looking at the top of his head, "what did y'have t'give?"

Davy frowned, puzzled, "What d'you mean?" he asked.

Ted looked up quickly and pursed his lips, "Ah mean," he replied heavily, "what did y'have t'give t'get th' deal?"

Still unsure of his ground, Davy bit his lip, "Well er, nothing," he replied hesitantly.

Ted was unconvinced, and it showed, "You sure?" he looked sideways at his young employee. "No discounts, free gifts, part exchanges, etc. etc.?"

"Oh," replied Davy, his face brightening, "Ah took a motorbike in part exchange."

Ted nodded, sighing resignedly; he had seen all of these young eager beavers before. He had, in fact, been one himself once. "You may not have noticed, son," he said, "It being only your second day an' all that, but it's cars we sell in this showroom, not bloody motorbikes." But as Davy's face fell, he relented a little, "So what is it an' how much did y'give f'r it?"

Somewhat subdued now, his enthusiasm faltering, Davy mumbled, "It's a 250 Beezer an' Ah gave fifteen quid f'r it."

Ted laughed and the tension eased, "Well, Ah s'pose that's not so bad then, but y'll have t'get rid of it y'rself so Ah suggest that y'ride it over t'th' auction at Leeds on Saturday morning an' dump it."

So it was that on the following Saturday Davy duly climbed aboard his newly acquired steed and, giving the kick start a hefty thump, he was surprised to discover that it fired up immediately.

However, it took him very little time to realise that as he proceeded westwards towards Leeds that the engine, situated as it was between his legs, was very much offbeat. Instead of operating with a healthy roar the piston seemed to traverse the cylinder, within which it was, of course, permanently confined, with an asthmatic shudder.

This unusual aberration, at speeds over fifteen miles per hour, set up a vibration which threatened to loosen his back teeth. So intent was he on keeping the machine on the road, whilst at the same time focusing his shuddering vision and hanging onto the madly vibrating handlebars, that he failed to notice the effect that the machine was having in the general direction of his loins.

Until, that is, the pressure on his flies became almost unbearable. "My God," he said to himself, rather shocked, as he closed the throttle and looked down, "Ah can't ride all th' way t' Leeds in this sort o' state. Ah'll need t'stop an' get sorted out."

He waited patiently until everything had subsided and returned to normal before setting forth once more. But, being just a young lad, and healthy at that, it wasn't very long before the motor cycle's vibrations began to have the same effect thus forcing a premature halt once again. So in this stop/go manner he finally arrived at the auctions, much disconcerted.

He was waiting at the bus stop for the return bus to York when, as luck would have it, the owner of his place of employment passed in his Jaguar. Recognising his newest employee, he stopped his car and offered a lift, which was gratefully accepted.

His employer, a bluff genial man in his late sixties opened the conversation in the usual manner. "So what were you doin' in Leeds this mornin', then?" he asked.

Davy told him and explained about the motorbike.

"What," said his boss, "an' y've let a good bike like that go f'r next t'nowt at th' auction. We'd better get it back," he grinned, "Ah could do wi' summat like that meself, at my age."

Gerry was suitably amused at the tale, "Ah can see what y'meant, about it bein' th' best bike y'ever rode," he chuckled.

"Aye," his host replied, his grey eyes twinkling mischievously behind his glasses, "An' Ah know what my owld boss meant an' all now," he said.

The hour was well past midnight but there were still a few hard-core drinkers left at the end of the bar when Andy, Davy's son and cellarman, unbolted the front door in order that Tom Dandridge could be poured out into the night. He had only opened the door a crack when he suddenly slammed it shut again, his face aghast.

"Whasamarra, son?" Tom slurred, almost losing the end of his nose in the door, "Ah'll need t'be gerrin' home. Th' missus'll be gannin' daft be noo......." His memory when drunk was extremely questionable for he had never married.

Cutting him short Andy grabbed him by the arm and propelled him back into the bar. As he re-entered the room his father took one look at his face and asked, "What's up?"

"Bloody jam san'wich, that's what's up," his son replied in terse, quiet tones. A 'jam sandwich' was the local term for a county patrol car, the sort with a large yellow stripe running along the side.

"Where?" enquired Davy urgently whilst at the same time turning to the last of the late night revellers. "C'mon, now lads, drink up. Get them bloody glasses off my bar. You heard what th' lad said, th' bloody law's outside."

There was a sudden draining of glasses and a concerted rush for the toilets as his words hit home. Andy took another look through a chink in the heavy curtains and groaned at what he saw. "He's right outside, facin' th' pub with his headlights flashin' an' the blue light goin' round an' round," he let the curtain fall back into place. "Ah think it's a raid, Dad. What th' hell are we goin' t'do?"

"Get rid o' this lot out th' back way f'r a start," his father replied quickly, "even if it does mean them walkin' home over th' fields," and he started towards the gents. He was stopped short as a thunderous hammering threatened to cave the front door in. "Aw, God, it's too late," he groaned. "Y'd better let them in, lad," and he braced himself for the inevitable.

With a sinking feeling in the pit of his stomach Andy went to do his father's bidding. As he unbolted the door for the second time in as many minutes it was suddenly thrust aside and he was confronted by the hugely grinning and bearded face of Graham Henshaw, the local police patrolman, "Evenin' Andy," he bellowed, for he was not renowned for his reticence. "Ah thowt Ah'd just pop up an' let y'have a look at me new patrol car. A beauty, i'nt she?"

"Henshaw, you, you, bastard," Andy ground out through clenched teeth, "y've just about given me father an' me a bleedin' heart attack apiece."

"Why?" bellowed Graham, his large frame seeming to fill the empty bar, "There's nobody here who's drinkin' after time noo, is there? Why, what have we here?" he chortled, leaning an elbow on the counter, "not members o' our illustrious cricket team hidin' in th' bogs?" as, one by one, the members referred to appeared, like rats from a hole, looking entirely sober, and very sheepish.

"Er, well, Graham, it's like this y'see...." Davy began but Graham cut him short.

"Say no more, landlord," he boomed, holding up a large hand, palm outwards, as if in benediction, "Ah can see y've been holdin' a private party, just a few friends like, an' what's wrong wi' that y'might ask?"

"Aye, aye, that's th' way it was," Gerry Dixon agreed eagerly as he vainly attempted to prop up the cattle dealer, who, of all them, was quite beyond caring who it was that had descended upon them so suddenly, having passed out completely some minutes before.

As the large policeman left Andy whispered to him as he opened the front door, "Don't think y've heard th' last o' this you blue arsed bugger. Ah'll get you back, just see if Ah don't," and he closed the portal finally on a bellow of laughter and a flashing blue light.

It wasn't until several weeks had passed that Andy was able to exact his revenge for the fright he and his father had been given but the policeman did eventually appear, having reserved a table for a night out with friends.

Andy returned a pile of empty plates to the kitchen and grinned broadly at his mother as he placed them in the sink. Recognising the smile she asked suspiciously, "What have you been up to now?"

Her son laughed quietly, "Ah've just locked Henshaw in the gents," he said, "t'pay him back for what he did to us th' other night."

Davy had recently installed a brass bolt on the outside of the gents' toilet door as a precaution against any intruders getting into the bar from that direction. Glennis was about to remonstrate with her son and suggest that he release what after all was a paying customer when Graham's voice boomed out behind her, "By, Glennis, that was a smashin' steak. Definitely up t'your usual standard."

Andy's jaw dropped, "How, how...?" he began but thought better of it and went to survey the suspected damage. As he had surmised, the big policeman had wrenched open the door in his usual manner, completely unaware that it had been bolted from the other side.

The bolt, ripped from its fastenings, hung forlornly by one last screw. "Aw, Ah give up," Andy moaned and went to resume his duties behind the bar.

7

All God's Creatures

James and John Bishop were two elderly brothers who kept a smallholding of about eight or ten acres a little over a mile from the boundary of High Cornhill. They had never married, preferring instead to remain true to their bachelor existence.

In fact James, the elder, and smaller of the two, was an avowed misogynist with a sour disposition, a man who was quite happy, for the most part, to keep his neighbours well away from his front door. His brother on the other hand was a gentle, unassuming man who, as he had done all of his life, allowed himself to be ruled completely by his autocratic sibling.

They weren't exactly friendless but the number of people who were of a sufficiently steely nature to withstand James' withering sarcasm and caustic tongue were, needless to say, few and far between.

They didn't socialise but about once a week John could be spied tramping the road to Low Cornhill, his shopping bag on his arm, for the few provisions they required from day to day. Very occasionally a scattering of local children would pluck up sufficient courage to call, particularly on a warm summer's evening and John would delight them all by sitting on the door step and playing his piano accordion, for he was in fact a renowned musician and had played at many a ceilidh in his earlier years.

They eked out a living by keeping pigs, chickens and a few rabbits. They also grew their own vegetables in a large plot at the back of the house and sold the surplus, which kept them in tobacco and the occasional dram.

Their main source of income, however, was horses, as they kept a number of quality brood mares and had, over the years, gained an enviable reputation as breeders of bloodstock. They also bought and sold horses and could often be seen at the sales bidding for any likely nag that they felt they might be able to turn a bob or two on.

James stormed into the house one morning, his normal sour expression contorted with fury and his small, wiry frame convulsed with anger. He tore the greasy cap he wore from his head, exposing a shining bald pate, and hurled it across the room, narrowly missing his brother's nose. John looked up from the paper he was reading, his expression one of mild concern; he was accustomed to his brother's sudden and explosive rages. "What's up?" he asked.

"What's up, what's bloody up?" James snarled in his rasping voice, lips drawn back, exposing broken, yellowing teeth. "That bloody cockerel, that's what's up. Look at this," and he pulled up the right leg of his dungarees to show a skinny white calf with two red punctures in the flesh that were just beginning to turn red and ooze blood.

John scratched an eyebrow, "Got y'agin, 'as he?" he quoth laconically, stating the obvious.

"Aye, he might 'ave," James snarled in response, "but Ah'm goin' t'mek sure it'll be his last. Where's that bloody gun?" and he yanked open the door to the understairs cupboard where they kept the family shotgun.

"Ah've hidden it," confessed John calmly, laying down his paper.

"Hidden it, what th' hell for?" James's anger became boundless, the colour rising in his cheeks and his flinty blue eyes flashing sparks.

"Because," responded his brother heavily, "Ah knew that it would come t'this one day an' that you might be tempted t'do summat y'd regret. We're all God's creatures, James an....."

"Be damned t'hell an' back again f'r th' auld woman that y'are," roared James suddenly, frustrated. "If Ah canna get it wi' th' gun Ah'll wring it's damn' neck," and he shot back out into the yard again, slamming the door hard behind him.

John took up his paper again, knowing that he had not long to wait. The cockerel, a large, white bird was the feathered equivalent of his brother; the exact match both in temperament and personality. The only difference being that James hadn't been known to attack anyone physically, although if you had been on the receiving end of one of his verbal harangues it certainly felt like it. About fifteen minutes later an exhausted figure staggered into the living room, narrow little chest heaving, and collapsed into the only easy chair.

"Y'll gi' y'sel a heart attack, man, if y'keep this up," John commented from behind his newspaper. He rose from the table and crossed the room to the range. "Y'll be wantin' a cup o' tea after all that, Ah s'pose?" His mild manner never appeared to alter no matter what histrionics his brother seemed to perform and as he had grown accustomed to them over the last sixty-five years he was by now singularly unimpressed. He did however admit to himself that his brother had a point as he had been attacked at the rate of about two or three times a week. Their white cockerel, seemingly, bore a grudge against the whole world and he had made James the main object of his one-bird vendetta.

They had raised this particular feathered fiend themselves from a chick and it soon became apparent that it was far more than a mere barnyard fowl, being one part vulture, one part golden eagle and one part bushwacker. It claimed the whole of their land as its domain and it had a nasty habit of lying-up in clumps of stinging nettles, under bramble thickets, behind trees and then, when it was least expected, it would leap out to the attack, sinking its long, vicious spurs into whatever part of the anatomy was nearest. Ben, the poor old Welsh sheepdog, was a favourite target of this unprincipled assassin and he daily lived in mortal fear of his life, slinking about with one eye over his shoulder and his tail between his legs.

"Ah knew y'wouldn't catch it," said John, handing his brother a steaming mug, "so Ah don't know why y'bother."

James accepted the tea, noisily drawing in air with the first mouthful. "Ah'll get it one o' these damn' days, you mark me words. Just let it ambush me once more, that's all," he said, his eyes glinting with the thought of revenge.

John shook his head sadly, "We're all God's creatures, James an' he deserves his place on earth th' same as you an' me."

"Aye, that's as mebbe," James returned sardonically, "but Ah'll stop 'is clock f'r 'im one o' these days an' that's f'r sure."

He had never really agreed with his brother's religious principles putting them down to the fact that he had always, even as a boy, been a somewhat sickly creature and he felt that he used his religion as a crutch. He couldn't deny, however, the strength that his brother seemed to gain from his faith. He, on the other hand, had always relied upon himself, being totally self contained and self sufficient, needing no one. It had been James alone who had carried them through their worst moments such as when both parents had died within a year of each other leaving them destitute and in danger of losing their home. That had been over fifty years ago but ever since John had relied upon his brother for all things, always sheltering in his shadow.

The following morning John arose a little later than usual. He had not had a good night and as he came downstairs he heard James, who was already up, busily raking out the ashes of the fire and putting the kettle to boil. He looked up as his brother entered the living room and, although he made no comment, he was concerned at what he saw. John, panting slightly with the exertion of descending the stairs sat down heavily on the nearest kitchen chair, his face grey.

"Y'don't look so grand this mornin'," James said, keeping his tone light in order to cover his concern. "Not had a good night?"

"Aw, Ah'll be alright, soon as Ah've had a cup o' tea." John dismissed James' query with a frown.

And so it turned out for within half an hour he was feeling remarkably improved; so much so in fact that, breakfast over, he announced that he would collect the morning's eggs. He picked up the collecting basket and was soon busy filling it with the warm produce of about two dozen chickens, which had been laid conveniently in the large henhouse in a double row of nesting boxes, the previous occupants of which were, by now, scratching around contentedly in the sun- dappled enclosure.

Having nearly filled the basket with the morning's offerings he proceeded next door to the smaller henhouse. This was very low and cramped and had been erected originally only as temporary accommodation; the intention being that they would dispose of it when they extended the larger henhouse. Needless to say this had never been done so every morning John had to bend his back and practically crawl into this secondary chicken coop. So intent upon his task was he that he completely failed to notice the cockerel which had taken up an ambush position in a nearby clump of nettles. The sight of John's unprotected posterior framed in the henhouse doorway was a target that was just too tempting to resist and so, without a sound, the barnyard bruiser leapt forward, wings flapping and savagely sunk needlesharp talons deep into his supposed enemy's backside. Shocked beyond belief, his unfortunate victim cannoned forward and landed face downward in his basket of eggs. At the same time his head came into sharp contact with the row of nesting boxes bringing a further cascade of eggs down upon the back of his neck, covering him in yellow yolk and eggshells.

His brother had observed the whole unhappy incident through the kitchen window and, rather than offer assistance, he dived into the understairs cupboard and pulled out the shotgun. He had discovered it some days previously hidden under a pile of bedding at the back. He loaded the weapon and stepped outside, his face grim. John hauled himself wearily to his feet, egg yolk and chicken manure dripping down his face and caking his hair, eyes protruding owlishly from a sticky mask of the stuff.

The cockerel in the meantime, extremely proud of its small victory, had flown to the roof of the large henhouse, and was strutting its stuff and crowing wildly, wings outstretched and with its neck craned heavenwards, a confident image of total triumphalism. It was about to let forth with yet another scream of unmitigated delight when James let it have it, with both barrels.

It met its extremely sudden and ignominious end in mid-crow, disappearing in a cloud of white feathers and landing flat on its back at the other side of its former home. Feathers that had once adorned its proudly pouting chest now floated slowly to the ground in a minor blizzard. In the silence that followed the explosion John sadly admonished his brother, "Aw, man, y'shouldn' ha' done that," he said, with a sorrowful shake of his head.

"Ah knaw, Ah knaw," James snarled in reply, "y'don't have t'tell me, we're all God's creatures," and he went inside and slammed the door.

As may have been gathered, John wasn't one for complaining, no matter how ill he felt and at times he felt very ill indeed; rheumatic fever as a child had left him with a weakened heart. So when in the the morning his brother arose and found him sitting in the easy chair next to the fire place he was immediately aware that something was seriously wrong.

"Eh, what's this then, couldn't sleep?" he enquired, frowning.

John's gaze was wan, his complexion waxen and he returned his brother's gaze through tired eyes, "Knaw, Ah was feelin' a bit poorly in th' night an' Ah thought Ah'd be better off in th' chair be th' fire."

"Man, y'look terrible." James's concern was genuine and not

misplaced for indeed his brother had the look of death about him; his cheeks and eyes so sunken that his face was practically skull-like.

"Ah'll make y'a cup o' tea then Ah'm away f'r th' doctor." He placed the kettle on the embers as he spoke and then bustled about the room setting out two mugs on the table. He heard John give a deep sigh behind him but thought little of it. Turning away from the table he leant forward to pick the now boiling kettle from the fire. As he did so he gazed directly into his brother's lifeless face, the light fading from his eyes. He left the kettle as it was, oblivious to the steam pouring from the spout. Reaching out a gnarled hand he gently gripped John's shoulder as if by the contact he might rekindle his waning spirit, but it was not to be. "If anybody was one o' God's creatures, bonny lad," he whispered sadly, "it was you."

8

Hell Hath No Fury

It was early autumn when Katherine first arrived in the village as a young bride and the hedgerows were hung with that season's rich fruits. Blackberries, hips and haws were abundant and all around her the fields were alive as the country folk worked to gather in the last of the harvest.

The cottage that she and her new husband, Paul, had bought was tiny, just two up and two down but, all being well, they planned to enlarge it when they could afford to. They had bought it primarily for its potential. Paul was training to be a solicitor in Durham and he had all of the ambition and drive that seemed to be intrinsic to his profession. They were very happy: in fact, the first ten years of their marriage, she had to admit, were blissful. But that was so long ago now, a lifetime and a war away and things had changed. Those who still remembered them spoke of them but occasionally, and then only in whispers and in dark corners.

She stepped out of the big cast iron bath tub and reached for the large white towel that she had hung on the back of the door. Behind her the water gurgled musically as it whirled its way into nothingness. She wrapped herself in the towel's enfolding warmth, revelling in the sensuality of it, curling her toes against the bathroom rug upon which she stood. She slowly began to rub herself all over, feeling her skin begin to glow. When the water's wet sleekness had been dried from her body she let the towel slip to the floor and gazed at her reflection in the full length mirror.

Her image gazed back sadly, the eyes large and rather mournful betraying in retrospect the merest hint of the girl she had once been. Her hair was still thick and dark, its natural curl buoyant with hardly any grey. "I've been lucky with that," she thought as she ran her fingers through it, tossing it lightly. As she raised her arms she noticed that the flesh beneath them was just beginning to sag a little. "Hmm, little wonder," she murmured, "at forty-eight." Turning sideways she turned her critical eye upon her profile, examining the line of her breasts. "Not too bad there anyway," she nodded approvingly, "and the stomach's still flat enough." She dressed slowly, her thoughts wandering like flotsam caught in a tide, "If that's not a sign of advancing years, I don't know what is," she warned herself, shaking a mental finger. She was startled out of her reverie by the sound of her husband's voice, its tone peevish, calling up the stairs.

"Katherine, Katherine. Are you ready yet? If you don't get a move on we'll be late."

She pulled a face, muttering, "I don't know why we have to go to this party. He never seems to really enjoy himself and I'm the one that usually ends up apologising." They had been invited to dinner at the 'big house', as she referred to it, the Maddisons, one of Paul's major clients. She never wanted to go with him these days; she had had enough over the years of his drunken sarcasm and mean temper. He changed when he had had a drink and his drinking had become gradually worse until now there seemed hardly a night went by but that he wasn't either out at the pub or drinking in the house. Either way, it usually amounted to the same thing, unless he passed out first; a row and tears caused by his bitter tongue. She hated him for it. Sighing, she switched off the light and picking up her wrap from the bannister she walked slowly down the stairs.

Dinner at the Maddisons was always a somewhat grand affair, with rather too many guests for it ever to be considered intimate. But Deborah Maddison was an exceptional hostess who took a great deal of care over the lavishness and variety of her menus. Her husband, Freddie, a self made and very successful entrepreneur, paid equal attention to the content of his cellar, which was his pride and joy. He could, unfortunately, be the most monumental bore on the subject of wine, however. A fault his friends seemed to forgive him gladly, largely due to the quality of his hospitality.

It was beginning to get late. The evening had been convivial and the pace leisurely and now neckties and waistcoats were beginning to be loosened as the liberal flow of liqueurs and spirits began to have a noticeable effect. Katherine found herself trapped by a garrulous and slightly inebriated solicitor who proceeded to extol the many virtues of the Bahamas where he had recently spent his honeymoon.

Paul, much as she had anticipated, had deserted her earlier in the evening and she saw him now, hands gesticulating fiercely, at the other end of the drawing room involved in what appeared to be an increasingly heated argument with their host. Seeing the signs and realising the dangers she graciously extricated herself from the verbal clutches of her companion, practically stopping him in mid-flow, and glided gracefully across to her spouse. Taking him by the elbow and mustering her sweetest smile for the benefit of their host she said, "I think it's time we went home, Paul, don't you?"

Angry as he was, her presence appeared to fuel his anger further, taking her completely by surprise. "Why th' hell can't you just leave me alone, just for once, woman?" he hurled at her, his face red. As he spoke he shook off her restraining hand violently, pushing her backwards and causing her to lose her balance. In a panic-stricken attempt to save herself from falling, Katherine made a despairing grab for the sideboard next to her.

Her effort went unrewarded as her fingers made contact with a tray of drinks and glasses which she swept to the floor as she fell. The resulting crash was awe-inspiring but the sudden silence that followed it was worse: it was deafening. She rose slowly to her feet, her face set in an emotionless mask, and with dignity preceding her every step, she left the room, looking to neither right nor left, leaving her husband to apologise for the debacle.

The short walk home past the Swan and across the green was made in total silence; her cold anger and his guilt working hand-in-hand to reinforce the barrier that had become so much a part of their lives. She knew now that, finally, she had reached the end of their journey together. Whatever love she once bore him had totally and irrevocably turned to ashes in her mouth. It wasn't until they were safely inside their own home, in their bedroom to be precise, that Paul began to mumble a half-hearted apology.

"Don't," Katherine hissed at him through clenched teeth, "there is nothing that you can say that will ever erase the indignity of this evening from my mind. It was shameful, humiliating and, and I hate you for it."

She sat down upon the bed and gazed around her helplessly, her mind a whirlpool of pain and despair. Vaguely, she saw all of her familiar things; the furniture, her dressing table adorned with the usual intimate female prerequisites, the pictures, the ornaments but mainly she saw the books - stacked in piles around the walls. It was Paul's all-consuming passion.....collecting books, which he stored wherever he could find a space. Passion was something that was lacking in her own life; not that she wasn't warm, not that she couldn't be aroused, as now, but these last few years Paul had grown colder and, as she confided to her friends sadly, he had all of the sexual sophistication of a small dog.

All of these thoughts ran unbidden through her mind in the few seconds that she sat there and merely served to exacerbate her ire. Suddenly, she swooped down upon the nearest pile of books and picking up two of them she hurled them at his head, screaming, "I hate you, you bastard. Just get the hell out of my life." Then she flung herself face down upon the bed and lost herself in a storm of weeping.

The following weeks were sheer hell, for neither of them was willing to make amends to any degree. They lived their lives apart, Paul having moved into the guest room, and spoke to each other only when absolutely necessary. Their estrangement was complete.

Katherine had been making plans to leave for some time and had eventually decided to move nearer her sister, her only living relative, who lived in Scotland. Having made up her mind to go she still hoped that they might at least part as friends, although in moments of lucidity she was prone to admit the idea's hopelessness, Paul by now having become more or less completely withdrawn, spending most of his spare time with his books and his whisky. Indeed, he had even begun to turn the smallest first floor bedroom into a library, something which he had been promising to do for years.

A week or so before the date of her planned departure Katherine, overcome with curiosity, decided to investigate the extent of her husband's endeavours during his absence. She entered what had once been the playroom and found it totally transformed. The walls were completely covered in heavy oak panelling. The single window had also been panelled over, blocking out all natural light and creating a womb-like ambience. She gently closed the door behind her and noticed that it closed with a solid thump. She felt entombed; all extraneous sounds were completely absent. The room had been soundproofed. She reached behind her in the darkness and switched on the light. The shelves lining the walls were empty, awaiting their final accolade, the preservation of a decade's diligence.

The solitary, deep buttoned leather armchair, beside which stood a small table with a reading lamp, gazed back at her silently. She sat down slowly as the realisation finally struck home; this was a space in which she had no part, in which she could not share, "Rather like this marriage," she thought bitterly. When the tears did come they came slowly at first and then in a torrent until she was certain that the sounds of her agony could be heard throughout the house. But nothing penetrated the graveyard silence.

Four days later her suitcase was packed and she was ready to leave. Standing sadly in the quiet hallway she gazed about her, "Twenty-two years," she thought, "and for what?" Only the gentle tick of the hall clock answered her. Slowly, as she stood among the ashes of her marriage, she allowed the flame of her anger to intensify, burgeoned as it was by her bitterness.

The memories washed over her but they weren't memories born of happiness, as she felt they should have been. Instead she recalled the arguments, the humiliation heaped upon her by her husband's often loutish and drunken behaviour and the deep sadness that had permeated the last few years. Gathering her resolve and with her mouth set in a hard line she took a step towards the staircase at the top of which she knew her husband sat in his room among his books. Slowly and reluctantly she began the final ascent to say goodbye.

She reached the door and knocked. There was no reply. She tried turning the handle but it wouldn't yield; it had been locked from the inside. She called out softly, "Paul", and then louder, "Paul", but the heavy portal remained dumb, the new dead lock gleaming like a brassy eye. She felt defeated.

Her anger suddenly fanned itself into fury, "To hell with you, then," she thought and walked along the corridor to her own bedroom. Without quite knowing why and in complete command of her emotions, she opened a drawer in her dressing table and removed the key that she found there. She returned to what was now the library and inserted it into the old original mortice lock; Paul hadn't seen fit to remove it during his alterations. The sound of it turning was the most satisfying sound of her life. The telephone began to ring as she descended the stairs but she ignored it. Slipping the key into her pocket she left the house for good.

9

Not in my Backyard.

The 'Not in my Backyard' syndrome or nimby, as it is known, that has dominated British social life in recent years, whether it be concerned with bail hostels, homes for the mentally ill, nuclear waste dumps or incinerators is, to a very large extent, based upon fear; fear of the unknown and uncertainty as to how these measures may impact upon individual lives and futures.

It was not so as far as the residents of High Cornhill were concerned. Their nimby culture was based upon nothing more than sheer bloody mindedness and an inherent dislike of authority.

"Bill, do me a favour will you, an' get some glasses in from outside?" Davy and his staff were distinctly harassed this warm August evening as the 'Double Duck' was full to bursting. In fact it was positively overflowing, with people sitting on the benches in the late evening sunshine and spilling onto the village green. Bill did as he was asked; always willing to help a friend in need was Bill.

"Y'knaw Davy," he voiced an opinion on his return, a stack of empty glasses in each hand, "Ah swear this place gets busier ev'ry year. Each summer seems t'bring in more an' more visitors. Ah swear Ah look for'ard t'th' winter when we can get the place t'oursel's again."

"Aye, it's alreet f'r th' likes o' you, me friend," Davy replied sardonically, "but Ah've got t'grab a livin' when Ah can. So let them all come, the more th' merrier. Yes sir?" He turned away from his conversation to serve yet another thirsty customer.

It did appear, however, that Bill was right in his assumption and that from June onwards the flow of summer visitors increased steadily, particularly at weekends.

The stream of ramblers and walkers, cyclists and tourists shattered the normal calm, peaceful existence with the steady tramp of their booted feet and the roar of their internal combustion engines. A great deal of the attraction lay with the village's location, set as it was in the heart of the Durham countryside, and the spectacular views it commanded. But, there was no getting away from the fact that the pub and its incipient hospitality was also a great draw and they came from far and near to sample its many delights.

The short term influx of so great a number of people began to have a noticeable effect upon the local plumbing, which simply wasn't designed to cope with such crowds. In fact, the only public loo there was as such was in the pub itself and at times queues would magically appear and bodies would line the corridor walls as though waiting to make confession.

At a corner of the village green stood a wartime relic; a reminder of days gone by when this little island stood alone against the might of Hitler's armies. It was a concrete pill box or machine gun nest and it commanded the junction of the two small roads that ran through the village. Obviously some bygone planner in his wisdom must have thought that should we ever have been invaded by the mightiest army in the world at that time then it was clearly destined to be stopped dead in its tracks by this sole means of defence. It had long since been made redundant and bricked up and was completely ignored by everyone. However, its day of glory was not yet over; the local planning authority were about to see to that.

Lizzie Donkin was, to put it kindly, an exceedingly curious woman, in both the pragmatic and the arcane sense of the word. Curiosity was both her strength and her weakness. In fact, had she been a cat instead of an old woman, she would undoubtedly have succumbed to the usual, well-worn maxim.

She had lived in the village all of her life and brought up a large brood of children. A widow now, her family grown and left, she had time on her hands and she filled her days by intelligence gathering. She was a woman who liked to know what was going on. She had a particular regard for 'them buggers up at opp'n cast,' referring to the systematic rape of the landscape that was happening just over two miles away.

She had already crossed swords with them when they had applied for planning permission to liberate coal from fields at the rear of her cottage. She had heard a whisper on the wind and had raised the alarm, organising protest meetings and had generally stirred up such a hornet's nest that the company had, in the end, come to the decision that the game just wasn't worth the candle and had given in.

This hadn't satisfied Lizzie, however, for she was fully aware that if they thought that they could get away with it they would try again elsewhere. She had learned from past experience that forewarned is forearmed so she kept a watchful and careful eye upon the local planning register.

It was during one of her periodic visits to the planning office that, whilst leafing through the most recent records, her eye fell upon an entry that immediately aroused her curiosity. "So that's what they think they're goin' t'dae, is it?" she thought to herself. "Ower my deid body," and she hurried off home to relight the beacon of protest.

That night in the pub, where most of the village had gathered in response to Lizzie's clarion call, the talk was all of rights and protest and general disapproval.

"Ah divn't care if they cover it in gowld leaf, we aren't havin' it here." Big Jack Lawson was adamant.

His near neighbour, Miss Jennings, a strait-laced, priggish and somewhat intolerant schoolteacher with whom he had been known to have certain disagreements in the past, spoke up. "I agree entirely. Speaking personally I would feel affronted having to look upon that, that, monstrosity from my sitting room window. I mean, what would my guests think?" and her eyes glinted with the light of battle from behind large, protective lenses.

And so the discussion went on back and forth, uniting friend and foe alike in common cause until finally Bill spoke up having, in his usual quiet manner, listened carefully to everything before venturing his own opinion.

"Well," he began, "it appears that we are all, more or less, agreed. We don't want it here. But the question is, what are we goin' t'do about it?" He threw the query across the room where it was taken up in a general chorus of suggestions, the loudest emanating from Big Jack Lawson who was all for 'burnin' th' bloody plannin' offices doon.' He was renowned as something of a hothead.

Davy raised his hands in a calming gesture, "Hold on, hold on, everybody. Just a minnit, will you?" Eventually, having reduced the decibel level to a dull roar, he turned to Bob Dixon. "You work at the council offices, Bob. Can't you put a word in f'r us?"

Bob shrugged his shoulders, "Ah'll try, o' course but Ah must warn y'that once them daft beggars have made up their minds, it's hard t'shift 'em." His tone was not at all hopeful.

"Aye, point taken, but y'll have a go, eh?" Davy asked.

Bob nodded.

"Just you tell 'em from us, Bob," it was Big Jack from the back of the room, "we'll hae nae public piss hoose on our village green, an' they can mak their minds up t'that."

There was a general roar of approval as Miss Jennings covered her eyes with a hand and shook her head helplessly, "I will never become accustomed to this uncouth lout," she thought despairingly.

And that, in a nutshell, was the upshot of Lizzie Donkin's catlike curiosity. The local authority proposed to build a small public toilet on the village green to cater for the influx of summer visitors. They did not, however, propose to spend a great deal of money designing what might have been considered by the populace to be a socially acceptable structure, had their opinion in fact been sought: a structure that would be pleasing to the eye of whoever beheld it: a structure that would blend aesthetically with its surroundings. That, in everyone's opinion, would be just too easy. Instead, they intended to redevelop that symbol of democracy's struggle for freedom, the wartime pillbox, and convert it into an alternative to the 'Double Duck's' hard-pressed plumbing. It wasn't so much this stark fact in itself that, if the truth were known, caused so much dissent. It was the fact that they were going to do it without so much as a 'by your leave,' that was getting up everyone's nose.

Two days later Bob Dixon reported back, his face glum. "Ah'm afraid it doesn't look like we'll get anywhere wi' this lot," he admitted. "Ah've spoken t'just aboot everybody Ah can think of but they all seem t'be o' th' same mind."

"An' what mind's that?" Bill asked in a tone that indicated he was well aware of the answer.

Bob shrugged, "They feel that it's essential not only t'th' well bein' o' the local community, us, but they are very concerned wi' th' amount o' summer visitors t'th' village."

"Did y'not tell them, man, that we want none o' it?" Big Jack growled, scowling.

"Well, what th' hell d'you think?" Bob replied with asperity. "O' course Ah did, man, but it's like bashin' y'heid off that wall. They're just waitin' f'r the next plannin' committee meetin' an' then it'll get rubber stamped."

"Damn th' bastards t'hell." Big Jack roared, his voice rising above the sudden babble that had erupted at Bob's disappointing words.

After waiting some moments for the noise to subside the messenger continued. "All that they could suggest was that we all go home an' write letters o' protest to anybody that'll listen, like our local cooncillor or MP, but we haven't much time left."

"Letters me arse," Big Jack snarled quietly to Davy and Bill. "You just leave this t'me, Ah'll sort them buggers oot, don't you worry."

The following evening found him in Low Cornhill in the snug at the Oak Tree huddled around a table with two other men of similar ilk. They were big, broad and tough-looking. Not the type to be accosted on a dark night unless, that is, you had a couple of Rottweilers for company.

"Okay then, y'knaw what t'dae," and as both nodded shaven skulls in agreement he pushed a wad of money under a beer mat across the table. "Ah'll see y'aboot two, then," he said, rising to his feet. His companions said not a word, being taciturn men.

A huge roaring noise filled the night air coming ever closer from the direction of the open cast site and a harsh, bright light cut a swathe through the darkness. Davy, not yet asleep looked out of his bedroom window and saw, to his astonishment, a most remarkable sight.

Big Jack stood at the edge of the village green, his hands in his pockets, whilst a massive monster of a machine, with an enormous steel bucket at the front edged with dragon's teeth, lurched and nodded its way toward him on gigantic balloon tyres. The driver sat high in his yellow cab, dwarfed by the mass of metal that surrounded him whilst the large searchlight above his head lit the scene as though it were day. It came slowly to a halt at the edge of the green and the driver, opening his cab door, yelled above the engine's mighty roar, "Is that it?"

Big Jack, laughing wildly now and intoxicated by the noise, waved him onward, "Aye, that's it," he shouted, "tear the bugger doon."

The monster needed no second bidding. It lurched forward, the hardened steel teeth on the bucket tearing into the reinforced concrete of the pillbox as though it were paper. It devoured it utterly, like some prehistoric dinosaur, reducing it to a mass of rubble and steel reinforcement in a matter of minutes scattering dust and debris far and wide whilst Big Jack looked on and danced with glee.

For a short while the earth shook to the monster's roaring voice, the calm night filled with the menace of it and then suddenly, as suddenly as it had arrived, it departed, its destruction completed, its voice dwindling back into the night whence it came.

No one saw or heard a thing.

10

Horses for Courses.

Davy stood at the low wall that bounded the rear of his property and gazed at the expanse of green field that he also owned. The expression upon his face, far from being benign as one might expect of someone who is lord of all he surveys, was serious. He rubbed a hand across his chin and turning to his wife, who was busily hanging out washing in the yard behind him, he said, "Look at all this bloody grass, Glennis."

She stopped what she was doing and came and stood at his side, "Umm, what about it?"

"Well, it's gettin' very long, i'nt it?" returned her husband, "an' you seriously don't expect me t'cut all o' this field wi' that little lawnmower o' ours, now do you?" He gazed at her mournfully the problem, to his mind, insuperable.

"I s'pose," Glennis made a tentative suggestion, "that we can always ask Bill to put some cows in again."

He sighed, "Ah don't see that we've much option but really, a herd o' black an' white Friesians don't exactly enhance the image o' th' pub, do they? An' another thing," he went on in the same mournful tone, "they make such a mess. Ah mean, y've got t'be careful where y'put y'feet where cows are concerned, haven't you?"

She knew exactly what he meant having seen him slip in a fresh cow pat only recently as he let their boisterous new Doberman off its leash; a sight which she found infinitely amusing until she came to wash his grey slacks.

"So y'see, Bill, although Ah don't mind cows as such, they do make summat o' a mess, don't they?" Davy recounted his dilemma to his friend that same evening.

Bill nodded. He was in fact in whole hearted agreement but having worked with a Friesian milking herd all of his life the mess associated with them was of little consequence to him, he was quite accustomed to it. He often recounted how his mother would make him keep the cows in the milking parlour until they had all finished unloading their stomach contents before she would allow them to pass her front door. He downed his pint and pushed his glass forward for a refill. As it was being pulled, he said, "Ah tell y'what, Davy, Ah just might have th' answer t'your problem. Aye," he nodded sagely, "an' it just might be th' solution t' someone else's problem an' all."

Davy raised questioning eyebrows as Bill placed coin of the realm into his outstretched palm.

"There's a young feller, Ah knaw," his friend explained, "well, he's really a friend o' th' lasses, he was askin' just th' other day if Ah had any grazin' f'r his horse. Ah think he's gettin' a bit desperate 'cos it must be costin' an arm an' a leg t'keep it in livery. Ah'll tell him he can keep it in y'r field if y'like. Kill two birds wi'one stone, so t'speak."

Davy considered the suggestion, "It sounds like a good idea t'me, bonny lad, as long as he realises that it's still his total responsibility. He can have th' grass be all means but he'll have t'look after it himsel'."

"Oh, y'needn't worry on that score," Bill was quick to assuage any fears, "from what Ah knaw o' this lad he wouldn't let anybody else take care o' his horse. Anyway," he took a long pull at his pint, "Ah'll bring him th' morrer's night an' y'can have a word wi' him." He wiped his mouth with the back of his hand.

It was just after opening time when Bill returned the following evening, with a companion. The place was empty, Davy having just opened the doors.

Bill quickly made the introductions, "This is Harry Robertson, Davy," he said, "th' young lad wi' th' hoss Ah was tellin' y'about."

Davy's proffered hand was taken firmly by a young man of medium build who stood a little under six feet in height. He was, Davy judged, no more than twenty-five years old. He wore a languid air as easily as he wore the faded and stained waxed jacket that hung around his shoulders.

"Ah'm glad t'meet you, Harry," Davy said in welcome.

The calm blue eyes gazed back at him steadily and he smiled as he said politely, "How are you, Mr. Dobson?"

"It's Davy," came the instant reply, "an' Ah'm fine, thanks. Bill here tells me that y'r lookin' f'r grazin' f'r y'r hoss?"

The young man nodded, "That's true, and the sooner the better. It's an expensive business keeping her in livery. Even though she's at a friend's place it still costs an arm and a leg."

Davy was sympathetic. "Well, if y'just follow me, lad, it might be that we can do each other a favour," and he led the way through the kitchen and out to the back of the pub.

Harry was impressed with the field and was quick to say so, "It's ideal, Davy. More than big enough for my mare. But what about a water supply?"

"Ah've got just th' thing, young man," replied his host and ducking into the shed he pulled out a cut down beer keg and a long hosepipe. "Y'll need t'fill this up about every other day, Ah reckon but if y'r comin' up on a reg'lar basis that shouldn't be a problem."

"No, indeed, that's fine," Harry was obviously delighted. "I'll come up every day, if that's alright, just to check on her and to hack her out. Now," he went on, changing the subject, "what about rent?"

"Rent?"

"Yes, of course, you'll require some remuneration, surely?"

Bill winked at him as Davy responded with a laugh, "Naw, naw, lad, don't be so daft. You keep th' grass down f'me, that's all th' rent Ah'll need."

"You've got yourself a deal, Mr. Dobson," Harry grasped the older man's hand warmly.

Later, they sealed their bargain over a pint or two of best ale at the bar. "So what kind o' hoss is it that Ah'll be harbourin'?" Davy asked casually. He knew immediately that he had made a mistake for the young equestrian's eyes lit up, rather in the same way a new father's do when asked about his first-born, and he set off at a gallop. It wasn't long before Davy suddenly realised that he had to change a keg and that Bill had milking to see to.

Later that same evening Harry made arrangements with his friend to pick up his horse the following day. He had hoped to borrow their horse trailer but on arriving he was informed that it wasn't availiable.

"Oh, well, not to worry," his natural optimism refused to be dampened, "I'll just hack her over. The exercise will do us both good. Hopefully I'll be able to arrange a lift back to pick up my car later."

"Okay," agreed his friend, Steven, "just park it in the corner of the yard, it'll be fine there. Er," he continued, his tone apologetic, "I'm afraid I haven't had time to get her in for you, Harry. D'you think you could go and get her yourself?" He chewed at his bottom lip knowing full well that he should have had the horse groomed and ready as he had arranged. He was obviously not the most reliable of people.

But as Harry was a fairly easy going type he simply shrugged his shoulders, "Yeah, no problem. Just tell me where she is....."

Steven cleared his throat, "Right," he said, suddenly at pains to be helpful, "she's down in the hollows with one or two others. Here," he turned and picked up a halter and a bucket containing pony nuts, "you'd better take these with you. Just whistle for her like you used to and she'll come, okay. Right then, I must get on," and he left Harry to walk the half mile to the field where he knew his mare to be.

The hollows were, as the name implied, at the bottom of a steep grassy incline. As he reached the top of the hill and gazed down into the valley he realised that the 'one or two others' Steven had mentioned were in fact a sizeable herd of thirty or forty assorted animals. He paused for a moment and silently cursed Steven, his easy going nature deserting him temporarily. "Now what?" he thought, scanning the peacefully grazing herd from his vantage point. "I certainly can't pick her out from here," and he began a slow descent of the steeply sloping hillside, all the while trying in vain to pick out his mare.

Halfway down, still unable to identify his horse, he stopped and sticking his fingers in his mouth, he whistled. Immediately forty pairs of ears pricked and several heads were raised, turning in the direction of the piercing sound.

"C'mon, girl," he called several times, hoping she would recognise the sound of his voice. But no single animal left the security of the herd. Frustrated, he rattled the feed bucket. There was an instantaneous response and several horses started in his direction. As soon as the rest of the herd realised what was happening they followed suit and Harry was suddenly faced with exactly what he didn't want, a surging mass of horseflesh coming towards him at a canter. "Oh, hell," he swore but stood his ground as the first horses reached him and started milling round, each one looking to get its nose into the bucket first.

He was jostled and pushed, snorted at and leant on and was in very real danger of either having his feet crushed by the mass of uncaring hooves or being sandwiched between the flanks of two half ton goliaths. Amidst this frantic melee he tried vainly to separate one from the other whilst searching for his own steed.

Then suddenly, just as he thought he would have to relinquish the bucket and retreat, there she was in front of him. He recognised her immediately by the white blaze on her forehead. "Good girl, good girl," he crooned as he put the head collar over her head, by which time he had abandoned the bucket and left the rest of the herd to fight it out between them.

As he groomed her he talked to her constantly, "These last six weeks separation seem to have done you good, lass, you've put on a bit of weight and I swear your mane and tail have thickened." She was a young horse, a Cleveland Bay cross, big and rawboned with a dark, healthily shiny coat. There wasn't another soul around when finally Harry mounted and rode her out of the yard, hooves ringing on the flagstones.

Once out of the gate he turned her head towards High Cornhill never realising just what sort of ride he was about to have. He had gone no further than about a mile, along a narrow lane, and was just beginning to settle her when suddenly she shied at a piece of old newspaper lying in the ditch, jerking herself across the road and very nearly unseating her rider. "What th' hell?" Harry cried, startled as he fought for control. It seemed that she was about to take off for places unknown and indeed, if he hadn't quickly been on top of the situation, that is exactly what would have happened.

He gentled her down to a walking pace again but instinctively he could tell that she was very much on edge, her head erect and muscles tensed ready to fly. Being a young horse she had a tendency to be flighty but this was worse than he had known. "What th' hell have they been doing to you, girl?" he mused, keeping her on a short rein as she tiptoed along.

After a further five minutes or so she was just beginning to relax a little, although Harry, his nerves still taut kept his knees jammed firmly into the kneeroll of the saddle. He leant forward to give her neck an encouraging pat when suddenly, unseen by either of them, a tractor from beyond the hedge to his right started up with a terrifying roar, black smoke belching skywards from its exhaust. This time there was no stopping her and she reared, front feet thrashing the empty air. At the same time she pirouetted on her hind legs away from the source of her terror and as soon as all four feet hit the ground, she bolted.

Harry, by some miracle, still in the saddle leaned backwards, hauling on the reins as hard as he could, to little effect. As she thundered along, the hedgerow whipping past and his eyes streaming, he knew he had very few options in his favour; he could either go with her and hope she ran out of steam quickly, which was highly unlikely or he could try and bale out, not wise on a Tarmacadam road.

He chose the third option and heaved on her right rein, turning her head hard towards his right knee. She followed, as she must and her mad, headlong flight was gradually brought under control, even though the narrowness of the lane made it that much more difficult.

Sweating profusely, terror turning his insides to jelly, he dismounted and holding her tightly by the bridle he snarled, "What th' bloody hell's got into you, damn it?" Her only response was to roll her eyes until the whites showed and she shuffled sideways. Realising that the tone of his voice wasn't helping he said soothingly, "C'mon, girl, hush now, there's nothing to be frightened of," and he walked her on, his hand on her neck until she calmed again.

Eventually he remounted and so they continued, both rider and mount, tense and nervous, ready to respond to the slightest hint of danger and twice more she reacted violently to a real or imagined threat. Harry was unaware of which, he was much too busy trying to keep his seat.

It took over two hours to bring his mare home and they arrived trembling and sweating. The mare was the more obviously distressed for white, foamy streams ran down each leg and her neck was lathered beneath the reins whilst her lips and nostrils were coated with a thick, white froth. Davy, watching from an upstairs window, saw them arrive and went down to assist. "By Harry lad, y'must o' galloped her all th' way. Sh's in a right state, i'nt she?"

Harry turned a bleak eye upon him, "Galloped her?" he said wearily, "It's taken all my time just to stay aboard, b'lieve me. I don't know what they've been doing with her at that livery," he went on, his voice rising angrily, "but I know someone who's going to get the thick edge of my tongue the next time I see him." He hauled the saddle off the mare's steaming back as he spoke and hung it on the gate.

"Ah s'pose y've left y'car at th' yard, eh?" Davy asked.

"Umm, that's right," Harry nodded, slipping the bridle over the animal's head. "I don't s'pose.....?" he looked askance at his friend.

"Aye," Davy said, his expression patient, "Ah'll run y'back. Just show me th' way."

About an hour later Harry was back where he had started from. As they drove into the yard he caught sight of Steven in animated conversation with a woman, his hands gesticulating wildly. He got out of the car, leaving Davy in the driving seat, gazing upon the scene with amused interest, his elbow resting on the rolled down window. As he walked across the yard, determined to give Steven a peace of his mind, Harry heard the female practically scream, "Well, where is she, then, 'cos she's not in your bloody field where she's supposed to be?"

Steven was about to reply in an equally heated manner when he suddenly noticed Harry striding purposefully towards him. "I don't know," he said quietly, biting back his response, "but I think I've got a damn' good idea." Before Harry could get his shot in Steven turned to him and asked, with just the merest hint of sarcasm, "How did your ride go, Harry?"

Slightly taken aback by the immediacy of the question, Harry paused. Then he said, a glint in his eye, "Funny you should ask that," he began through tight lips, "because it was, to say the least, bloody awful, not to say downright dangerous."

Steven, his anger at being berated by his client undiminished, let fly, "I'm not surprised, you damn' fool," he snarled, "you took the wrong bloody horse."

Harry felt his own anger collapse suddenly, its keystone removed by Steven's hot words. It was replaced by a sinking feeling in the pit of his stomach and he began to wish he was somewhere else, fast. His mouth opened and closed twice, "Whaaaat?" he gasped, stunned.

"That's right," Steven didn't try to hide his disdain. "Your mare's still down in the hollows, where this lady's ought to be. Her horse has never been away from this yard. She does all of her riding on our land......"

"Jesus Christ Almighty," the 'lady' interrupted, "so it was you. Can't you tell the difference between your own horse and someone else's?" and she waded into Harry, her high pitched falsetto rising at times to an almost unbearable decibel level. She called him all the names she could lay tongue to whilst all that Harry could do was stand and take it with as much dignity as he could muster.

"Oh, God," he thought, his mind whirling under the onslaught, "tell me this isn't true someone. Tell me it isn't really happening, that it's just a nightmare." But there was no respite. This woman, her vindictiveness boundless, was determined to have the skin stripped from his bones for abducting her beloved mare. That is until Davy, taking pity on his friend, and having more than enough of her unbridled ranting, stepped in.

"What's up?" he asked in his broadest Yorkshire accent.

"It's this fool here," snapped Harry's antagonist, her eyes flashing sparks, "he can't tell the difference between his horse and mine."

"Aye, well, anyone can mek a mistake, lass," Davy defended his friend stoutly.

"Not like this, they can't," the woman snapped, whipping round to Harry again. "I'm going to sue you for....."

"Well you an y'husband did, Mrs. Somerville," Davy replied softly. The mention of her name stopped her in mid-flow and she turned her attention back to Davy once more. "Like the other week," he went on, his manner conversational, "when you forgot t'pay th' bill in my restaurant. Y'must remember," he nodded, smiling benignly, "Ah had t'stop y'in't car park just before y'drove away. A mistake y'said, aye, that were it, an honest mistake that anyone could mek," the smile never left his face and his grey eyes twinkled. "Payin' for th' meal had obviously slipped y'mind, eh? Well, never mind," he shook his head sympathetically, "me young friend here'll arrange t'fetch your hoss back an' we'll say no more about it." But the woman wasn't listening and Davy grinned broadly at her retreating back as she stormed out of the yard without another word.

Harry looked as though he had just gone three rounds with Mike Tyson and was relieved to get away with nothing worse than a broken jaw. He threw his companion a glance of pure gratitude, "Thanks Davy," was all he said.

Davy dismissed the gesture with a shrug, "My pleasure, bonny lad," he replied with a grin. "Ah've been waitin' f'r a chance t'get even wi' her an' her husband f'r a while now. Ah'm not th' fust publican they've tried t'rook an' Ah dare say Ah'll not be th' last either, Ah'll bet." They started to walk towards the car, Steven having left in search of his client. "It's a damn' good job that hoss stealin's not a hangin' offence any more," Davy chuckled, "else she'd a' had y'hung, drawn an' quartered be now."

Slightly shamefaced Harry hung his head. "I can see how it happened, trying to get my horse separated from that mob, and she does look very like mine......." his voice trailed off into a lame silence.

"Y'don't have t'explain owt t'me, lad," Davy laughed as he climbed behind the wheel, "but Ah'll guarantee it'll be a cauld day in hell afore y'live this'un down."

And so it was, for the villagers affectionately nicknamed their newcomer Hossthief Harry, a name with which he was greeted every time he entered the bar.

He soon became a familiar sight around the village and its environs for he exercised his mare regularly, taking full advantage of the surrounding countryside.

"Goin' out again, lad?" Davy enquired on opening the pub door and finding Harry about to mount.

"Aye," he replied, swinging his leg over the saddle, "I thought I'd go down through the gladda and around by Mick Johnson's place." It was a route with which he was very familiar now.

"Well, y've a canny night f'r it," Davy replied as he raised his hand.

They had a good ride, the mare responding well to the gentle urging of hands and leg, the soft evening laying on them like a mantle. Dusk was just beginning to fall as they approached the last mile or so and the track ahead of them lay like a ribbon through the woods.

It was here that Harry always allowed her to stretch out and have her head, for she loved the chase. This evening was no exception and the mare, excited now, knowing what to expect, set off at a dead run. Crouching low over her neck to avoid the occasional low branch, Harry urged her on.

They came around a curve at a flat out gallop and took the hill in front of them. As they did so the saddle suddenly slipped sideways, catapulting the rider without warning out of the side door and throwing him to the ground with tremendous force. The long summer days had baked the track in places to the consistency of a Tarmac road. Fate decreed that it was one of these places that he should make contact with. And make contact with it he did; with his chin, which split open like an orange. Red and yellow lights exploded inside his head and he felt his back teeth collapse with the force of the impact. Stunned and shocked, but still conscious, just, he lay still for a few moments listening to the sound of his mount's retreating hoofbeats. Groaning loudly, and with a thousand drums beating a tattoo in his skull, he finally staggered to his feet and gazed, bemused, as the blood from his ruined chin, dripped in a steady stream onto his waxed jacket and from there to the ground. The one thought in his mind was to get home and find his mare before she did any damage to herself or anyone else.

The village lay about a mile away almost due north and he lurched and staggered in that direction, at times passing out for a split second but never falling and never quite relinquishing his grip on reality. He knew that if he did so it would be a long time before anyone found him out here. It was with consummate gratitude that he eventually spied the lights of the pub through the gathering dusk, lighting his way across the green and he maintained an unsteady and meandering course towards them. On reaching his perceived sanctuary he was greatly comforted to find his mare standing by the gate to the field, steam rising gently from her flanks. He teetered towards her, arms outstretched like some mad marionette and she stood quietly whilst he removed her saddle and led her through the gate. But the bridle proved to be too much of an obstacle and his head began to swim violently as he fumbled with the fastenings.

"Must get some help," he mumbled to himself, "can't get this thing off by myself." He tottered around to the entrance and tried to push open the door to the bar. He couldn't move it, it seemed locked or his remaining strength simply wasn't sufficient to open it. Summoning what willpower was left to him he gave an almighty shove. Too late he realised he shouldn't have gritted his teeth for the pain that shot through his jaw and into his brain was like a thousand red hot needles. He collapsed as the door gave way, finally succumbing to the devils that were dancing in his head.

He was surrounded by a white light of intense brightness, so intense that he found it difficult to open his eyes. When he did so he was surprised to find a beautiful but unfamiliar face bending over him.

"I've died and gone to heaven," he thought wearily, and closed his eyes again.

"Oh, you've woken up then?" The voice floated somewhere above his head.

"Where am I?" he said, attempting to rise.

"Durham General Hospital," said the nurse, pushing him gently back into a reclining position, "casualty department."

"But what about my horse?" Harry was completely bemused, "I must see to her."

"Don't worry about a thing, my love," the nurse replied kindly, "he's been taken care of."

"She," Harry mumbled, and wondered why it was he couldn't open his mouth properly.

"Oh, yes of course, she," his mentor agreed, her starched uniform rustling as she moved about him. As she worked, arranging sterile instruments and dressings on a little table by his couch she chatted, and he learned that he had been brought into the hospital some twenty minutes previously by two friends, ranting and raving, completely out of his head and cursing all and sundry for not getting him a drink of whisky.

"But I never drink whisky," he mumbled, puzzled.

"No, and I'll bet you don't swear either," returned the nurse, smiling.

"Oh, God," groaned Harry inwardly, "what th' hell's been going on?"

The nurse filled a hyperdermic syringe, "This is just a local anaesthetic, it'll make you feel more comfortable," and Harry winced as she pushed the needle gently into his jaw. As she finished, the door opened to reveal a ginger haired young man, complete with white coat and obligatory stethoscope, not much older than himself.

"H'mm, nasty," he said without preamble, gently pulling open the raw lips of the wound with a pair of tweezers, "I can see your teeth."

"Don't be stupid," Harry mumbled, "I had my mouth closed."

"I know," the doctor grinned, "but I could still see your teeth. Now listen to me," he was suddenly serious, "you've got an awful lot of muck in there so we'll need to get rid of it before I can stitch you up, okay?"

Whatever you say," agreed Harry wearily, too tired to argue.

So they scrubbed out the wound with a sterile solution and a toothbrush and they didn't stop until they were entirely satisfied that they had eradicated every foreign body.

"How did you do this?" enquired the doctor conversationally as he sewed away at Harry's chin like a demented tailor.

"Fell off my horse," Harry replied through clenched teeth.

"That's funny," chimed in the nurse, "we had a similar incident last Saturday night about midnight. A chap had fallen off a horse and smashed his face in."

"Funny time to be out riding, wasn't it?" Harry said.

"Oh, he wasn't riding," giggled the nurse, "he fell off the statue in the market place, stoned out of his mind."

"Oh, don't make me laugh," winced the patient as the last stitch went home.

11
The Mouse

Winter was late coming that year, for it seemed that autumn had no intention of leaving. When finally it did strike it came suddenly, without warning, cutting across the landscape with an icy scythe and reducing all living creatures to a state of mere survival.

James Bishop, in his lonely, isolated homestead struggled to keep his stock fed and watered. God knew that it would have been hard enough even with his brother's help but since his death, life had been arduous to say the least, for he had renounced the world at large almost totally and discouraged those who saw fit to offer their assistance.

But this winter was one which he could well have done without. He rose each morning about six thirty and long before he had finished his meagre breakfast he knew what to expect. The snow had been falling incessantly for eight days until now every time he opened the door of the house he had to dig his way out. Floundering through thigh-deep drifts that had gradually grown deeper, and had been sculpted into surrealistic curves and waves by the wind, his was a continuous battle, his determination often more than his physical strength, so that no animal in his care went hungry.

All of the horses were, of course, under cover in their respective loose boxes but nevertheless it was a problem keeping their troughs free from the all-encroaching ice. The sub-zero conditions meant that he was constantly having to break open one trough after another, his hands becoming wet and blue with the cold. Chilblains began to develop, the skin breaking open, leaving raw and weeping wounds, so that gripping anything became extremely painful yet still he could not stop. He felt at times like the 'Flying Dutchman' of old, doomed to go on, no matter what.

The loneliness wasn't a problem; he had been a loner all of his life but he missed his brother, especially now with so much heavy work to do. But he was beyond cursing his lot and simply accepted his fate with a resignation born of past experience. Sometimes though, at the end of the day, when he had collapsed wearily into the easychair by the fire, self pity would creep up on him and catch him unawares. That was the dangerous time, the time when he had to shake himself mentally and he would often snarl out loud, "C'mon, y'stupit auld bugger, gerra a grip o y'sel, f'God's sake," and then he would go and find something else to do no matter how tired he felt.

Before the onset of winter he had acquired a new thoroughbred colt which he intended to bring on and use at stud. He was a fine big animal, but young, with a nervous temperament which manifested itself in the flare of his nostrils or the sudden stamp of a hoof. It lived in the loose box at the end of the yard, farthest away from the house and shared its home, quite unbeknownst to its owner, with a mouse. It was just an ordinary fieldmouse, unpretentious and uninspiring with absolutely nothing to recommend it except an instinct for survival that the winter had honed to a fine edge. It was this instinct that had driven it indoors to escape the icy winds. It expected to remain there until spring with no greater danger to contend with than the occasional prowling cat, living on the hayseeds that fell from the colt's manger like manna from heaven.

James heaved open the half door, pushing against the built up snow, and stepped inside. He was greeted by the familiar odours of warm, pungent horse droppings and good meadow hay. Although it was dark he refrained from switching on the light as he was well able to see by the faint illumination of a myriad of stars that had dared to venture out this early in the evening, the snow clouds having dispersed for a while. He saw that the colt's stable rug had slipped to one side and he made to adjust it.

The mouse cowered under a small pile of straw, its eyes, like tiny black beads, reflected the starlight. It remained perfectly still, panic beginning to rise in its breast like quicksilver, the only discernible movement being the rapid pulsating of its flanks as fear transfixed its body to the floor. Suddenly, a huge snow covered boot crashed down near its head and unable to contain the urgency of its fear further, the tiny animal leapt forward and upward, desperately scrambling up the colt's hind leg. Both animals reacted instinctively, the colt's though was blindingly swift and devastating in its result for, suddenly alarmed, it lashed out with both hind feet causing the rug to slip over its quarters.

That first kick missed him as he was standing to one side but as the colt panicked and kicked and kicked again at the terrifying encumbrance clinging to its hindquarters James was driven, horrified, into the farthest corner of the stable. Fear now engulfed him as it had the mouse mere seconds before and he heard himself through his terror, as if from a distance, screaming as he pressed himself closer to the wall and vainly tried to protect his head from those murderous, flashing hooves. Sparks flew from the walls, briefly but brilliantly illuminating the scene as steel struck flint as the colt continued in its desperate attempt to free itself. Through the awful horror of it all the sudden realisation dawned that he was going to die, that this animal, unless by some miracle it were forced to stop, must surely kill him.

Through this nightmarish scene came the sudden flash of steel, cold and grey in the starlight and then the world exploded as he was struck by both hooves almost simultaneously. The first struck him on the forehead, a glancing blow but opening a wide gash which allowed the quick rush of blood to flow freely into his eyes. The second strike was the more devastating for it struck him just above the knee, shattering the old bone as though it were an icicle.

It had started to snow again and the wind, moaning softly, blew a light dusting of flakes into the stable, whirling them in frantic eddies across the floor. The old man groaned and tried to open his eyes but the left eyelid refused to move. His senses having been dulled by pain and exposure, he was unable to understand this at first; then he realised that blood from his head had congealed around it.

He slowly pushed himself into a sitting position and the night dissolved into a fantasy of brilliantly coloured lights that exploded somewhere out there in the darkness. Feebly he pulled a large handkerchief from his jacket pocket with which he attempted to remove some of the blood. As he did so the wound opened once more and blood began to flow freely again in a bright, red stream. He tied the handkerchief around his head and gradually the flow eased. He tried to move his leg and felt suddenly sick as the grinding agony of it tore at his throat. He leaned back against the wall fighting the nausea and waited for his senses to return to normal before taking stock of the situation.

The colt had vanished, smashing the stable door to matchwood in its headlong flight. He shivered as the wind became suddenly stronger, blowing through of what remained of the door. "Well, Ah canna bide here an' freeze t'bloody death," he said aloud, suddenly shattering the silence, "Ah'd better be mekkin' a move," and he began to haul himself slowly towards the door ignoring the agony that bit and tore at his leg like some ravening animal.

By the time he had reached the threshold he had started to perspire freely, in spite of the cold, and his head wound had begun to weep again staining the handkerchief with its crimson brightness. He peered outside and the wind tore at him with a ferocity that froze the breath in his lungs but, summoning every last vestige of his strength and calling himself all of the names he could lay tongue to, he pressed on, plunging his hands deep into the soft, powdery snow, dragging his useless body behind him.

The longcase clock in the corner of the living room ticked solemnly, beating out life's seconds with metronomic insistence. The fire crackled softly to itself in a self-satisfied way, sending shadows leaping and dancing across the ceiling. Outside, the wind, growing ever stronger, rattled at the windows, demanding entrance. Ben, the old sheepdog, lay curled in the easychair by the fire, ears pricked, alert to any sound that would herald the return of his master.

It took him all of an hour to drag himself to the bottom of the yard where he lay gasping in the shelter of a low wall. He was completely spent, whilst his hands were blue from the cold of being constantly buried in deep snow. His head throbbed incessantly and oozed blood from beneath his makeshift bandage and his shattered leg kept screaming at him, begging him to stop.

He was beginning to grow light-headed; whether through the pain or loss of blood he was unsure and he was too weary to care. He closed his eyes and groaned. Tears of self pity welled from beneath the lids and trickled slowly down his face, freezing on his, rough, stubble covered cheeks. When he opened them again it was to see his father standing before him, dressed as he always remembered in polished high boots, moleskin trousers, hacking jacket and flat cap.

"Y'allus were a soft bugger our James," said his father, although his lips never moved. "H'way, man, y'can see th' hoose from here. It's only another fifty yards so get y'sel a move on."

As the image of his father faded from his befuddled mind James raised his head and peered over the low wall. There, beckoning him onward, like the finger of God, was the light from his own living room. Once, twice, three times he plunged his frozen hands deep into the snow again and three times he slowly heaved his broken body on before finally collapsing face downward, the blood from his head turning the freezing whiteness crimson.

"Hello, James, anybody about?" Bill Stobbart called. He had driven up from the village in a tractor, much against his better judgement but at Sarah's insistence, to check on the wellbeing of his neighbour. He half expected to hear the usual snarling reply from one of the loose boxes but, encountering only a deathly silence and noticing the absence of chimney smoke, he began to feel uneasy.

He waded across to the house and peered through the nearest window. Seeing nothing he made his way round to the back door which was unlocked. He stepped into the scullery and was struck by its icy coldness. "There's been no fire in here for a while," he thought grimly. He was about to step outside again when Ben bounded from the living room, his mouth agape and tail wagging furiously. Bill bent and patted the dog fondly, "Hello, boy," he said softly, "where's that auld devil at, Ah wonder?" and he let the collie into the yard ahead of him. Ben bounded through the snow, delighted to be free of the confines of the house , and ran up the yard whining, searching for his master, Bill as close behind him as the drifts would allow.

They came upon the broken stable door swinging gently in the breeze, the loose box empty. "Aw, shit," Bill swore, "this doesn't look too good." He turned and peered back down the yard to where Ben was now frantically digging in the snow, his high pitched whining echoing in the silence. By the time Bill had floundered his way to him the dog had exposed the heel of a boot and part of one leg. Quickly, knowing what to expect, Bill threw the snow aside as fast as he could and it wasn't very long before he had unearthed James' body, stiff and stark, lying where he had fallen, face down.

"Poor auld sod," Bill breathed sadly, "what a way to go." He grasped the body by the shoulder and turned it over. As he did so he noticed something clasped in the crooked, clawlike fingers of one hand. He managed to free it with some difficulty and saw that it was the frozen body of a tiny fieldmouse. "It must have crawled in there t'get th' last o' th' warmth," he muttered, casually throwing the small body across the glittering, final page of James Bishop's life.   .

12
One-Two Tommy.

A cottage, stone built and solid, as were the rest of the houses, stood alone in about acres of land about a half mile from the western boundary of the village. The road that snaked its way across the fell until it disappeared into the Wear valley, ran past the front door. It was home to but two people; Jessie McDonald, a single mother, and her son Tommy.

The cottage had originally belonged to Jessie's parents and when, in the fullness of time, they had both died she had continued to live there, changing practically nothing; except for the sudden and unexpected addition of a male child.

As a young girl she had been well liked by her neighbours and popular with her contemporaries but as she grew she began to feel more and more apart from them. This was due in the main to the fact that she was totally committed to caring for ailing and elderly parents whose demands became more and more persistent until she was barely able to leave the house, particularly when her mother became bedridden.

Eventually, as is the nature of things, both her parents died within two years of each other. This left Jessie the freedom to do exactly as she wanted but as she had become so accustomed to her solitary existence she neither needed nor sought the company of others. Where her son came from was a complete mystery. Much wild speculation heralded his arrival and for years afterward. Some said that he wasn't her son at all but a distant relative whom she had agreed to raise for a small gratuity, others that he was simply adopted. Only Jessie herself knew the simple truth and she wasn't prepared to tell anyone. No one knew that he was the product of one wild fling which occurred shortly after the death of her parents. She was free then and she did exactly as she wanted; for a short while at least.

Because of his mother's somewhat separate existence, which on the whole the villagers respected, Tommy grew up a lonely little boy, quiet, shy and reserved. He was blonde and blue eyed with a round, rosy, open countenance and he was nearly always to be seen with a small smile hovering near the corners of his mouth, as though he were privy to some secret joke. But the one thing that placed him apart from his fellows more than anything else, certainly as a child, was a terrible speech impediment. A thickening of the tongue, the locals called it. He could barely string two words together without an enormous effort and yet, as they quickly discovered when he began attending the village school, he was bright, intelligent and quick to learn.

These two things, his intelligence and his speech impediment, made him the butt of cruel, childish mockery which had its inevitable effect, for the older he grew the more introverted and silent he became until practically the only people he would speak to were his teacher and his mother. It was whilst he was at school that he was given the cruel sobriquet of One-Two Tommy because the children would inevitably begin counting every time he tried, and failed, to begin a sentence. As a result he had few friends. The only one he could completely rely upon, and who was a staunch supporter all of his life, was Ernie Blakey, himself underprivileged and somewhat deprived, his father being a farm labourer with little interest in anything other than his work and the pub.

As he blossomed from infancy into childhood his mother began to realise that there was something rather special about her disadvantaged son. This realisation went beyond the normal love and maternal instinct that most mothers bear their offspring for she knew, simply by studying him closely, that he had an almost uncanny affinity with the animals that surrounded him and were part of his life. They seemed to trust him instinctively; even those animals that had a natural distrust of man, being wild, such as badgers or foxes, lost their inherent suspicions in his presence, becoming docile and compliant. Seeing all of this his mother likened him to St. Francis although that was a thought she kept strictly to herself, not wishing to be thought either irreligious or superior.

When he was about eleven years old she bought him a pony and he quickly became an expert rider, teaching himself by study and practise the complete art of horsemanship. He could often be seen galloping around their small acreage performing the sort of tricks from the back of his pony that are normally reserved for circus stuntmen.

But, more than this, horses became his passion and his life, and he learnt everything he could about them, from their psychology to their anatomy and when he left school he contributed to the family's meagre income by training young animals for those who had neither the time nor expertise.

It wasn't long before his reputation as a gentle but expert handler became widespread and owners would come from as far away as Newcastle to entrust their precious animals to him. He had learnt at an early stage in his career that horses have their own language and communicate with each other through signs and body language and this he used to fullest advantage.

To the uninitiated, and to those whom he occasionally allowed to watch him at work, it appeared as though he bewitched those horses in his care for it wasn't very long before even the most recalcitrant and intransigent animal was listening and obeying his every instruction. Magic had nothing whatsoever to do with it; it was simply a case of understanding and communicating with his horses. This way he gained their trust and respect. He never 'broke' a horse in his life believing that a broken animal is of no use to anyone. He was never able to accept people as readily as he did their animals and often his stammer, which precluded normal conversation, meant that his mother had to act as interpreter, particularly when anyone he hadn't met before came seeking his help.

Help was the farthest thing from Josh Chisolm's mind when he came storming into the 'Double Duck' one evening, his face red and furious.

"You look like y'could do wi' a drink, lad," Davy greeted him as Josh bellied up to the bar.

"Aye, mek it a double Scotch." Josh scowled, his heavy brows meeting in the middle of his forehead. Never known for his light hearted bonhomie he was in a worse humour than usual.

"What's up?" Davy asked conversationally as he pushed the whisky across the bar.

Josh shook his head angrily, "That bloody awkward bitch o' a mare o' mine, that's what's up," he snarled, draining his glass in one and thrusting it back at the landlord for a refill. "That's the third time this week she's had me off. Ah swear sh's f'r th' bloody knacker's th' next time."

Knowing how much he had paid for the horse, for he had told anyone that cared to listen, and how little he liked losing, Davy doubted the perspicacity of this last remark. He did his best to contain a smile as Josh expounded.

"D'y'know what sh's done this time?" he asked of all and sundry and no one in particular. "Sh's got a neat trick off now, be God," he went on without waiting for a reply. "Sh's found that if sh's quick enough she can wipe y'out o' th' saddle be duckin' under th' lowest branch o' that big chestnut tree doon in th' gladda...."

"An' don't tell us," interrupted mine host, "that's just what's she's done?"

Josh scowled into his drink as he waited for the general laughter to subside. As it did so, a voice spoke up from the far end of the bar. "Y'should go an' see Tommy McDonald, Josh. He'll be able t' sort her oot, nae bother." It was Ernie Blakey.

Chisholm gave a derisive snort, "One-Two Tommy," he snarled, "dinna mek me laugh. Y'seem t'f'get, Ah went t'school wi' that stammerin' fool." He had little time for anyone less fortunate than himself.

"Knaw, Ah hadn't forgotten," Ernie said quietly, "nor have Ah forgotten that it was you that called him One-Two Tommy in't fust place."

Josh shrugged off the implied criticism and again downed his whisky in a gulp.

"Ah'll tell y'what, Josh," Ernie went on in the same quiet manner, "Ah''ll lay y'two hundred quid that Tommy can sort y'mare oot an' have her behavin' like a real lady in six weeks, how's that?" and he put his pint down on the bar with a decisive air.

Chisholm stared back at him, contempt and disbelief vying with each other for domination of his features. "Where th' hell ha' you got two hundred quid.......?" he began.

"We'll mek it five hundred, if y'want," Ernie interrupted softly.

The bar went suddenly quiet, realisation dawning that this was deadly serious. Everyone waited for Josh to make his move. Not a man to back away from a challenge, especially in front of so many witnesses, he slammed his tumbler down hard, "Reet," he said, his mouth set in a grim line, "y're on. Y'can come an' pick her up th' morn's neet. But, six weeks mind, and nae mair."

The bar was suddenly agog with anticipation as he stalked out, slamming the door behind him.

"Well, what d'you think o' her?"

Ernie and his friend were leaning over the bottom half of the loose box door where Chisholm's mare had been installed earlier that evening.

"Sh,'sh,'sh's a,a,a b'b'bonny lass, reet enough," Tommy stammered admiringly. "M'm'm'must be worth a b'b'bob or two, eh?"

His friend nodded, "Aye, but can y'dae owt wi' her?" he said.

"Aw, c'c'c'c'mon, Ernie man, y'y'y'y'knaw b'b'better than that." The reply was in no way boastful, merely matter-of-fact.

Ernie dragged his gaze away from the horse and looked at his friend full in the eye. "Listen, Tommy," he began, "this could be the opportunity t'get one ower on that big ignorant bast'd, wha'd y'say? Teach him a lesson, like," he grinned at the thought.

"H'h'h'how d'y'mean?" asked Tommy, glancing sideways. They had been friends for so long now that the question was really superfluous.

"Well," he smiled archly, "it all depends on how y'train this hoss, don't it?"

Tommy scratched his cheek reflectively, his own, secretive smile spreading slowly across his face like the ripples on a pond, "Aye, it does that," he conceded.

He began work early the following morning, the mist rising from the valley floor as he led the mare out into his small yard. He was fully aware that he had would have to establish his supremacy over her quickly if he was going to get her respect. He knew her for what she was; a horse that understood firm yet gentle handling. Chisholm, he knew, had none of the subtlety required to get the best from this type of thoroughbred. The harder he fought her the harder she responded, neither one of them giving an inch. Tommy was confident of gaining her co-operation but she had to know just who was master and accept his role as such. Only then, when she was malleable, could he work with her and bring to fruition the plan he and Ernie had discussed between them.

He began by lunging her in the paddock and, although not enjoying it exactly, she responded to his soft commands reasonably enough. To the untrained eye she appeared to be moving smoothly and easily as she circled him. Tommy, however, was perfectly aware from the set of her head and her ears, by the occasional swish of her tail and the tenseness throughout her body, that she was prepared to rebel at any moment.

He halted her and brought her to stand. As he approached her, gathering up the lunge rein and speaking softly in a continuous monotone, she stood, head erect and tense, one eye upon him the whole time. He slowly reached up to her head and unclipped the rope stepping back and away from her as he did so. When working with animals his stammer completely disappeared. "Walk on, girl," he commanded firmly. The mare didn't respond, simply standing and watching him. He repeated the command, this time flicking the end of the lunge rein towards her. She started and, flinging her head high, she shied. Tommy immediately got behind her and flicked her again, deliberately driving her on. This time she set off at a fast trot, circling him and keeping well away from what she perceived as danger. He drove her round the paddock, all the time talking to her and occasionally flicking out the end of the lunge rein to keep her moving, driving her on, away from him.

At the end of about ten minutes of this treatment he knew that she would be ready to come to him of her own accord, if he gave her the right signals. All horses are gregarious and are governed by the herd instinct therefore they will always want to congregate, particularly if invited to do so.

Being the supreme horseman that he was Tommy was well aware of this and gradually he ceased driving her away. Slowly, slowly she allowed her speed to fall as Tommy stood in the middle of the paddock without moving, simply watching her.

When she had come to a complete halt he stepped towards her gently, leaving the lunge rein on the ground. Before he reached her he stopped and turned away from her, walking slowly back towards the centre of the paddock. Four times, exhibiting infinite patience, he did this. On the fourth attempt the mare, accepting the invitation to join him, extended through his body language, followed him. She stopped, her head inches from his shoulder. Reaching up, he caressed her head and ears, softly blowing into her nostrils as he did so. He walked away from her; she followed. When he stopped, with his back to her, she pushed him with her head. He grinned, knowing he had her now and quietly turning he blew once again into her nostrils, clipping on the lunge rein as he did so. Taking her back into the centre of the paddock he once again put her through her lunging exercise. This time she was completely different, relaxed, ears pricked forward, stepping out as though she was thoroughly enjoying herself.

With much fuss and praise he brought her back into the yard and tacked her up. As soon as he had swung his leg over her back she became once again the highly strung, excitable animal that was the product of Josh Chisolm's rough wooing.

"Aye, Ah thought that's how it would be," he muttered, swinging left out of the yard and picking up the track that led into the gladda. He had deliberately chosen this route for he had been told by Ernie of his mount's dangerous habit when riding through this small valley. The track wound its way through mature woodland, the trees close and overhanging with occasional oases of verdant green lying between. Above his head the spring birdsong echoed through the surrounding timber as every ornithological Romeo gave voice to his passion.

A small stream lay across their path and beyond that the way lay through a broad meadow where bright yellow buttercups and skyblue cornflowers vied with each other for attention as they danced and curtsied among the tall meadow grasses that bowed gracefully with the breeze.

They followed the path which took them close to the vicinity of the biggest tree in the valley, the same massive chestnut that had so discomfited his mount's previous rider. "Y'll not be daein' th' same t'me, mind girl," Tommy thought to himself as they approached the enormously heavy lower branches that swept close to the ground as if in homage.

As horse and rider drew nearer to the wide, overhanging canopy the mare suddenly tensed and set off at a fast canter towards the nearest branch. Tommy didn't fight her or try to turn her, instead he let her have her head, knowing full well what her intention must be. He was more than a match for this kind of equine sculduggery and, slipping one foot from the stirrup he leaned far over to the side, hanging along her neck like a Red Indian. Swinging back into the saddle after they passed beneath the tree he knew she was surprised to find him still in place upon her back for she jerked to a sudden stop, stamping and snorting.

"Okay, bonny lass," Tommy said out loud, "if that's th' way y'want t'play it, it's okay by me," and he turned her head and urged her into a canter once again, heading in the reverse direction. Again she tried the same trick and again he foiled her in precisely the same way. They ran towards the tree for the third time but on this instance Tommy had determined that she needed to be taught a sharp lesson, even though it went much against his grain to hurt her in any way.

She was just about to pass under the branch yet again when he pulled her head round hard to the left. Follow she must, unable to resist the unrelenting pressure of the bit and she cannoned into the massive, gnarled bole of the chestnut, coming to a sudden and shocking halt. It took courage to carry out this kind of manoeuvre on a swiftly moving horse for it was impossible to predict with absolute certainty just what the outcome would be.

He was also immediately sorry for what he had done and he leapt from the saddle as she staggered backwards, eyes rolling, to check that there was no serious damage. He discovered nothing more serious than a large swelling between her eyes which he knew he could reduce with cold water compresses as soon as he got home. He crooned softly to her, stroking her velvet nose until she had recovered her composure.

She seemed to bear him no illwill and appeared to accept her accident for what it was, an everyday hazard that was best avoided. As soon as he remounted he knew that he had won this round also. She was now totally his and he trotted her round and round the big tree without her once attempting to remove him from his seat. He was her undisputed master and she was willing to respond to whatever he asked of her. Her reward was unremitting kindness and unstinting patience and for the next six weeks they became one harmonious whole, forming a lasting bond of affection.

Nearly the entire village turned out the evening Tommy brought the mare to the field at the rear of the 'Double Duck' and the air was alive with the thought of the five hundred pounds that was the understood wager between Ernie Blakey and Josh Chisholm. As Tommy neared the gate, his mount under perfect control, her neck arched beautifully and her small head tucked in, Ernie called out, "Now then Tommy, lad, let's see what y've done wi' 'er, eh?"

Tommy merely smiled his slow, secretive smile and held his peace. As soon as he reached the centre of the field he began putting the mare through her paces. Nothing too complicated at first, merely exhibiting the fact that she was under control and responding to his every signal, whether from hands, leg or seat. He walked around the field twice and then halted her. She stood absolutely still, her head erect, the only movement the occasional swish of her long, luxuriant tail. He dismounted, leaving the reins on her neck, and walked away from her. Still she didn't move, not a muscle. He walked all the way to the far side of the field and then turning, he whistled softly twice. She immediately responded and stepped out, covering the ground between them. He whistled again, a single low sound. She stopped stock still. Putting both fingers to his mouth he gave forth with a loud piercing shriek that cut through the air like a knife and could be heard down in the valley.

The mare kicked up her heels and cantered towards him like a two year old. The crowd went wild, clapping and cheering as he mounted once again. He cantered her round in a wide circle, sitting deep in the saddle, his body moving in perfect unison with hers. He brought her back to a trot and executed a beautiful half pass, her front feet crossing each other cleanly as she moved sideways through the dressage movement. To complete his little exhibition he cantered her over from the far side of the field towards the crowd and brought her to a halt in front of her owner. As he reined in, the mare rose on her hind legs, front feet pawing at the empty air as she completed a perfect pirouette and came down on all fours again with her backside towards him.

There was immediate and spontaneous applause from the villagers and Jack Lawson called out, "Well, it's obvious what sh' thinks o' you Josh," to guffaws of rough laughter. As the noise subsided slightly there were more calls for him to 'show us th' colour o' y'money', and, 'h'way, Josh, even you should be able t'ride her noo, man.' Through all of this Tommy stood silently at the mare's head, the reins held loosely in one hand, his smile one of quiet confidence. Scowling, Chisholm walked over to where he stood and, grabbing the reins, prepared to mount. As his left foot went into the stirrup, the animal shied sideways, her eyes rolling in alarm.

Three times he tried to mount and three times he was left hopping around on one foot. Finally Tommy held her head and with much heaving and puffing Chisholm finally settled himself in the saddle jerking at her head as he did so, trying hard not to let his neighbours, who were much amused by his antics, see how rattled he really was.

He dug his heels into her flanks and commanded her to walk on. Instead of the expected response she began to shuffle backwards and the more he attempted to move her forward the more she did the opposite.

"It's the front end y' r s'posed t'foller," Gerry Dixon yelled from the back, which naturally had the effect of convulsing the crowd even further.

His face darkening and with his jaw set, Chisholm eventually got her moving in the direction she was expected to move in and she appeared to settle down. He squeezed harder with his legs, asking for a trot and raised himself from the saddle in anticipation. The mare, her quarters bunching, suddenly leapt forward and set off at a dead run, catching her rider completely unawares. Before he had time to realise what was happening she had come to a sudden halt, shooting him forward up her neck and very nearly causing serious damage to his manhood on the pommel of the saddle.

With tears in his eyes, the laughter of the village ringing in his ears and his face bright red from humiliation, to say nothing of the severe pain in his loins, Josh slowly dismounted. He walked painfully back towards the crowd, who, thoroughly enjoying the spectacle of a neighbour making a complete and utter fool of himself were, to a man, convulsed.

"Okay, okay, Tommy, you win," he said, holding out his hand. "What th' hell ha' y'done t'her? Sh's worse wi' me now than sh' ever was afore."

Tommy said not a word, merely smiling as he shook Chisholm's hand.

Ernie Blakey broke in, a grin on his face as wide as a water melon, "Ah telt y'he could dae it, didn' Ah? Under Tommy's hands sh's a perfect lady but Ah doubt you'll ever get th' best out o' her, eh?"

Chisholm nodded ruefully, "Aye," he agreed, "y'just may be right on that score. Ah s'pose y'll be wantin' y'money now, then?" He reached into his jacket pocket as he spoke.

But Ernie waved a hand dismissively, "Naw, naw, keep y'money, Josh, Ah don't want it," he said.

"Eh, why not, man. Ah'd have tekkin' it off you?" Josh couldn't believe his luck.

"Aye, well, that's as mebbe," said Ernie. "But Ah'll tell y'what though, we'll scrub th' bet an' y'can sell th' mare t' Tommy, how's that sound?"

Chisholm turned to the man that had made him look like such a fool, "Is that it, then, Tommy?" he asked, his voice hard. "Is that what y'want?"

Tommy nodded his golden head and opened his mouth to speak, "Ah'Ah'Ah'........." he stammered.

"Shit, Ah might o' knawn," Chisholm spat, barely concealing his contempt. "Y'did all this, made me look a fool, just so's y'could get y'grubby little han's on me hoss. Well, listen t'me, One-Two Tommy," he snarled, his lip curling, his face thrust to within inches of the smaller man's, "it won't work. Th' hoss is not f'sale, t'you or anybody else, understand."

"You always was a fool, Chisholm, Tommy needed nae help from anybody in that direction. It was you an' y'big gob that got y'into this, an' nowt else." It was Bill Stobbard, speaking over Tommy's head who had long since given up trying to get his brain and his mouth into synchronization. "Now," Bill went on, "Ah suggest that y'either pay y'gamblin' debt t' Ernie here or tek Tommy's offer. Ah'm sure he'll gie y'a fair price for th' hoss, 'cos there's one thing sure as God made little green apples, YOU won't be ridin' her again Ah'll bet, not from what we've seen t'night."

There was a murmur of assent from the assembled village and Chisholm, suddenly realising that any sympathy he may have had had vanished, like snow on a June day, capitulated, his bluster gone. "Aye, alreet, tek th' bloody hoss," he growled sulkily, "we'll talk aboot th' price t'morrer," and he shouldered his way through the press and stumped off homeward into the gathering darkness.

Later that same evening Bill and Ernie stood at the bar of the 'Double Duck' Tommy between them. As the fourth pint was slowly consumed Bill asked the question that had been plaguing him all night. "Just how did y'do it, Tommy?"

Tommy looked questioningly over the rim of his glass, "Do what?" his eyes asked.

"Get that bloody hoss t'do what it did t'Chisholm. Man, it was bloody marvellous."

But One-Two Tommy smiled his slow, secretive smile and held his peace.

89

13

A Case of Mistaken Identity

Big Jack Lawson had been constantly in and out of work most of his life. As a result he had experienced more financial ups and downs than most but during the boom years of the late eighties he had earned quite a lot of money as a shovel driver on the nearby opencast. The hours were long and the work arduous but the compensation was, of course, the financial security that this afforded him. He was, as we have already seen, a big drinker and inclined to hotheadedness, especially when he had had a few but his one stabilising ambition in life was to own a car. Not just any car, mind you, but one which complemented his bulk, for he had absolutely no sense of status.

"By, but it's a grand motor that," said Billy Freeman, lost in admiration at the big, gleaming Rover saloon that stood importantly outside the 'Double Duck'.

"Not bad, eh?" replied Big Jack, trying not to sound overly proud, which in fact he was.

Billy stuck his head through the door of the bar and called, "H'way out here an' see what Big Jack's just got hissel'."

An immediate chorus of contempt was hurled at his head from all and sundry.

"Piss off," said Davy, grinning, "he's been in here for the last hour already braggin' about it," and as Jack followed Billy into the bar he thrust a foaming glass at him. "Here Jack," he said jovially, "have a pint on me to wet the cylinder head."

"Ah just hope it's big enough, Jack." Ernie Blakey laughed from his usual perch at the end of the bar.

"W'd y'mean?" Jack responded innocently, wiping the foam from his upper lip with the back of his hand.

"Well, th' last time Ah gave thee a lift t'work y'couldn't get y'big fat arse outa th' seat as Ah recall." Ernie replied to hoots of laughter all round. He drove a beat up Cavalier with bucket seats which had proved something of an embarrassment to Jack in the past.

And so the new car became a distinctive addition to village life; its proud new owner could be seen most weekends washing and polishing for all he was worth. 'More than he ever does here,' quoth Elsie, his wife, on many an occasion. Jack was also a keen football supporter and he looked forward eagerly to Saturday when he would drive to Newcastle to support his favourite team. That is, until one fateful Saturday morning he opened his garage to find his car missing.

His jaw dropped, his eyes bulged he turned round twice in the driveway as though trying to convince himself that he wasn't just dreaming; and then he exploded. He hurled invective at the sky the like of which hadn't been heard in the village since the night Josh Chisholm's grandfather had fallen into the communal cesspit whilst returning home drunk from the pub. Elsie, convinced that he was having some kind of seizure rushed outside to find him kicking the garage door as hard as he could. Miss Jennings, the spinster schoolteacher who lived next door, looked out of her front window and placed her hands over her ears as the thunder of his rage echoed around the green.

"Jack, Jack," cried Elsie, appalled, clutching ineffectually at his arm, "whatever's wrong?"

"Wrong, wrong, woman?" her husband roared, "some bast'd's pinched me bloody car, that's what's wrong," and he stormed off to the pub to use the telephone.

"Well, the good news is, Mr. Lawson, that we have found your vehicle." The fresh faced young constable gazed earnestly across the table at Big Jack. Big Jack thought he should still be in school.

"Good," he grunted ungratefully, "an about time an' all."

"But I'm afraid there is some damage," continued the officer, hastening to add as he observed the colour spreading in a crimson flood across Jack's ugly features, "Not much, but they have broken the rear quarter light and the ignition lock."

"Th' bast'ds," spat Jack, his big hands flexing as he imagined them around the neck of whoever had had the audacity to touch his beloved motor. "Ah swear t'God if Ah ever get me hands on them, they're broon breid."

The young constable had had enough experience to realise that it

91

was useless to argue with someone of Jack's volatile nature when in this mood. He rose to go, picking up his hat from the table, "You can collect it at your convenience, Mr Lawson," he said. "The finger print boys are done with it." He turned at the door, "And if I were you, I'd invest in an alarm system for both your garage and your car."

"Huh," snorted Jack, watching the blue uniform disappear down the path from the parlour window, "he must think Ah'm made o' brass or summat."

"Nearly a hundred an' fifty quid," Big Jack answered Davy's query as to the cost of the damage. Slamming his pint down on the bar top he repeated for the umpteenth time, "If Ah ever get me han's on 'em......."

"Aye, well, y've got t'catch them fust," Bob Dixon interrupted, "an' that won't be so easy, now will it?"

Jack looked glum, staring into his half empty glass, "Naw, Ah s'pose not. Th' polis aren't hevvin' much luck neither even if they did use me car t'knock off the Co-op doon in Low Cornhill. Ah dunno," he went on sadly, shaking his head, "y'd ha' thowt they would have left some clues f'them flatfoots t'go on, noo woudn' yer? Well, they won't get it a second time, mark my words."

"Why," Bob asked, "have y'put an alarm on?"

"Naw," Jack grinned broadly, "summat ev'n more effective than that," and he reached into his pocket and pulled forth the high tension lead which normally connected the coil and distributor.

"Without this," he said, placing the black connector on the bar, "naebody can mek me car go."

Less than a week later his car went walkabout again. It's perhaps best left to the imagination as to the immediate effect this had on Big Jack. Sufficient to say that no one had the courage to speak to him, let alone enquire after his car, for several days afterwards.

However, the police again located it and this time before the local villains had had chance to use it for any nefarious purpose, and they duly returned it to its rightful owner, again not without a certain amount of minor damage.

"Reet," Jack swore silently to himself, "that's th' final straw. If them daft buggers can't stop'em, then Ah will, by God."

From the information gleaned from the police he surmised that both thefts had occurred between the hours of two and four a.m. He therefore resolved to mount a one man vigilante patrol between the same hours every night for the next month or so, or until he caught the thieves in the act. He was fully aware that it meant losing a great deal of sleep but he was quite determined and no amount of persuasion from Elsie could make him alter course.

So every night he rose about one thirty, donned warm dark clothing and skulked about the village until he was practically frozen to death. Needless to say, this exercise did very little for his temper and by the time he was well into the second week he and Elsie had stopped speaking. He pressed on gamely however, refusing to be daunted, even though he was beginning to doubt if the thieves would ever make a reappearance.

Then one night, about the seventeenth of his solitary patrol, he was returning home by his usual route, keeping in the shadow of a high wall and creeping silently along the grass verge, when he noticed something odd, something he couldn't quite make out in the darkness.

There seemed to be a shape, a bulk of some kind, a shadow, slightly darker than the surrounding trees that hadn't been there at the beginning of his vigil. He crept closer, holding his breath, stopped once more, peered intently through the thick darkness until his worst suspicions were confirmed. It was a van, dark blue in colour, parked in such a position as to be almost invisible surrounded as it was by shrubbery. It was only about fifty or sixty yards from his house. His eyes glinted in the night and he practically drooled with expectancy. "Reet, y'bast'ds," he whispered to himself, "Ah've got y'now."

Throughout his patrolling he had always armed himself with a short, steel fencing spike. It was about three feet long and about one inch in diameter with a sharp point at one end. He normally used it for boring holes to erect fence posts but in this instance it made a formidable weapon if he had to tackle more than two or three. Less than that number and he was quite confident that he could sort them out without resort to any kind of 'equaliser'.

He crept through the grass, keeping low the whole time, hoping for the element of surprise. But it was he who was surprised for, as he yanked open the passenger door, practically dragging it off its hinges in his eagerness, he realised that the vehicle was quite empty. Disappointed, but with his fighting spirit undimmed, he softly closed the door again. Stepping round to the front of the vehicle he inserted the fencing spike through the radiator grille and pushed. The radiator gave way with a satisfying gurgle and warm water splashed onto his boots. Then he did the same to all four tyres. "They won't be goin' far in that th' neet," he chortled softly before settling down to wait for the owner's return.

It wasn't long, no more than five minutes, before he heard a rustle in the grass and a soft footfall assailed his listening ear. A dark hooded figure loomed out of the blackness carrying something heavy in front of him. Jack waited perhaps two or three seconds until the figure had passed his hiding place before launching his attack. With a snarl that would have done credit to an enraged grizzly bear he grabbed his unlucky victim by the back of his dark coat and spun him around, at the same time slamming him hard against the side of the van. His opponent reacted by dropping whatever he was carrying with a tremendous crash, right on Jack's foot. The result was that Jack was forced to abandon his furious assault for he was more concerned with his injured appendage, which was causing him to howl like a banshee and hop about like a one legged kangaroo. Seizing his opportunity, the cause of all this pain and suffering decided he would finish what Jack had started and threw a roundhouse right that connected sweetly with Jack's left eye, pitching him flat on his back. Before he could even think about rising his assailant had dived on top of him, pinning him to the ground and effectively turning the tables.

"Noo, what th' bloody hell's all this about?" he panted as he sat astride Big Jack's heaving torso.

"Ah'll show y'what it's all aboot just as soon as Ah gerrup," Jack swore loudly. "Ah'll teach y't'gan aboot at neet robbin' innocent folk, y'bast'd," and with a tremendous heave he sent the other man flying.

"Howld, howld, y'stupit bugger," he shouted, holding out his hands defensively as Jack came for him again, "Ah'm the bloody milkman. Ah'm not tryin' t'rob anybody."

This statement brought Jack up short, the words penetrating his fighting rage as though fired from a gun. "What?" he said, incredulity replacing madness, "but, but if y're th' bloody milkman, what th' hell are y'daein' oot at this time o' th' mornin'?"

The milkman, observing that his attacker was beginning to calm down, rose to his feet brushing detritus from his clothes. "Ah wanted t'get finished a bit earlier t'day," he began by way of explanation. "Ah don't usually get here until about five but Ah've other things t'do t'day."

"Aw, shit," Jack swore softly, looking shamefaced. "Y'won't be finishin' at all, bonny lad," and he showed the milkman the damage he had inflicted upon his innocent van.

Jack didn't get to bed again that night. Instead, he spent the time he should have been sleeping delivering the milk in his car. No easy task with only one eye.

The thieves never returned to High Cornhill. The assumption was that they were probably scared off by rumours of a nocturnal maniac that roamed the village whilst normal people were fast asleep in their beds.

14

Hinge and Bracket

In the early thirties, during the slump, life was very hard for most of the village folk, with little work and even less money. It was a time when the community spirit was never more evident as each helped his neighbour in whatever way he could. Therefore, when it was rumoured that a retired banker from Sunderland planned to move into the village and build a brand new house, providing work for at least those blessed with carpentry and construction skills, instead of resentment, a certain air of relief was felt.

The house took over a year to build and very grand indeed it was, being by far the biggest dwelling in the village, with three storeys, a large garden, several very fine reception rooms and eight bedrooms.

At the rear were stables and a huge garage, fronted by a cobbled yard. The whole house was surrounded by tall, shady conifers which created a secluded and private atmosphere.

Nearly everyone in the village benefited in some way, either directly or indirectly, from those that assisted in its construction to the domestic staff that were recruited from the surrounding area. It was regarded by just about everyone as a blessing, at a time when such things were very scarce on the ground.

The original family that lived there did so for nearly a quarter of a century but eventually, as death took its toll, and without the benefit of progeny, the house became a victim of passing time, remaining empty for a number of years, shuttered and forlorn, prey to the vagaries of the English weather and the destructive tendencies of man.

The garden became weed-ridden and overgrown and children playing in the grounds broke many of the windows. Holes began to appear in the roof where tiles were blown off by chill winter winds and grass grew between the cobblestones of the yard.

The authorities, as authorities are apt to do, became rather concerned about the dilapidated state of the property and urged the executors of the old banker's will to either renovate it or dispose of it. So eventually, the house was placed on the market but was in such a poor state of repair that it excited little interest.

A venerable Morris Minor wheezed into the village and drew up outside the big house. Lizzie Donkin, from her front window across the green, espied two ladies of middle years leave the car and walk up the short gravelled driveway. At the large front door the taller of the two took a key from her handbag which she used in an attempt to gain entry. But the lock refused to budge, no matter how hard she tried, it being several years now since it had been subjected to any kind of intrusion.

"Here, my dear, let me try," said the smaller one, pushing past her larger friend. But she too had no luck whatsoever; the lock remained firmly in place.

"Ah, well," said the tall lady, defeated temporarily, "let's look around the back. There may be a way in there." And so they proceeded to explore the rear of the property. To their delight they discovered a ground floor window that, although broken, permitted careful access. Between them they dragged an old packing case they found in the garage across the yard and, standing on it, they climbed in. Not without some difficulty and much heaving and straining.

Slightly dishevelled, their hair awry, they found themselves standing in what was once the kitchen. A door in one corner, hanging drunkenly from its single hinge, opened onto a corridor, dark, dank and musty smelling, along which they proceeded with infinite caution, not knowing what they might find. At the end was yet another door and, on opening it, they passed into a large, bright and airy room, that had once served as the dining room. It had seen better days and was in keeping with the rest of the house as the walls were water stained and peeling and the decorative plasterwork that had once decorated the high ceiling now littered the floor in large white chunks, like oversized hailstones.

"Oh, Katherine," exclaimed the small lady, clapping her hands in delight, "isn't it gorgeous. It must have been so lovely once," she added wistfully.

Her companion, who was made of more pragmatic material, sniffed, "that's as maybe, Georgina," she replied in a voice that was deep and masculine. She peered about her through heavy spectacles with the disapproving air of a schoolteacher, "but what I'm more concerned about is the cost of renovation and repairs. Just look at the place, it's falling to pieces," and she kicked out at one of the lumps of plaster lying on the floor which left a white scar on her smart court shoe causing her to tut with annoyance.

Nevertheless they stayed for about an hour and explored the property from top to bottom, eventually leaving the same way as they had arrived.

Mr. Sidney Grisedale was an estate agent with a small office in the nearby market town of Castleton. How he had landed the plum commission to sell High Cornhill's most prestigious property was unclear. He leaned back in the leather upholstered chair behind his large ostentatious desk and beamed at his visitor. "Well, Miss Parnell," he asked, "What d'you think? A very nice property, isn't it?" His manner was an admixture of overbearing confidence and a certain sly obsequiousness. He was definitely not the kind of man to inspire anything but contempt in the breast of Miss Katherine Parnell. He was not, however, alone in this for she exuded liberal doses of this emotion to most of mankind.

"Mr. Grisedale," she began primly, her eyes glinting icily behind her heavy glasses, "the information you were kind enough to send us waxed lyrical, if not to say effusively, about a prestigious property set in the idyllic surroundings of the Durham countryside. It failed to mention the fact that half of the roof had blown away, that water, as a consequence, had flowed unimpeded down the walls for several years, that the windows were broken, that the ceilings had fallen, that........." her voice had lost its insular calmness and had begun to rise as she recalled in detail the many faults she had noted.

Grisedale's smile remained glued to his face like a mask, fixed and grinning, the muscles atrophied. "Er, a little artistic licence," he began apologetically, interrupting his visitor in full flow.

"I haven't finished," snapped Miss Parnell, who regarded any interruption as an affront to her intelligence. "Dry rot, wet rot, weeds like palm trees, rising damp, need I go on?"

By now the smile had completely vanished, routed by the litany of complaint. "Well, of course I agree with you, Miss Parnell," he began again, hesitantly, "to a certain extent, but the price does reflect the fact that certain repairs will be necessary......."

Miss Parnell drew herself up to her full sitting height and in doing so thrust out her bosom, a bosom that commanded Grisedale's full attention, sitting as it did in front of its owner like a mantleshelf, "Some repairs, Mr. Grisedale?" she interrupted him, completely impervious to the fact that he may have shared her own aversion to being rudely halted in mid-flow, "some repairs," she repeated, hammering home her advantage, her voice rising imperiously, rather in the manner of Lady Bracknell in 'The Importance of Being Earnest', "In my opinion the property needs gutting and major construction work carried out immediately if the house isn't going to collapse, which, of course, will require a great deal of money."

Before Grisedale could make further comment Miss Parnell opened the cavernous black handbag she always carried and produced a white envelope. "Please convey this offer to your clients, Mr. Grisdale. The address and telephone number of our hotel is included. If we do not hear from you within two days we will assume that our offer is unacceptable and we will return home. Unless, that is, we have located another property in the meantime. Good-day to you," and she swept haughtily from the office, like a galleon in full sail, whilst Grisedale struggled to extricate himself from behind his walnut desk.

Within the time stated, the two ladies were pleased to learn that their offer had indeed proved acceptable, Mr. Grisedale coming to their hotel in person to impart the good news. As in times past the village and its inhabitants benefited once again from the old house as a small army of artisans were recruited locally and slowly, over the months, it was restored to its former glory.

Although perceived by most as slightly eccentric, a condition which occasionally encroached upon village life, they nevertheless in time became to be highly regarded by the locals who affectionately referred to them, when out of earshot, as Hinge and Bracket.

The stronger character of the two was, by far, Miss Parnell, who took the lead in most things and decisions, particularly the more important ones, were most definitely her domain. She brooked no interference from anyone and was inclined to needlesharp waspishness if she felt that her plans had been thwarted in any way; definitely no lady to cross swords with.

Her companion, Miss Reynolds, on the other hand, was demure, inclined to frivolity, with a simplistic, childlike regard of the world which enabled her to perceive good in everyone. Her baby blue eyes, froth of blond curls and warm nature quickly made her everyone's favourite, bringing the paternal instinct out in the male population whilst at the same time her childish demeanour seemed to pose no threat to the women of the village.

As girls they had both been pretty, although in Katherine Parnell's case the adjective, handsome, may have been a more appropriate description. If their background was ever enquired into, a habit which they both actively discouraged, they merely described themselves as teachers; although teachers of what exactly was never actually defined.

It soon became apparent that both ladies were, in fact, accomplished musicians. Miss Parnell played violin whilst Georgina Reynolds offered equal virtuoso accompaniment upon the piano. They were prone to musical evenings in their recently refurbished drawing room and, at one time or another, most of the village had been invited to a soiree or two; that is to say those with at least the merest hint of musical appreciation, Big Jack Lawson and his ilk wouldn't have been so inclined even if they had had an invitation.

Approximately every three months or so carefully calligraphed invitations would be sent out to a select few. To be honest, not everyone actually enjoyed Brahms, Beethoven, Schubert and the like but no one ever refused as the ladies' hospitality was famous, Georgina quickly establishing herself as a pastrycook par excellence; her vol au vents surpassing adequate description.

As the years passed the two spinster ladies became a totally integrated, not to say, necessary, part of village life, wholeheartedly supporting all of those activities so beloved of country women such as the WI, church fetes, Christian Aid and other multifarious good works. Life for them was lived upon a sea of calm tranquillity, much as it should be for two retired ladies of exemplary character. Until, that is, the day they received a devastating piece of news through the post.

Miss Parnell, sitting at her breakfast table in the conservatory, was the first to realise the full and shocking implications of the letter she had just opened. She froze rigid in her chair, unable to speak at first, the colour draining from her cheeks leaving her face an alabaster mask. Her companion, noting the sudden change in her appearance, was quick to voice her concern.

"What is it, my dear, whatever's wrong?" she asked earnestly, replacing her china tea cup carefully in its saucer.

Still unable to articulate even a sound Miss Parnell, her hand shaking as though plagued, passed the single sheet of paper across the table.

Fishing her spectacles from her handbag Georgina read: 'I am sorry to have to inform you that the above company went into liquidation on July sixth of this year. Whereas everything possible is being done by myself to secure shareholders' assets it is highly unlikely, judging from our initial investigations, that there will be sufficient capital realised from the sale of the company and its assets to reimburse any individual with a financial interest. I will, of course, keep you informed as to the ongoing situation on a monthly basis. In the meantime, should you require further information please do not hesitate to contact me. Yours Sincerely, G. A. Montague, Montague, Duke and Cohen, Chartered Accountants.'

Miss Reynolds slowly tore her eyes from the cold, unfeeling lines of type and looked up, shock paralysing her cherubic features, "What....., what does it mean, Katherine?" she whispered fearfully, although even with her simple grasp of things she knew instinctively that disaster was contained in the words she had just read.

Her companion was in no mood to spare her feelings or to give her a soft landing, "It means, Georgina, as I read it anyway, that our so-called 'safe' investment has turned out to be no such thing after all. It would appear, therefore, that we have lost almost all of our original capital." Her voice became harsher, more strained as she continued.

"Our money has disappeared as if it never had existed." She clasped her large, masculine hands in front of her as she gave a mirthless laugh. It seemed that she was mentally strangling the quick talking salesman who had originally persuaded them to invest almost ninety percent of their hard earned savings in this off-shore securities company.

"Oh, God, oh God," wailed Georgina, finally succumbing to the weight of misery that now engulfed her, the tears coursing down her china-doll cheeks, "what are we going to do?"

Katherine Parnell's Methodist stoicism became apparent once again as she grimly tightened her jaw and threw her friend a look that would have sliced through case hardened steel.

"Well you are going to stop all of that nonsense for a start," she snapped, "and then we are going back to work."

Georgina felt as though she had been slapped, "Work," she croaked, appalled, "but...but, how can we, at our age?"

101

"We cannot sit here and wait for divine providence, Georgina." Miss Parnell used a tone of voice that she would normally have used for a reluctant pupil. "It is up to us, and us alone, to rectify this, this, unfortunate situation, agreed?"

Georgina nodded dumbly, dabbing at her eyes, knowing that, as usual, her friend had assessed the situation and had come to an immediate decision. She was happy, again as usual, to let her do so. "So.. so what is it you propose?" she asked resignedly, her expression doleful, the corners of her mouth turning down.

"Do, do, Georgina?" Katherine's voice betrayed her exasperation at her friend's lack of understanding. "We are going to do what we know best, of course," and before she could be interrupted yet again she went on, her sense of purpose gaining momentum with every syllable.

"Listen, we have a large, well appointed house with many rooms, some of which we use but rarely. With some minor adjustments we can utilise everything here for our purpose. Do you not see?" she began to glow with enthusiasm, the light of battle shining in her eyes, "we can be back in business in a matter of weeks."

But Georgina remained unconvinced, refusing to be carried along on her friend's tide of optimism. She looked at Katherine through bewildered eyes, "I...I still don't see how?" she faltered, "we really are far too old....."

"Oh, please, Georgina, use your head for once." Katherine was becoming angry now, her waspish nature showing, "We will simply bring younger people in to assist. We have our contacts, do we not?" Her hot gaze bored across the intervening table, brooking no further argument. Georgina, as she always did, gave in. "Right then, let's get on. Your address book, please," and she held out her hand.

Autumn had returned, the harvest was in and Bill and his men were hard at work ploughing those fields that had been earmarked for winter wheat. He arrived back at the farmhouse late one evening, long after darkness had fallen and as he sat down to his evening meal he said to Sarah, placing a hand in the small of his back and stretching, "Y'knaw, Ah think me back's worse than ever this year." He had suffered recurring back trouble for years, like most farmers, the result of sitting for hours in a twisted position pulling a plough behind a tractor.

"Well, you should go and see about it, then," Sarah said, not unkindly, placing his dinner in front of him. "it will only get worse if you don't."

"Ah'll tell y'what," replied her husband, catching her around the waist, "after Ah've had me dinner Ah'll go an' have a hot bath an' then y'can gie me a massage, how's that?"

"And we all know what that can lead to," Sarah smiled at him.

"Aye, wi' a bit o' luck," Bill nodded, his mouth full.

A few days later Sarah was leaving the post office in Low Cornhill when her eye fell upon a small advertisement placed in the window. It read, 'Banish tenseness, back pain, muscular problems. Relax in the hands of our expert masseurs in a genteel and discreet atmosphere,' and it gave a telephone number to ring. She made a note of it and passed it on to her husband that same evening. He, in his usual manner, put it to one side and completely forgot about it until Sarah found him rooting though the sideboard one evening, silently cursing under his breath.

"What on earth are you looking for?" she asked calmly, eyeing the mess he was making and knowing who would be clearing it up.

"That damn' phone number," her husband growled.

"Which 'phone number?"

"Th' one f'r that bloody massage parlour, me back's killin' me. Ah, found it," he concluded triumphantly, holding aloft a scrap of paper. Picking up the telephone in the hall he dialled quickly. A few seconds later Sarah heard him say softly to himself, "Well, Ah'll be damned," and then, louder, "Yes, yes, that's right, an appointment, f'r me back........"

A little later that same evening he came downstairs dressed in casual slacks and sweater, "Ah'm just goin' t'that new massage place an' Ah might just call in at th' pub on me way home," he announced to his wife who was busy at her ironing board in the kitchen.

"Alright, my love, I'll not wait up for you." It was some minutes after he had gone that she realised that she hadn't heard the car leave.

Bill walked up the drive of the big house and rang the front door bell. It was opened almost immediately and he was ushered into the drawing room by a bosomy, long haired beauty who couldn't have been more than twenty five, he reckoned. The sleek dress she was wearing hadn't been bought in a local branch of Doggarts neither, he surmised silently. A breath of exquisite Parisian perfume enveloped him as she bent towards him and murmured softly, "Mr. Stobbart, if you would care to make yourself comfortable on the sofa I will just go and make sure that everything is ready for you." She glided out of the room on a perfumed cloud, the only sound was her silk stockinged thighs rustling slightly.

He gazed around him at the expensive furnishings, some of which were genuine antiques, and settled lower in his seat. He had been in this room on many occasions but now, somehow, it all seemed so different. It was that girl, he decided, she had leant everything a pervasive atmosphere of sensuality. It made him feel uneasy. His thoughts were interrupted as another guest was shown into the room. He looked up as a familiar voice boomed at him, "Oh, hello, Bill, what th' hell are you doin' here?" It was Archie Greenside, another landowner from the other side of the valley.

"Oh, hello there, Archie," he replied quickly, "Ah've come t'get me back fixed. It's bin givin' me gyp lately...."

The newcomer laughed loudly, "Oh, aye," he said, smirking, "Ah thowt all o' this might be a bit close t'home f'r you like, if y'knaw what Ah mean?"

Bill looked blank. Mystified, he could only shake his head, unable to grasp the significance of the remark. Suddenly the door opened yet again and Miss Parnell appeared, dressed in something long, black and formal. "Mr. Greenside," she gushed warmly, not noticing Bill at first, "how nice to see you again," and then, surprised, "and Mr. Stobbart too, well this is a pleasant surprise. I do hope that my niece is looking after you?" They both nodded their assent, so she went on, speaking directly to Archie, "You have called for your usual service I presume, Mr. Greenside?"

Archie nodded again, "Aye, that's right, Miss Parnell. Ah'm booked in wi' Deidre, t'night. Top floor, as usual."

Katherine Parnell nodded in a regal fashion, "Good, good," she murmured. "Now, if there's nothing further I can do for you gentlemen, I must return to my other guests," and with a gracious smile, she was gone.

His face an artistic study in amazement, Bill caught at the sleeve of his friend's expensively cut jacket, "what th' hell's goin' on,

Archie?" he hissed expressively. "An' what's so special about th' top floor?"

"Have y'not bin here afore, then, Bill?" Archie answered the question with one of his own.

"O'course Ah have," Bill replied testily, "but only t'one or two o' their musical evenin's. Ah came here th' neet 'cos Sarah saw one o' their adverts in the post office window an' Ah thought Ah could get me back massaged. Ah told you......."

"Aye, Ah knaw," his friend replied wryly, "it's bin givin' y'gyp lately. Y'never knew that they did this sort o' thing an' all?" he asked incredulously.

Bill was becoming more and more exasperated, and it showed, "What sort o' thing? What th' hell are y'on aboot, man? Like Ah said, Ah came here f'r a massage but Ah didn't even knaw it was Hinge an' Bracket's place until Ah rang up earlier."

"Oh, they dae more than just a massage," Archie said, grinning expansively. "Massages are on th' second floor. It's what goes on on th' top floor that matters."

"So what th' hell does go on up there, f'r Chris' sake?" Bill almost screamed at him.

Archie clicked his tongue disapprovingly, "Y'shouldn' even ask. An' you a married man, an all." He remonstrated mockingly. He had recently been divorced.

Bill's eyes widened, "Jeesuus," he swore, his breath whistling between his teeth, "If y're tellin' me what Ah think y're tellin' me Ah'm out o' here, an' damn' quick. Our Sarah'll murder me just f'r thinkin' about a place like this." He had begun to sweat, little beads of perspiration appearing just beneath his hairline.

"Ah, ah, just a minute, old son. "It was Archie's turn to grab Bill's sleeve. "Y'll have signed the visitors' book?"

Bill nodded.

"Aye, well," Archie's tone was serious now as he gazed into his friend's face, "all th' guests are asked to remember that discretion is of the utmost importance, knaw what Ah mean? Mum's th' word, eh?" and he placed a finger to his lips.

"There's been an awful lot of comings and goings in the last few weeks across at the old ladies' place," Sarah observed casually as she and her husband relaxed one evening about a month later in front of their sitting room fire. "I couldn't help noticing," she went on, her knitting needles poised in mid-air as she studied her pattern with a frown, "the variety of big flash cars that keep appearing on their driveway. Still, it's little wonder I s'pose"

Bill wriggled deeper into his chair and raised his copy of the 'Farming Times' a shade higher. He grunted non-committally in response.

"Well, have you seen the three, or is it four, girls they have staying over there? Absolutely gorgeous, all of them. Their nieces, they tell me. Now one of those might do your back the world of good, my love," and she giggled at the thought.

Bill's face was suddenly suffused with colour. He cleared his throat, opened his mouth, and then thought better of it.

15

A Day at the Seaside

"Well, where's it t'be this year, then?" Tom Dandridge posed the perennial question as he walked into the bar of the 'Double Duck'. It had fallen to the cricket team, as it did every year, to organise the annual outing for the village.

"Ah can't see what's wrong wi' goin' back t'Whitley Bay or Cullercoats mesel'," quoth Big Jack Lawson, gazing round at the assembled company. "We had a grand time there last year."

"Now what th' hell would you knaw about that, eh?" Ernie Blakey grinned, "y'were pissed oot o' y'skull most o' th' time as Ah recall. It was you we had t'go back for 'cos y'd passed oot in one o' them promenade shelters."

There was general laughter all round as Jack mustered the grace to look embarrassed. "Ah wasn't pissed," he defended himself, "Ah was just tired, that's all. Ah'd had a hard day, man."

"Aye," Billy Freeman called from his end of the bar, "a hard day proppin' up just about ev'ry bar on the North East coast."

As the laughter subsided, Davy, in his usual position, one foot resting upon the low sink, asked, "So, has anybody got any ideas, or do we make it Whitley Bay again?"

There was a rousing chorus of assent as they all agreed that the seaside offered just about everything for everyone; it had sand in the shape of a broad clean beach, an amusement park and shopping arcade if it was raining. But best of all, certainly as far as the village's male population was concerned, there was an abundance of good pubs. In the long practised traditions of eighteen carat male chauvinists the men travelled in the lead coach, accompanied by several cases of Newcastle Brown Ale, whilst the younger members of the village and their mothers followed in a second conveyance.

The only time during the day in which they became a whole was when everyone assembled on the beach for an organised picnic lunch, after which, those that were able retraced their steps to the seafront hostelries, such as the Gibraltar Rock and the Sea Hotel, whilst those that weren't slept it off on the sand, usually to be buried by their offspring. The more responsible members of the party, however, such as Davy or Bill did spend the greater part of the day with their respective spouses whilst those of a more single minded nature, Jack Lawson, Josh Chisholm, Tom Dandridge et al were off their starting blocks even before the coach wheels had stopped turning.

One that fell into the former category, although unmarried, having been widowed for some years, was the club's life president, Sam Kilpatrick. Although now well over eighty years of age he lived alone in a small cottage in the centre of the village and had most of his everyday needs catered for by the ladies of the community, who were happy to keep his house clean and his shirts washed and starched, just the way he liked them. For Sam was, and always had been, a perfect gentlemen in the old fashioned tradition; a much loved relic of those bygone days between the wars when chivalry and politeness weren't denigrated in the way they are today.

He had been an active sportsman all of his life, playing cricket for the village for over forty years and had only recently given up playing golf, a decision forced upon him by the necessity of having to undergo operations to replace both hip joints.

He had the mental attitude and general bonhomie of a man of half his years and was gifted with the mind of a trained accountant, sharp and precise. If any fault could be levelled at him it was that, once a year, he liked a drink. He seemed to conserve all of his natural alcoholic inclinations for the day of the annual outing; the remainder of the year, even at Christmas-time, he was as sober and upright an example to everyone as a village elder aught to be. But once he got away from home with the cricket club members he really let his hair down.

Being the president, and an octogenarian, he was naturally feted and cosseted and made much of and he invariably ended the day having to be carried home and put to bed. This particular practice had been going on for as long as anyone could remember and was therefore regarded by all and sundry with rather amused indulgence. Even his wife, when she was alive, always turned a blind eye, although she herself rarely ventured on these seaside excursions.

She had always been there, however, to see that he was safely tucked up in bed upon his return. In spite of this annual inebriation Sam never ever forgot the fact that he was a gentleman and even when he collapsed at the feet of the wife of Davy's predecessor he did so with consummate grace, attempting, as his knees slowly buckled, to raise his hat.

A finger of sunlight traced primrose patterns upon his bedroom wall as Davy slowly opened his eyes. The day of the outing had finally dawned and blue skies augured well for it. He slipped quietly out of bed, not wishing to disturb his still sleeping wife and stretching mightily, he walked across to where his dressing gown lay. As he did so he glanced out of the window, which looked out onto the field at the back of the pub and gave a magnificent panoramic view across the whole of the valley.

"Bloody Nora," he swore softly then, moving back to the bed he called out urgently, "Glennis, Glennis, wake up," as he shook his wife by the shoulder.

She, thinking the place was on fire, immediately sat bolt upright, her blond hair like a haystack, "Whassamarrer?" she slurred, her voice thick with sleep, her eyes unfocussed.

"It's the little hoss," her husband hissed at her, aghast, "Ah think he's dead."

Harry Robertson had by this time acquired a two year old black gelding which he kept in the field along with his mare.

"Wha' d'you mean, y'think it's dead?" Glennis replied unbelievingly, fumbling her arms into her own dressing gown.

"Go an' tek a look f'r y'self," Davy replied, his normal imperturbable manner disintegrating rapidly, "he's layin' flat out wi' th'mare standin' ower him an' sh' looks very sad t'me."

Glennis peered out of the window but, without her glasses, it was just too far to make anything out clearly.

"What're we goin' t'do? What on earth are we goin' t'tell Harry? What....?" Davy was becoming even more agitated.

Prevarication wasn't something Glennis was renowned for. "Oh, stop dithering, Davy," she snapped at him, "and go down there an' have a proper look. It might be nowt nor summat."

"Aye, aye," replied her spouse, heavily, "'appen y're reet, pet."

He stepped outside into the still, calm morning and looked over the low wall that bounded the field. The mare hadn't moved. She was still in exactly the same place, standing with her eyes closed, her head drooping, her nose practically touching the gelding's flank. He heaved himself onto the wall in order to improve his view but, as he straightened, his left foot slipped on a small piece of moss, casting him ignominiously into a clump of stinging nettles.

"Bugger an' blast it," he roared, the nettles performing their customary unsociable function.

In the stillness of the morning his voice crashed across the hill top like a thunderbolt from the gods. The mare's head jerked up suddenly and, startled out of her wits, she turned in her own length and set out for far distant horizons at breakneck speed. The gelding leapt to his feet as though springloaded, every primaeval instinct lending wings to his feet and he followed her, tail up, head erect and together they pranced along the farthest fence, clearly demonstrating their intense displeasure at being woken in such an unseemly manner.

"Dead, eh?" Glennis sniffed scornfully as she administered to her husband's hot and painful hands and feet. "I don't s'pose it ever occurred to you that they may just be asleep......?"

"But sh' looked so sad, her head hangin' down like that," Davy interrupted defensively.

His wife, who had been raised on a farm, gave a long suffering sigh, "Horses can sleep standin' up y'know." She shook her head, unable to comprehend her husband's ignorance of such matters.

"Can they?" Davy stared at her blankly, "Well, Ah never knew that."

The sea was at its pristine best as the crowds thronged the promenade and beach of Whitley Bay. It seemed to reflect the mood as it sparkled under a benevolent sun and tiny wavelets unceasingly nudged the shore. The bay stretched as far as Cullercoats in a giant horseshoe, the tip of which was marked by the white monolith of St. Mary's lighthouse.

"Would y'look at that?" Davy remarked admiringly as, breathing deeply of the ozone laden air, he gazed out over the blue North Sea. "There's nowt like it, is there?" he went on as he and Glennis and Bill meandered slowly across the grassy cliffs having left the bus and its horde of passengers some minutes before. The journey

110

coastwards, in one coach this year owing to their being fewer passengers, had been light-hearted and noisy with most of the men seated at the rear, the obligatory crates of brown ale conveniently placed.

By the time they had reached their destination more than half of the dark brown bottles were upside down; the life president having kept pace with the best of them. He had disappeared in the direction of the nearest toilet as soon as he had alighted, slightly the worse for wear, although only those who really knew him could tell just how far gone he was. Bill kept looking back in the direction of the coach expecting the old man eventually to appear from the car park. When, after ten minutes or so, there was still no sign of him he decided he must go back. "Well, y'never know wi' auld Sam, 'specially when he's had a drink or two," he apologised to his companions.

Arriving back at the bus Bill was quick to discover that there was no sign at all of the life president, in fact, there was little sign of anyone as all of the occupants had dispersed in the general direction of the beach or the town. "Damn it," he swore silently to himself, his frown deepening, "where th' hell can he have got to?" and he shaded his eyes scanning the wider area of the car park and cliffs. Unable to detect the vaguest hint of the old man he set off again intending to rendezvous with his friends when the sudden thought occurred to him that Sam might just have gone into town for he could be wayward under alcohol's benign influence.

As he passed the entrance to a vast undercover amusement arcade the sound of a high pitched whoop of pure glee brought him to a halt in mid-stride. He recognised the voice. Threading his way through a constant ebb and flow of happy youngsters he eventually located the source of the sound through the general mayhem. Behind a broad pillar stood a single, computerised, electronic, state of the art box of tricks of which Bill had little knowledge and even less interest. What was of interest, however, was the fact that Sam was driving it and as he pushed his way through the crowd of ten and eleven year olds that surrounded him, their eager faces fixed determinedly upon the multi coloured screen, he saw that the life president had his hands wrapped firmly around the controls as he gazed in a near trancelike state at the electronic gizmos that flashed and screamed at mesmeric speed from the heart of deep space as represented by, what was to Bill, nothing more than a sophisticated television set.

"Here they come again, Terry," Sam yelled excitedly to the diminutive companion at his side as literally dozens of virtual reality, computer graphic spaceships hurtled towards him, all guns blazing, from the centre of the screen. "Take that, an' that, an' that, did you see that? Oh no you don't," his commentary, as he successfully manipulated his own spacecraft through the marauding hordes, whilst at the same time destroying in spectacular pyrogenics as many as he could, was unceasing.

"Go on, Sam, get that 'un, aye that's it, shoot the buggers out o' th' sky," Terry screamed ecstatically as more reinforcements were sent hurtling to their doom in rapid succession.

Disbelievingly, Bill shook his head, a wry smile on his lips. Tapping Sam lightly on the shoulder he growled, "C'mon, y'owld idiot, leave that t' th' kids."

Sam turned at Bill's light touch, his eyes alight behind his spectacles. "Oh, hello, Bill," he grinned, "have you ever tried one of these things? You should, y'know, they're marvellous, great fun and absolutely harmless."

"Ah'm not so sure about that," he smiled in response, "H'way outside, man. Th' sun's splittin' th' trees an' th' beer's gettin warm. Y'shouldn't be cooped up in a place like this t'day."

"No, no, of course not, you're absolutely right," Sam agreed. "Well, boys, it looks like I'll have to be getting along." This was met by loud moans from his tightly packed audience. "But here, before I do," and he delved deeply into his trouser pocket for a handful of change, "have a few rounds on me."

"Mister," said the undersized Terry, grinning, "f'r an auld feller y'don't half play a mean machine."

"It's the brown ale y'know," Sam remarked as they stepped once more into the sunlight, leaving the cool, dark environs of the amusement arcade behind them.

"What is?"

"That keeps your reflexes sharp," replied Sam, a steely glint in his eye as he recalled just how many enemy ships he had destroyed with such devastating precision.

"Ah'm s'prised that y've any reflexes at all th' amount of ale y've supped already," Bill smiled at the little man as they walked toward the cliff top path.

"And we have still the rest of the day untouched," Sam replied eagerly.

As it happened he was just a little premature in his eagerness to take the day by storm for Glennis had other plans and insisted that they spend at least some time together. Davy knew exactly what that meant. Shops, particularly of the antique variety, of which she was so fond. He pulled a face at the thought but Sam, ever the gentleman, lent his wholehearted support.

"After all," pointed out, "without the ladies....."

"Aye, aye, we know," Bill interrupted, with the air of a man about to be hanged, "where would be?"

"Exactly," replied Sam, taking Glennis by the arm and turning his face once again in the direction of the town.

By lunchtime they were all beginning to feel a little jaded and, thinking that he had done his bit for one day, Davy suggested that a little liquid refreshment might be in order and the 'Rock of Gibraltar' was mentioned. Glennis declined suggesting that they meet again in an hour for a picnic lunch on the beach, near the steps.

"Good, lass," Davy kissed her cheek gratefully, "just a couple an' then we'll be down."

"Just as long as it is only a couple, mind," replied his wife with mock severity although Davy was under no illusion as to the consequences should he spoil her day through his neglect. It was a sentiment with which Sam agreed wholeheartedly.

They entered the bar to discover half of the cricket team already installed and, judging by their appearance, they had been installed for some time. Bob Dixon, on catching sight of the newcomers, lurched unsteadily across the floor and put an arm around the life president's neck.

"H'way, Sam, me ol' mucker," he slurred, "let's you an me have a drink. Noo, what'll it be bonny lad?"

"Oh, it's alright, Bob, thank you, but we three will just stick together." Sam was at pains not to allow Bob's drunken enthusiasm to get the better of him.

But Bob was not to be put off so easily and he wagged a wavering forefinger under Sam's nose. "Never let it be said," he announced, "that Ah wasn't able t'buy me mates a drink. Landlord," he called, turning too quickly and nearly overbalancing, "a drink for these gentlemen, if y'please."

They accepted with good grace and after they each had consumed three pints the spectre of Glennis waiting by the steps began to haunt them, at least it did Davy and Bill for by this time Sam was just beginning to get his second wind and so, very apologetically, he asked that he might be excused.

"Okay, Sam, whatever y'say," Davy agreed, "but mind, don't forget that th' bus leaves at six sharp. An' that goes for th' rest of you lot, an' all," he raised his voice above the babble.

"Wha's that, Davy lad?" a voice he recognised as Big Jack's came at him from somewhere over by the pool table.

"Th' bus leaves at six, if y'r not on it, y'walk home."

A chorus of ribald and derisory comments was hurled at their backs as they left.

For Bill and Davy the rest of the day was spent quietly enough doing what most people do when spending a day by the sea. As the time came for them to leave Glennis decided that they should have one last cup of tea at one of the outdoor promenade cafes and then make their way to the bus. They hadn't been at their table long when several members of the cricket team appeared. The last time they had been seen was in the 'Rock'.

"Heyup, Davy lad," Bob Dixon called out as they all took their places at nearby tables, "have y'had a good day then?" His lunchtime drinking session seemed to have left him a little the worse for wear but he was enunciating more clearly.

Davy returned the good natured enquiry with a laugh, "Aye, but not as obviously as you lot have, eh?" he said.

"Well, thanks very much," Glennis interjected half seriously.

Her husband quickly smoothed her ruffled feathers, "Now, now, my love," he said patting her hand, "y'know what Ah mean."

"By th' way," Bill chipped in, "where's our illustrious president? Ah don't see him wi' you lot."

Bob frowned hard, trying to get his creaking brain to function in a more orderly manner. Turning in his chair he called out, "Jack, have y'seen owt o' Sam?"

The cry was taken up and it soon became clear that Sam was missing once again.

"Your turn this time, Ah think," Bill grinned across the table as he reached for the milk jug. "We'll just finish our tea then we'll meet you at th' bus."

Davy groaned as he rose to his feet. "Okay, where did y'last see th'auld goat?" he addressed the assembled company. He gathered from the chorus of information that Sam had definitely been with them all when they left the pub but somewhere between there and the cafe he had gone missing. He set off alone to retrace the route and it wasn't long before he spotted Sam in the middle of a group of children enjoying the dying minutes of their day in the paddling pool.

"Sam," Davy called as he approached, "c'mon man, y'll miss th' bus."

The president looked up, a broad smile on his face, having just been thoroughly soaked by a small boy. "Ah, Davy, my man," he intoned expansively whilst at the same time gesturing generously with an open palm, to the point where he nearly fell over. Davy could see that he was well gone by now. "C'mon in, the water's fine," and he giggled delightedly at his feeble joke.

"No Sam," Davy was determined, "you come on out. The bus leaves in about five minutes."

Sam sighed but seeing that further argument was useless he waded across to the edge of the pool. Clasping the outstretched hand that was offered he heaved himself out of the water. As he did so Davy realised that, although he had rolled his trousers up he had completely forgotten to remove his socks and shoes. He squelched out onto the surrounding concrete apron and gazed down at his feet in dismay, "Oh, dear," was all that he could think to say, alarm spreading across his face as he gazed down at his ruined footwear.

Davy began to chuckle gently at the old man's consternation, "You're a daft auld beggar, Sam," he said fondly, at which Sam began to giggle tentatively. Soon they were both roaring with laughter as they made their soggy way back to the bus.

The journey home was companionable, if noisy, as each related their individual adventures of the day. Sam, a bottle of brown ale clutched in one hand, chatted and sang happily nearly all of the way home. Davy and Bill took him to his cottage and saw him safely inside. As they turned to leave, having deposited him in his favourite armchair, he said cheerfully, "Thank you once again, my friends. We'll do the same again next year, I have no doubt."

A little over three weeks later Sam passed away peacefully in his sleep much mourned by all of those whose lives he had touched.

16

Drink and the Devil

When the Co-op in Low Cornhill closed its butchery department the local residents were left at a loss for they were definitely not accustomed to travelling far in pursuit of their Sunday roast. They need not have worried, however, for the manager, Joe Fletcher, regarded the Co-op's loss as his opportunity and with his savings and a small bank loan he opened a new shop in what had once been the Post Office. Over the years, with prudence and careful planning he gradually built a thriving little business which more than satisfied his customers' needs. Tom Dandridge, the cattleman, supplied most of his beast and as their relationship matured they became firm friends. It was Tom who brought him the news one day that a butcher's shop was for sale in the nearby dormitory town of Newton Moor, a suburb of the city. It was peopled with a majority of high earners who liked to live well and soon Joe was the proud owner of two butchers' shops.

He gradually formed the habit, about once a month, of spending the day in the company of his cattle supplier visiting the various auction marts throughout the North in his quest for prime beef cattle and fatstock.

Now this was all very well as far as it went but one of Tom's endearing little habits was to visit every pub that was associated with each cattle market and as they visited three, sometimes four, marts in a day they naturally consumed a proportionate amount of alcohol. A lot of business is done outside of the main ring.

Tom, whose routine this had been for most of his life, could take it in his stride. Unfortunately Joe, who wasn't blessed with his friend's iron constitution, could not and inevitably he would arrive home much the worse for wear and have to be put straight to bed to sleep it off. Nothing wrong in that you might say; once a month isn't going to kill anybody. This was not the view taken by Joe's spouse, a staunch Methodist, who regarded drink with a horror that can only come from a deeply held religious conviction. She also regarded Tom as the devil himself and blamed him absolutely for leading her husband down the stoney path to eternal damnation and wouldn't have him in the house at any price, preferring to pick her husband up off the front door step than have, 'that man' sully the unctuous atmosphere of her parlour.

Tom being Tom of course, regarded this attitude with great amusement as it merely served to incite his sense of mischief even further and he looked forward to his monthly excursions with even greater eagerness. But he didn't have to face the music. It was always poor old Joe who had to bear the brunt of his wife's severe disapproval which usually manifested itself in one of two ways; either total silence for a number of days, the length of time directly proportional to the amount of alcohol consumed, or a most unholy row, depending on what was said on his arrival home. One would have thought that familiarisation of an event that occurred with such monotonous regularity, combined with a little love and understanding, not to say a leavening of humour, might have imbued a certain acceptance, if not exactly tolerance, within the good lady's breast; but religion, drink and the devil are a toxic and explosive mixture.

"Ah now, our Ada's not that bad, Tom," Joe defended his wife's honour as he wagged a slightly unsteady finger under his friend's nose. "Apart from her gettin' het up at me takin' th' occasional drink sh's allus bin a good wife t'me." His bald head shone under the lights of the 'Double Duck' as they both sat in a corner putting the world, and in particular, Joe's domestic problems to rights. It was a Friday night and as such it was most unusual for the two friends to be out together but Tom had called at the shop earlier in the day and they had agreed to meet that night, 'just for a couple'.

"Oh, don't get me wrong , Joe," Tom's reply was earnest in the extreme as he strove to ameliorate his initial unconscious criticism. "Ah can see that sh' has. All Ah meant was that Ah'm glad sh's yours an' not mine, that's all. 'Cos let's face it, man, it's me sh' blames for you gettin' in th' state y'dae. Ready f'r another?" he finished artlessly, draining his glass.

Joe nodded. It never occurred to either of them that a solution to the problem would have been to modify their drinking habits. Perish the thought.

The evening drew to a close and they wandered out into the night, Joe pulling his car keys out of his pocket as he did so.

Tom's expression grew a little anxious, "Are y'sure y'can manage now, Joe?" he enquired as he watched his friend struggle to insert the key in the lock.

With all of the bravado born of drink Joe dismissed his concern. "Aye, aye, dinna fash y'sel,man," he said, finally opening the door and climbing into the driver's seat. "It's only a mile doon the back road an' be th' time Ah get home sh'll be in bed an' asleep, wi'any luck."

The cattle dealer stood under the stars and watched as the headlights carved a meandering course down the hill.

Some five days later Tom stuck his head around the back door of the butcher's in Low Cornhill.

He found his friend wielding a boning knife with great dexterity. "Now then, Thomas," Joe greeted him, continuing his deft knifework. "Just gie' me a sec an' Ah'll put th' kettle on." Here in his own domain he was an entirely different character. Here he was master, dressed in white smock, white hat and blue striped butcher's apron and as such he was the epitome of efficiency and brooked no slackness.

"So," Tom remarked, a steaming mug in his hand, "how did y'get on t'other neet?"

Joe looked puzzled.

"It wasn't exactly a straight line y'was drivin' when Ah last saw yer," he said by way of explanation.

"Oh, that," Joe replied, enlightenment dawning. "Aye, well, y'd better come outside an' Ah'll show yer." His friend detected a distinctly sheepish air.

Out in the lane at the back of the shop stood Joe's smart Volvo estate; or at least it would have been smart except for the deep scratches down both blue flanks.

Tom whistled appreciatively. "How.....?" he began.

"Parkin'." Joe replied enigmatically, nodding.

This took Tom completely by surprise and he stared blankly at the butcher.

Inside once more Joe sat down and, picking up his mug of now lukewarm tea, he began. "Ah thought Ah'd got away wi' it 'cos, as

Ah'd hoped, sh' was in bed an' asleep when Ah got in. That much Ah do remember."

Tom nodded, "Aye, so what happened?"

Joe shifted his position and looked embarrassed. "It was th' followin' mornin' that all hell broke loose," he said.

His friend uttered not a word, a slow, expectant smile spreading across his face.

"Ah'd parked th' bloody car in th' hedge, hadn' Ah?" Joe blurted out, his face reddening.

Tom could hardly contain himself, "What, nose fust?" he chortled.

Joe nodded, wilting under his discomfiture and then, as Tom's guffaws grew in intensity, he joined in and soon they both had tears running down their faces. "Aye, but that's not all," Joe gasped, wiping a damp eye with the corner of his apron.

"Y'mean there's more?"

"Oh, aye," Joe's voice was laden with doom. "It was Ada what found th' bloody thing. Sh' needed it t' go shoppin' but sh' couldn't get the doors open, y'knaw how thick our back hedge is. What's more, neither could Ah."

"But y'must o' got out o' it th' night afore, man?" Tom gurgled helplessly.

"Why aye, man, that's just th' point," Joe had started to laugh again, "Ah couldn't remember f'r th' life o' me just how Ah'd done it. It was all locked up an' everythin'. Ah had t'get one o' th' lads from the farm t' tow it out wi' a tractor afore we could oppen th' doors."

The cattle dealer collapsed completely at this, his huge stomach vibrating to his unbridled bellows of laughter, his mouth agape as he gasped for air. Ted, the front shop assistant left his post, anxious to know what all of the noise was about.

Tom waved him away weakly as he wiped the tears from his eyes, "Naw, naw, lad, it's allright. It's just this daft beggar o' a boss o' yours, he'll be th' death o' me yet."

"Huh, Ah mightn't," Joe grinned, "but if our Ada gets her hands on you, she most certainly will be."

They therefore decided, in the best interests of all concerned, that they would discontinue their monthly excursions, at least until the heat had died down. They hardly saw each other, except in the course of business, for at least three months, Tom keeping a very low and discreet profile. However, all flesh is weak and eventually Joe again succumbed to the devil's temptation. As he opened the door of Tom's battered Landrover he issued a stern warning. "We are not, under any circumstances, going to touch a drop, understand?"

Tom merely grinned, nodding. His excuse for a conscience had had some effect on him and he agreed to support his friend's newly acquired temperate attitude. And so it was that they visited four marts in all, bought some fine beast and arrived home sober but satisfied.

Tom was feeling rather smug as he drew the car up to the path in front of his friend's house. So much so that, having spied Ada busy in the front garden hoeing a border in the evening sunlight, he decided to take his courage in both hands and make his peace. After all, it was a long time since he and her husband had had a drink together therefore he deemed it safe. A low wall, a new addition, bounded the road, atop of which was set a row of smart, hooped railings. Tom climbed out of the driving seat and, greeting Ada in a friendly manner, he leaned a casual elbow nonchalantly on top of the new fencing, a pose he hoped would put her at her ease. It immediately collapsed beneath his weight, pitching him face downward in the dirt.

"You drunken pig, Tom Dandridge," the good lady screamed and brought the handle of her hoe down with a sharp crack on the back of his unsuspecting head.

"Oh, Ada.....!" cried her horrified husband, too stunned to move.

"And don't you dare speak to me, Joe Fletcher. Every time you go out with this, this, drunkard, you come back in this sort of state," and with tears of anger in her eyes she stormed off into the house.

Tom sat up, looking bemused and nursing his bruised skull. "What th' hell happened?" he croaked.

"Aw, man, it's all my fault," Joe apologised, struggling to get Tom's bulk off the ground. "Ah shoulda warned y'about these damn' railin's."

"Why, what's wrong wi' them?" said Tom, shaking his head in an attempt to clear it.

Joe pulled them back into an upright position, "Look, they're plastic. They only look like steel."

"Well, Ah'll be....." Tom stuttered, still rubbing the back of his head. He gave a rueful smile, "Well, that's poetic justice f'r yer, isn't it?" he laughed.

17

A Child Crying

Religion did not play a major part in the life of the village which, if one thought about it, was surprising. It was surprising because of the fact that the predominant teaching institution in the area was a large Catholic seminary.

Its huge, Gothic structure, sited prominently on a hill, dominated the surrounding landscape and every evening and at regular intervals during the day the solemn tone of its bell could be heard drifting across the fields summoning the faithful to prayer.

It had stood like an island, surrounded by its own sea of magnificent parkland, for over one hundred and fifty years and although numbers were now in serious decline it had in the past proudly sent forth a vast quantity of humanity duly ordained to proclaim the word of their particular God.

It was every Catholic mother's ambition, especially in those days when families of ten children or more were commonplace, to have her eldest son attend this alma mater and, after a given number of years, emerge from its chrysalis duly transformed into a dull, grey moth, more than capable of buckling on the armour of selfrighteousness and descending upon the heathen hordes, to smite them hip and thigh.

One such family was the Charltons and they boasted no fewer than three priests and two nuns to say nothing of a missionary bishop among their ancestors. It was inevitable, therefore, that young Matthew should eventually be deposited upon this ecclesiastical door step and left in the tender care of those whose duty it was to uphold the religious, moral, spiritual and intellectual well being of those innocents left so freely in their charge. The year was nineteen thirty three and Matthew was thirteen years old.

At first he fitted in fairly well with the strict regime of study and prayer having been conditioned by his mother practically from the day he was born as to what to expect, his destiny having already been decided for him. It was no worse and no better than he had anticipated although whether he was ever going to make a priest or not was a matter of no small conjecture, both for him and his tutors.

He was there for almost two years before his and Tony's paths crossed. Tony came from the South and had been public school educated. It had been entirely his own decision to study for holy orders, much against the will of his domineering father, a prominent City lawyer. It spoke highly of his single minded determination to succeed against the might of parental authority.

He was a year older than Matthew and he seemed to him to be very worldly wise and sophisticated with his posh Surrey accent and smart clothes. But what impressed the impressionable Matthew most was his irrepressible humour and his never ending fund of anecdotes of the girls he had known and the wild parties he had been to whilst at school. He was altogether, Matthew thought, a dashing, handsome figure, always laughing, always up to something but never losing sight of his one ambition, to become a priest. The two boys, each from opposite ends of the social spectrum, became firm friends and during their years at the college were inseparable.

"Religion is like life, y'know Matt. It's what you make it and its there to be enjoyed. I just can't believe God ever consciously wanted me to be miserable."

The boys were walking home through the darkened fields having had a rare evening out at the 'Double Duck'. They were discussing the possibility of bringing a little more levity into religious teaching as a serious philosophical proposition. They were also late as it was well past ten o' clock, which for them was the witching hour. To compound the felony they had also been drinking under age although Tony was confident that he could argue that he would be eighteen in just six weeks; not so his friend.

As they approached the rear entrance to the college they saw, framed in the doorway, the light at his back, the dreaded figure of Father Patrick, the head of Religious Studies and their tutor. He was a strict disciplinarian whose temper was on a notoriously short fuse. He was issuing instructions to another figure whom they couldn't see but guessed it was the caretaker.

"Oh, hell," whispered Tony fiercely, dragging Matthew into the shadow of the wall. "What do we do now? As soon as he's finished he's going to go in and lock the door and when he finds us missing....."

The priest invariably checked the dormitories and rooms at night. The consequences weren't worth contemplating.

"What we need is a diversion of some kind," Matthew breathed, his mouth close to Tony's ear, "something that will get him away from that door whilst we nip inside."

"Good thinking," hissed Tony sarcastically, "like what?"

"Like this," Matthew grinned triumphantly, producing a fishing reel. He was a keen freshwater fisherman and had been given a new reel to try by a friend he had met in the pub.

Tony was unable to disguise his contempt. "What're we supposed to do with that," he sneered, "throw it at him?"

"No, you fool," Matthew was stung by his friend's sarcasm, "look over there." and he pointed to where about two dozen metal dustbins were stacked in rows, one on top of another. They had been emptied late that afternoon and were awaiting distribution the following morning. They sat upon a concrete apron about thirty yards from where the two boys were hiding.

"I'll nip across and tie one end of this line to the bottom bin," Matthew outlined his plan quietly, "then we'll get as close to the door as we can without being spotted and then pull the bottom bin away. Hopefully gravity will do the rest."

"Bloody brilliant," Tony's voice was full of admiration, "but we'd better get a move on, here I'll go," and grabbing one end of the line he shot across to the bin enclosure keeping low and avoiding the light. He was back again in less time than it takes to tell giving the 'thumbs up' Without further discussion they set off along the grass verge, their bodies pressed hard against the wall, their feet making no sound as they paid out the line behind them. Finally they halted at the corner of a bay window, which was as close to the entrance as they could get without being seen.

"Just in time by God," Tony whispered as Father Patrick and the caretaker began their mutual 'Goodnight.'

Without hesitation Matthew jerked the line as hard as he could. He was duly rewarded as the bins cascaded to earth, or rather, concrete. Startled by the sudden assault upon their eardrums in the quiet of the night the two men instinctively ran towards the sound. Quickly cutting the line with his small pocket knife Matthew took off and never once looked back, Tony close behind. Later, safe in their small beds, they chuckled softly to themselves at their cunning.

The breakfast bell was ringing stridently as the pair made their way towards the dining room the following morning. As they passed Father Patrick's door the priest stepped out into the corridor. His sudden appearance made them both jump. It was as if he had been waiting for them.

"Good morning, boys," he said pleasantly, smiling benignly upon them.

"Oh, 'morning Father," they chorused.

"You'll be off to breakfast, I s'pose?" Father Patrick not only had an annoying habit of stating the obvious, he had a slight Irish accent with which to do it.

They nodded.

"Good, good," his smile never wavered. "Well, eat hearty boys, you will need it." He turned to go, "Oh, be th' way, Matthew," he said, almost as an afterthought, "I have here something which may be of some relevance, considering your hobby." And reaching beneath his cassock he pulled forth a tangle of fishing line which he placed in his student's palm. "Oh, what a tangled web we weave," the boys heard him mutter as he stalked off up the corridor his black cassock flapping around his legs.

As the years passed their friendship, nurtured safely within the cloisters of religion and academia, flourished. By the time they had reached the ages of eighteen and nineteen respectively, when the college considered them to be more or less adults, they had moved into their own rooms and out of the common dormitory, as was their right.

The rooms they had been allocated were sumptuous by comparison to what they had been used to. Their only drawback, it seemed to them, was that they were situated in the east wing of the college, which meant that they had a fair way to walk to their lectures and the dining room. They very soon agreed, however, that it was a small price to pay for their privacy.

They each had an open fireplace, with a ready supply of coal during the winter, at the sides of which stood armchairs that had seen better days. A single, iron bedstead stood in one corner next to which was a desk with shelves above for books. A small wardrobe and handbasin completed the furnishings.

"Hey, how about this?" Tony grinned excitedly the first day he moved in, flopping into the armchair which groaned in protest. "Not bad, eh?"

"Umm, very nice, very nice indeed," Matthew replied mockingly, imitating his friend's superior accent, "but I think perhaps a Gustav Klimt above the fireplace or an Art Deco lamp for the desk would add just that touch of piquancy, don't you?" He didn't share Tony's love of modern art.

A cushion flew across the room thumping into the side of his head. "Okay, smartarse," Tony sneered, "you wouldn't know a decent bit of art if it came and bit you in the balls. Anyway," he grunted as the cushion was returned with good measure, catching him in the chest, "what's your room like, as good as this is it?"

"Come and have a look for yourself," Matthew replied, leading the way down the corridor. The room was very similar to the one they had just left apart from there being an extra door set in the wall near the bedhead.

"Where does that lead?" was Tony's immediate query.

"Dunno," Matthew shrugged, "it's locked. Daresay I'll find out soon enough, though."

It turned out that the door led into a storeroom where the college thespians kept their props. The key was always left on the lintel. His curiosity satisfied, and with his studies to keep him fully occupied, Matthew ignored the room altogether except when the players needed to be in it.

"Goodness, is that the time?"

Tony looked up from the book he was reading, glancing at the clock on the mantleshelf. "'Fraid so," he said, stretching. It was nearly one o' clock in the morning. "It's high time you and I were in our beds, young man." He adopted his usual paternal attitude towards his younger companion.

"Yeah, I guess you're right. I'll see you at breakfast," Matthew replied, gathering up the books he had been studying and draining the last of his wine.

Once in his own room he quickly got ready for bed. He settled himself beneath the covers laying his head on one hand, a habit he had had since a child, and waited for sleep to claim him. His mind was drifting softly, like a leaf falling to the ground, when suddenly he was jerked back to full consciousness by a sound; a sound that was devastating in its loneliness, heart-rending in its sorrow.

It was the sound of a child crying. It was soft, muffled, but he heard it distinctly and it emanated from beyond the door beside his head. He left the warmth of his bed and crossing the room he switched on the light. He turned and stopped, listening.

Yes, it was still there but quieter now, as though whoever it was, was trying to stifle the sound of sobbing in a pillow and, yes, he was certain now, it did come from beyond that door.

He reached for the key and inserted it in the lock. As he pushed and the door opened, light from his room flooding into the darkness, the crying stopped.

It was as though he stood before a wall; a wall of deathly silence. He stepped across the threshold, his heart beating madly against his chest. "Is anyone there?" he called softly, feeling slightly foolish, knowing that another presence was impossible.

There was no reply and all that he could make out in the gloom was a pile of old chairs and a stack of flats leaning against the wall. It was indeed just a stage storeroom, as well he knew. He was unable to see beyond the pool of light that spilt over from his own room and he really hadn't the courage to venture further so he retreated, closing the door softly behind him.

Not wishing to appear a fool he decided against mentioning his nocturnal experience, particularly to Tony, whom he knew would have scoffed mightily at the idea of anyone being so stupid as to believe that they heard a small child in the middle of the night crying in a store room. He simply put it down to his overworked brain causing an overactive imagination and duly forgot about it. For about a week.

At breakfast he dined alone to begin with, Tony having overslept. He came rushing into the dining room attempting to comb his hair with one hand whilst tucking his shirt into his trousers with the other. He held a letter between his teeth. Grabbing a cup of tea and a roll he joined his friend.

"Now then, what d'you think this is?" He posed the question whilst hastily scanning the closely written, light blue pages.

"Looks like a letter from your sister," said Matthew wisely, recognising the handwriting.

"How right you are dear boy." Tony chuckled, "She wants to come for a visit."

"Oh, yes," Matthew's interest quickened, "when?"

"Hah, I thought that would get you going, you dirty little devil. Fancy her, don't you?" His grin was wicked.

Matthew blushed, the colour running into his cheeks. It was true that he and Bernadette had got on well together on her previous visits for he warmed to her tomboyish character and winning ways. But then, he wasn't the only one, he was well aware. There was certainly no future in it for him, given his vocation but, if things had been different....., he left the thought unfinished.

She was just his age, a year younger than her brother but with the same sense of humour which beautifully matched her mass of dark curls and wide, generous mouth. He particularly liked the way she would sometimes look sideways at him, teasingly, her grey-green eyes twinkling as she lowered her eyelids. When she did that his heart truly melted within him. She hadn't visited for nearly a year, being busy with her own studies, so they looked forward eagerly to her coming.

At the appointed hour the two friends waited on the platform of Durham station for the train to arrive. As it thundered in amidst clouds of smoke and steam they caught sight of her hanging out of a carriage window as far as she could, waving madly. She ignored the steps, leaping onto the platform as soon as the train had stopped, no decorous descent for her, straight into her brother's arms.

"Tony, Tony," she laughed, smothering her brother's face with her kisses, "oh, I've missed you, how I've missed you."

"Hey, steady on, old girl," he said, half seriously, fighting her off but laughing at the same time "remember my calling."

"Well, if you don't want me, I know someone who will," she giggled mischievously and leaving her brother's half-hearted embrace she flung her arms around Matthew's neck and kissed him full on the mouth. He blushed to his hair instantly but his arms still slid around her beautifully slim waist.

"Pity you're going into the priesthood," Tony remarked with heavy irony, "you'd make a lovely couple.."

Matthew cleared his throat as he reluctantly released her, "Hrrmph," he said, his embarrassment obvious, "hello, Bernadette."

She insisted upon seeing their rooms as soon as she had arrived having had several guided tours of the college's magnificence on previous visits. They were soon installed in front of her brother's fire eating toast and jam washed down with liberal quantities of strong tea. Bernadette, who occupied the one and only armchair, pushed her shoeless feet towards the flames and stretched like a cat. "You have it made here, don't you?" she said, eyeing the two friends from beneath her long dark lashes.

Tony frowned, instantly on the defensive. "How d'you mean?" he asked.

His sister waved a deprecating hand around the room, "Well, all of this and so little work. You're obviously kept in the lap of luxury. They must be grooming you two for the papacy," she goaded him, knowing exactly the reaction she would get.

"Listen, you little minx," Tony rose to the bait as always, "what th' hell d'you think this lot is for, fun?" and he gestured emphatically towards his desk which was, as usual, littered with papers and books, some of which had cascaded onto the floor.

Her smile was wide, innocent, "It reminds me of home, actually, with you being your usual untidy self. C'mon," she said, quickly changing the subject in the annoying way she had, "let's go and have a look at your room, Matthew," and grabbing him by the hand she led him towards the door.

"I've seen it before so I'll just stay here and get on with living in the lap of luxury, if you don't mind," her brother's reply was sarcastic. "Leave your door open and remember your vows," he hurled at Matthew's retreating back.

"I haven't taken them yet, thank goodness," was the unbidden thought that rushed into his mind.

A bright fire welcomed them as they entered but Bernadette, walking into the middle of the room, turned to Matthew, her face serious, a look that was almost alarm showing in her eyes. She shivered, "It's cold in here, Matthew," she said.

He moved towards her, frowning, his eyebrows drawn down, "What's wrong?" he said, concerned.

The smile she returned was brittle, forced, "Oh, nothing, I'm okay, really," and again quickly changing the subject she pointed at the far door. "What's through there?" she asked.

He shrugged, "Nothing really, just a storeroom."

Before he could continue she asked, "Can I see?"

"Yes, if you like," and he reached up for the key above the door. As he pushed it open Bernadette peered past him but before it had swing wide she grabbed his wrist, her nails digging into the flesh, "Close it, close it, for God's sake," she hissed at him, the colour draining from her face and her eyes wide with terror.

Appalled at her sudden change Matthew did as he was bid, hastily slamming the door to. Turning, he grabbed at her shoulders, "What the hell is wrong, Bernie, what's wrong with you?" he cried, shaken.

She didn't reply, not at first, she simply stared at him, one hand covering her mouth whilst the air whistled harshly in her nostrils. He led her to the bed and she sat down whilst he waited for her to recover her more normal composure. A little over a minute had passed when slowly the colour began to return to her cheeks. She took hold of his hand; she was as cold as ice. She tried to speak but no sound would come. Instead tears welled from her eyes and poured unceasingly and silently down her face. Matthew took her in his arms and held her against him, her body racked as she shook uncontrollably. He considered calling out for Tony but then thought better of it as she became calmer. He didn't say anything, waiting for her to speak.

"Oh, Matthew, there is such utter and absolute sadness in there," she began, her voice hollow and filled with pain. "Call me mad if you will but I know that something terrible has happened beyond that door. I know, I can feel it and it has gone right through me to my heart." She shook her head sadly and tried to smile for him, "I...I, can't explain it. I just know, that's all."

Matthew returned her gaze for a long moment, pondering the question as to whether to tell her or not. Then he said slowly, "I've heard a child crying in there and it was one of the loneliest sounds I ever want to hear. God seems to have forsaken that child." His voice broke on the last word.

She gripped his hand again, "When?" she said, her eyes never leaving his.

"About a week ago. I had been working late and was just getting off to sleep when it happened."

"Did you investigate it?"

"Yes, of course, but I didn't find anything and it stopped when I opened the door. It just looked like it does now, just a storeroom."

Bernadette's next question caused him to bite his lower lip. "But has it always been a storeroom?" she asked.

He frowned, "Hmm, that's a thought," he said, "I seem to remember someone once telling me that all of these rooms had once been a dormitory. I'll check it out with Tony."

"No," she replied quickly, "don't mention it to Tony, he'd never understand. He'll just think we're both crazy."

"I think we're both crazy," Matthew suddenly grinned.

He received a wan smile in reply as Bernadette shook her head, "No Matthew," she sighed, "we aren't crazy at all. I told you, something terrible has happened in that room. Call it woman's intuition, call it some kind of psychic power, call it anything you like, I know, that's all. Oh God," she said, standing up and looking into the small shaving mirror that stood on the shelf over the washbasin, "look at my face. I must go and wash up and try and repair the damage."

That same evening Matthew left Tony and his sister at the 'Double Duck' where she was staying for the night and returning to his own room he took the key to the storeroom and searched the place thoroughly. What he thought he might have found he really had no idea but in the event he found nothing. After about an hour of fruitless activity he turned in. The usual night sounds of the college gradually subsided and as they did so he drifted into sleep.

It seemed that he was in limbo, that twilight world where everything seems to take on an unreal quality, neither sleeping nor waking, but somewhere in between. Suddenly, he couldn't breathe. He opened his mouth in an attempt to force air into his straining lungs but something, a force, a power appeared to be exerting tremendous pressure upon his throat. He thrashed wildly, madly, kicking and clawing at what he knew not and in the extremes of his terror he knew himself to be screaming silently for his mother.

In a wild, unbridled panic, he rolled onto his side, trying desperately to escape from the evil that threatened to engulf him, when, suddenly, abruptly, he was wide awake and lying on the floor. He had rolled out of bed. He lay for a long time against the side of his bed, chest heaving, trying to re-orientate his senses, trying to push the overwhelming sense of terror back into the darkness whence it came. Slowly he hauled himself to his feet, his limbs as leaden weights, and staggering across the room, he switched on the light. It was only then that he realised that his pyjamas were soaked through with sweat. He stripped them off and towelled down and, naked as the day that he was born, he sat in his armchair, buried his head in his hands and silently wept, allowing the terror of his nightmare, if nightmare it was, to flow from him through his tears.

Tony had gone to buy a paper leaving Bernadette and Matthew alone for a few moments on the station platform. She gazed earnestly into his eyes, her hand gripping his arm, "You heard it again last night, didn't you?" she asked. She had observed him closely all that morning and knew that something was very wrong.

He sighed deeply, his eyes reflecting his inner sadness. "I wish that were all it was," he replied, attempting a smile. And he told her exactly what had happened the previous night.

Her grip on his arm tightened, "Oh, Matthew you must get out of there. There's something evil about that room. I'm so worried for you." Her lovely grey-green eyes clouded over with concern.

He tried to make light of it, to laugh it off but it merely rang hollow; she knew how badly it had affected him. "Don't worry about me, bonny lass," it was the first time he had used the familiar colloquialism with her, "I'll be okay, you'll see. Ah, here's your big brother back so we'll say no more about it."

On their journey back to college Tony said conversationally, "What was the matter with Bernie this morning? She looked like she had lost ten bob and found sixpence. Come to think of it," he went on, turning to his companion and looking at him more closely, "you don't look so sparky yourself. You two haven't fallen madly in love, have you?" he asked, a mocking smile on his lips as he flicked idly through his paper.

Slowly the weeks passed and although he had no re-occurrence of his nightmare, for that was how he had come to think of it, there was hardly a night went by that at some point he wasn't awakened by that dreadful, heartbreaking sound of a child crying. It always emanated from the same place and try as he might he was never able to locate it, the sound ceasing abruptly every time he opened the door. It began to have an obvious effect upon him, both physically and mentally. He found that his concentration had gone and he was unable to study. At lectures he was often preoccupied and inattentive. He lost his appetite and became thin and pale but the crunch came late one evening when Tony walked into his room to find him standing in the middle of it, his eyes wild and staring, and with his hands over his ears.

"In Christ's name, Matthew, what the hell is the matter with you?" he shouted, aghast at his friend's appearance. For him this was the final straw for he had watched his slow deterioration over the previous weeks with something akin to horror.

"Yes, indeed in Christ's name, Tony," his friend replied weakly, slowly lowering his hands to his sides. Tony noticed that they shook almost uncontrollably although Matthew did his best to hide the fact. "I think that Christ has deserted me or I'm going slowly mad, or both." He was very close to tears.

"Here, old son, sit down, sit down and I'll get you a drink." He pushed Matthew gently towards the armchair and then ran back to his own room for a bottle of whisky. On returning he poured a generous measure into a tumbler and handed it to his friend. Matthew took a long pull at the glass and shuddered violently as the liquid burned its way down. Tony sat on the bed and waited.

After gazing long into the amber liquid before taking another drink Matthew lowered his glass and suddenly stopped, his hand suspended in mid-air, listening, "There," he whispered, staring in the direction of the storeroom, "can you not hear it?"

Tony remained blank and gazed at his friend in disbelief, "Hear it," he said, puzzled. "Hear what?" ·

"That child," Matthew wailed, his voice breaking, betraying his desperation, "that poor, benighted bloody little child. He's in there, crying his bloody little heart out. Can you not hear him, man? You must be able to, for the love of God, you must, you must," his voice trailed into miserable silence and he buried his face in his hands, his shoulders shaking.

But Tony heard nothing. Insisting that he take another large whisky, he stayed until Matthew had settled down to sleep watching over him as he tossed fitfully, muttering, until finally he seemed to capture the repose he was seeking.

"Now then, Tony me boy," Father Patrick greeted his student as he sat behind his big desk in his office, "you said you wanted to see me. What about?"

Although he had turned this interview over and over in his mind for two days now Tony was still at a loss as to how to begin. All he knew was that he had to get the priest's attention so, taking a deep breath, he plunged right in, "I think Matthew is going mad, Father," he said quietly.

He knew that he had succeeded in his intention for the priest leaned forward suddenly, resting his chin on his coupled hands, "Oh, aye," he said, peering at his guest over his half glasses, "and why would you be thinkin' that now, I wonder?"

Tony related everything that he knew about his friend's situation, what he had observed over the preceding weeks and he finished by describing Matthew's mental and physical condition.

The priest's battered visage had turned grave, "Aye, lad, we are not altogether blind here, in spite of what you young 'uns think. I have been aware of Matthew's condition for a little while now and I do intend to do something about it, even though, mark you, he has insisted that there is nothing troubling him when I've had occasion to ask. What's your opinion, what do you think is behind all of this?" Father Patrick invited his young protege to take him into his confidence with the question.

Startled at being asked to express his own view by someone who was, to all intents and purposes, of the other side, Tony could only stare at him for a second or two. As he considered his reply he began to feel even more unsure of himself. He cleared his throat, "Well, Father," he began, "he thinks that, or at least, he feels that......"

"Yes, yes, go on," his tutor encouraged him gently.

"Well," Tony began again, his normal self confidence deserting him for the moment. He felt incredibly foolish knowing what it was that he was going to say next. "He believes he can hear a child crying." It came out in a rush.

The reaction, or rather, lack of it, that appeared to emanate from the priest astounded him, for instead of incredulity, as he had expected, Father Patrick merely sighed heavily and stared hard at the top of his desk for a long time. Finally he looked up, gazing directly into Tony's eyes, his expression one of deep sadness. "I see," was all he said.

Confused, Tony stuttered, "What, Father, what is it......?"

But the priest interrupted him, standing suddenly, his tall figure looming over his desk, "Come with me, lad," he said, ushering Tony towards the door.

They left his study and made for the college library. The priest seemed to be in a hurry and Tony had difficulty in matching his long stride. It was a magnificent room, with a carved hammer-beam roof that arched high overhead, its oak panelled walls lined with tier upon tier of heavy wooden shelves that were home to thick, leatherbound volumes of ecclesiastic and scholarly works. Portraits of bishops and long-dead principals stared down at them from every available space whilst massive, heavily decorated furniture lay scattered about the thickly carpeted floor. Going to the far end of the room Father Patrick pulled a set of keys from his pocket and opened an oak door set in the wall. Tony had never been privileged to enter this small room before but he was aware that in here were kept the college records from the date of its inception. The priest, after switching on a light, ran his finger down the line of leatherbound volumes. Choosing one he sat down at the desk in the centre of the room and beckoned Tony to him. "Listen to me carefully, lad," he said seriously, "what I'm about to reveal must go no further than these four walls, understand?"

Tony nodded dumbly as Father Patrick opened the volume in front of him. He saw, inscribed in a beautiful, copperplate hand the legend, 'A Record of Students and Staff for the Year of Our Lord 1834'. The priest leafed carefully through the book until he found an entry dated 12th. October 1834. His finger came to rest upon the entry and his eyes bade Tony look. It read, 'Matthew Thomas Charlton, found hanged in his dormitory aged thirteen years and four months. God rest his soul'.

Dumbfounded, Tony could only stare at the words, reading and re-

reading them. Finally he looked up, "What, what the hell does it mean, Father?" he whispered fearfully.

The priest gave a deep, heartfelt sigh and placed his large hands flat upon the desk. "It means," he said sadly, half to himself, "that he has come back to us. And we thought we had laid the poor little divil to rest more than forty years since."

Tony shook his head, bewildered, "I'm sorry, Father, you're going to have to explain...." he began.

"Aye, aye, lad," the good priest returned, looking up at his student, "I'm goin' to have to do a deal more than that I fear. Sit down here," he went on, indicating the chair opposite, "and I'll try and throw some light on the matter. But mind," he raised a warning finger as Tony did as he was asked, "you're to say nothing, understood?"

Tony nodded his head briefly, "Yes, yes, of course, you have my word," he said.

Father Patrick sighed again and it was a sigh that was dragged from the very depths of his soul. He was obviously reluctant to begin but, mentally girding his loins, he sallied forth. "This poor little beggar was murdered," he began, tracing the name written in the book with a heavy finger, almost as though he were caressing it, "murdered be one of us, as surely as if he had put the rope around his neck himself. It's all there," he said, indicating the shelves behind him, "in his academic and social records from 1830, when he came here, until the day he died."

"What d'you mean, murdered by one of us?" Tony asked, grave faced. "A..a priest?"

"Aye, lad, exactly," Father Patrick replied heavily, "a priest. From my research I have discovered that the boy was systematically abused by a priest from practically the day he joined us until the day he departed this world. I know who the priest was and I also know that, apart from a severe reprimand by his bishop, the man got away with it almost scot-free."

"But, but that's dreadful, awful, Father," Tony was appalled. "Are you certain?"

"As certain as I'll ever be," Father Patrick replied. "You see, it's not the first time that young Matthew has disturbed someone's peace, his own peace notwithstanding. About forty years ago," he went on, his mind drifting back to the time when he was a much younger man, "he appeared to me. The room that Matthew now occupies was once mine. I know all about the poor wee lad for I researched his case long and hard because I wanted to do something for him. I wanted to lay his soul, his poor tormented soul, to rest so that he would have the peace he was due to, the peace that he deserved. Peace that he never got on this earth, not whilst he was with us anyway." He paused, letting the silence build between them, as he reflected. "I felt that I owed him that," he went on quietly, "to try and make amends, so to speak. I thought that I had succeeded too as he hasn't been heard of these last forty years or so. It seems that I was wrong," he concluded sadly.

Tony shook his head, his disbelief written in large letters across his face. "Are you telling me that, his ghost, his spirit......?" he began

The priest nodded emphatically. "As a priest, or would-be priest," he said, "you must believe in Heaven and in the Grace of our Lord and the life hereafter, surely?"

"Of course I do, Father, but I'm not so sure that I believe in ghosts. I mean, it's........"

"Why not?" Father Patrick practically snapped. "To me, this young boy has not, because of the way he died, attained that state of grace that allows him to pass beyond this world. He is still with us, and through no fault of his own." He leaned back in his chair and steepled his fingers. "If I thought that Matthew was in any danger I would never have let him have that room," he said, "but I thought that the wee laddie had gone, that we had laid him to rest years ago. But, I s'pose," and he sighed deeply again, his guilt apparent, "he would have found him eventually, wherever he was."

"So what do we do now, Father?" Tony, sensing the old man's guilt, buried his own scepticism.

The priest looked up, the light of battle glinting in his eye, "We exorcise him once again, lad, and lay his poor soul to rest once and for all, but this time," he pushed his chair away from the table and rose to his feet, "we do it properly. Now that he has made himself known to Matthew, who is, after all from the same family, a soul-mate, so to speak, we might just stand a better chance."

And so it was done, with all of the pomp and circumstance that the Catholic church could bring to bear but only Matthew knew with complete certainty, that his ancestor was at last with God. After the ceremony, which he personally found intensely moving, he went to the college's small grave yard. After much searching he eventually found what it was he was looking for buried beneath a bramble thicket, just beyond the boundary of consecrated ground and much weatherworn.

He stood in front of it for a long time, that old, weathered gravestone, reading the carved inscription again and again, 'Here lieth the mortal remains of Matthew Thomas Charlton, Hanged by his own hand, October 12th 1834. Aged Thirteen years and Four months. God give him peace.'

As the strain and the tension and the heartache of the last few months flowed from him, Matthew knew, at last, that his namesake had indeed found the peace that had been denied him for so long.

18
Sarah's Sheep

Bill Stobbart put his hand in the small of his back and, wishing that he had taken advantage of the 'massage' parlour when he had had the chance, he straightened painfully. It was 4.a. m. on a dark, bitterly cold February morning and lambing had just started.

He had been up nearly all night as the lambing shed was full of expectant ewes who were giving, or about to give, birth and, being the good shepherd that he was, his place was with his flock. Tonight had been as busy as he had known for almost a dozen sheep had produced lambs already with only one of them being stillborn. The distraught mother continually nuzzled her dead offspring, unable to understand why it could not rise.

"Don't worry, bonny lass," Bill told her kindly, "we'll find you a young'un soon." He was certain that there would be several orphaned or rejected lambs later. It was important that a lamb such as this would arrive soon for he needed the skin of the dead lamb before it grew cold and the mother lost interest.

He needn't have worried for Nature can generally be relied upon to maintain a balance in any situation and so it wasn't long before he had the rejected lamb that he needed. He expertly removed the skin of the dead lamb with his pocket knife and taking the other bleating infant between his knees he quickly slipped the empty skin over its head and legs.

This done he pushed it in the direction of the forlorn mother who proceeded to nudge it towards her dripping udder. Once she had accepted the lamb completely, which usually took no more than two or three days, the old skin could be removed.

At about 6.30 Sarah arrived with steaming mugs of soup and enough bacon sandwiches to feed a regiment. Rising from his knees Bill quipped, "By, are you a sight for sore backs, bonny lass," and he took the proffered sustenance from her. He was feeling good even though he had had a hard night of it. Everything so far had gone smoothly with few problems. "H'way, lads," he called to his two stockmen who were working at the far end of the shed, "breakfast's up."

Sarah sat down on a hay bale as she listened idly to the men's conversation, a whisp of straw between her lips.

"You'll look after any pet lambs we get, missus, you an' th' lassies?" Gilbert, their long-serving shepherd, enquired.

She sighed softly to herself. It was the same every year for there were always orphaned or abandoned lambs that needed a surrogate mother. She became very attached to these unfortunate animals and always found it hard to part with them when they had to go to market. She looked up and nodded, "Whichever you can't find a mother for you can give to me," she confirmed.

"And what about when they have to go for the chop?" Bill deliberately posed the question cruelly in order to test her resolve.

"I'm not as soft as you seem to think, Bill Stobbart," his wife responded spiritedly, "it's all part of being a farmer's wife," she cleared away the empty mugs and plates as she spoke.

Bill glanced across to Gilbert and their eyes met. No words were needed.

"How's it going, Dad?"

Bill looked up at the sound of his youngest daughter's voice. "Hello, Clare, love," he smiled at her fondly as she leaned over the gate of the lambing shed. "C'mon over an' see if y'want," and he offered a helping hand as she clambered over the top rail.

They were two weeks into lambing and he was pleased with the way things had gone up until now. The weather had been unseasonably mild and they had lost few lambs. There were some stillbirths, which was to be expected, and they had had a number of rejections but, all in all, it had been a successful lambing so far.

He was about to deal with an obdurate mother as his daughter arrived. "Y'see that ewe over there," he said to her, pointing to a mother who was resolutely refusing to allow her offspring to suckle, butting it with her head every time it tried, the tiny infant bleating continuously, "well, we'll just see if we can get it to take its baby, shall we?" and he whistled for Jed, his ever-present Welsh collie. Grabbing the ewe by the fleece at her neck he thrust her into a pen they had constructed from hurdles for just this purpose, the lamb following, its distress obvious. It was only big enough for two or three animals at the most. Clare watched as her father called, "Get by, Jed, get by," and the obedient animal leapt into the pen. As soon as its feet hit the earth again Jed went into a stalk, his belly low and ears pricked, in anticipation of his master's further commands.

"Oh, Dad, he's not going to hurt her is he?" Clare cried anxiously as the collie crept ever closer.

Bill laughed softly, "No, no, don't fash, sweetheart," he said kindly, "he wouldn't hurt her even if Ah asked him to. Just watch what happens."

As the collie circled her, the sheep, having nowhere to run, kept circling also, her head towards him. The lamb, completely oblivious to the dog, was all the while trying to gain access to its mother's udder, its cries piteous. Preoccupied with the collie as she was the ewe ignored the lamb at first but in the end it became so insistent that she suddenly turned on it and butted it away from her side. The infant, its legs knocked from under it, sprawled upon the floor, its cries louder now. Still Jed stalked the mother and once the lamb had recovered sufficiently from its maternal abuse, it tried again. It seemed to be as equally determined as its mother for the scene was re-enacted several times before Bill decided that the lamb had had enough and called Jed off. He entered the pen and retrieved the tiny starveling, "Here y'are, Clare," he said, handing it over to his daughter, "you'll have t'look after this'un, 'cos its mother surely isn't."

"What were you trying to get Jed to do, Dad?" she asked, as they made their way towards the farmhouse, the lamb cradled protectively in her arms.

Her father smiled ruefully and placed his hand on her shoulder, "Well, Ah was hopin' that th' dog might arouse the ewe's maternal instinct, seein' him as a threat, only it wasn't t'be, was it?"

Clare returned his smile, "Not to worry," she said, "It just means that we've another pet lamb to look after, doesn't it?" and she hugged the tiny creature delightedly.

Bill laughed out loud, "Well, there's not much wrong wi' your maternal instinct, Ah can see that," he chuckled. "Ah just hope y'mother can cope wi' five pet lambs t'feed, that's all. What're y'goin' t'call this un', then?" he asked as they entered the kitchen.

His daughter frowned hard, "Well," she said thoughtfully, "we've already got a Genevieve and a Giselle. What about Gertrude?"

"What about Gertrude?" They both turned as Sarah entered from the living room.

"Look, mum, another one," her daughter declared, holding out the small bundle for her mother's inspection.

Sarah raised her eyebrows but no objections as she gently took the lamb from her daughter, saying as she did so, "Go and get me the feeding bottle from the side of the stove, will you?" She looked at her husband and said softly, "I don't know whether we'll be able to save this little scrap. She looks too far gone to me."

But not only did Gertrude survive, she actually thrived and it wasn't long before she joined the tiny flock of pet lambs that enjoyed a far more privileged existence than the rest of the farmyard animals. They were hand reared, bottle-fed and, like all young, growing things, were constantly hungry.

Sheep are not noted for their high IQ, if anything being more noteworthy for their lack of adequate grey matter but Gertrude proved to be more intelligent, more resourceful and more resilient and had much more of a personality than any of her contemporaries. She was invariably the first to find the teat or feed bucket at feeding time and always seemed to be the ringleader of any misadventure that befell herself and her four siblings.

To begin with they were housed in a small shed near the farmhouse until they gained in strength and the weather became warmer. Under Sarah's careful ministrations they rapidly gained weight and it wasn't long before they were constantly at her heels as she performed her daily tasks around the farm. By the time they were a few weeks old Sarah had assumed her annual mantle of earth-mother and her miniature flock related to her completely.

It was a late Spring evening and the family were just finishing their dinner when the telephone rang, its strident tones cutting though their conversation. Lucy, Bill's elder daughter answered it. She grimaced as she handed the receiver to her mother, "It's Aunt Alice," she mouthed. Aunt Alice was Sarah's elder sister. She lived in Northumberland's stockbroker belt, having married well, and she had a tendency to a rather superior view of her social standing, in comparison to her rural relatives. Sarah was fond of her, but only in small doses. She took the 'phone from her daughter, "Hello, Alice," she smiled into the receiver, "how nice of you to call."

Later over a belated cup of tea she announced that Alice intended visiting them the following day. The chorus of moans from the two girls was entirely predictable whereas Bill, heaving a sigh of relief, said, "Thank goodness it's mart day, t'morrow. Wi' any luck Ah might not be back 'til sh's gone."

Sarah, frowning disapprovingly at this minor mutiny, retorted, "I knew I could rely on you lot for support. As usual, it will be up to me to entertain her all day."

"Which I'm sure you will carry out with your customary charm," Bill smiled at her as he settled into his armchair and picked up the 'Farming Times'.

A gleaming, white Mercedes rolled serenely into the farmyard as Sarah went about her everyday tasks, her five progeny milling around her legs. The heavily tinted windows prevented the easy identification of her visitor, but she made a fairly accurate guess as to whom it might be. Her eyes surveyed the sparkling chrome and pristine bodywork, "Ha, a good enough reason for a visit, I s'pose," she thought cattily.

The driver's door opened and a silk-stockinged leg was thrust forth but before its occupant could fully emerge a bright red thunderbolt in the shape of an Irish setter leapt from the back seat and into the sunlight. This particular hound had no conception as to the decorum required of visiting animals and as soon as its eyes alighted upon Sarah's sheep it hared up the yard towards them, tail and ears streaming in the wind. Their concerted and immediate response was one of utter panic and with one accord they turned and dashed up the muck heap, the setter, barking joyously, in hot pursuit.

Down the far side they flew, Gertrude leading as they made a direct line towards the back door of the farmhouse, which Sarah had forgotten to close. For five seconds there ensued the equivalent of a woolly rugby scrum as they all fought to get through the door simultaneously and then the dam burst and they scattered through the kitchen, down the hall and out through the front door, which had also been left open, it being a warm day.

Alice, all Amani suit and Raybans, her jaw sagging, half in and half out of her beautiful, new motor car could only stare in horror whilst her ungovernable animal created unholy mayhem around her. Her sister, seeing which way the stampede was heading, dashed across the garden and closed the gate to the field through which both pursued and pursuer had vanished. "At least they can't get any further," she thought grimly as she turned back to Alice who, red in the face, began to gush apologies.

"Just get your damn' dog back here, Alice," Sarah snapped, grim-faced, "we can't have him running around loose."

It was some considerable time before the setter finally responded to the plaintive wailings of its mistress and returned tail up, tongue lolling and with a happy smile upon its face. It was most put out when it was banished to the small shed for the rest of its visit.

When things had finally returned to normal and the two sisters had made up for the initial contretemps they settled down in the sitting room where Sarah served coffee. They were well into their second pot when Alice announced that she needed the loo.

"Oh, just use the bathroom in our bedroom," advised her sister, "it's nearest."

She had been gone but a few moments when an ear-splitting scream rent the air above Sarah's head. Leaping to her feet in alarm she dashed into the hallway, where she very nearly came into collision with Alice, who was leaping down the stairs in a passable imitation of a mountain goat whilst the bemused face of Gertrude peered around the newel post on the landing above her.

"Oh, oh, Sarah," her sister sobbed hysterically, her hand to her heart, "that smelly animal gave me such a fright. It was on your bed and as I walked into the room, it, it leapt at me."

Sarah sighed heavily and put her hand over her eyes. Leading her suburbia conditioned sister back into the sitting room she gently settled her once again into her seat. The sudden adrenaline rush had obviously banished any thoughts of the relief she may have needed from her mind. Shooing Gertrude out into the yard Sarah contemplated the redesigned pattern on her best bedspread with despair.

"So how did y'day go wi' your Alice, my love?" Bill, whose own day at the mart had proved profitable, was in a hearty mood.

The look his wife cast him as she turned from the stove where she was preparing dinner was positively malignant, "Don't even ask," she said through set teeth.

Throughout that summer the five pet lambs grew rapidly, and although they became a part of the rest of the flock they could often be seen off by themselves, grazing separately. They also invaded the farmyard at each and every opportunity looking for Sarah, and any free handouts that might be on offer.

"That's the third time this week Ah've put those lambs back in th' field," Bill complained loudly to his wife. "Ah swear t'God they could get out o' a locked box." As Sarah smiled sympathetically he went on, "Well, we won't be troubled f'r much longer, Ah'll warrant. Another month or two an' we'll have them away t' mart."

Sarah's lips compressed as she watched her husband climb into his Landrover and slam the door.

As luck would have it they didn't have to wait that long, not as far as Gertrude was concerned anyway. She arrived in the farmyard early one morning and was following Sarah about in her usual fashion but Sarah, being preoccupied with other things, shooed her away until, taking the hint, the sheep wandered off in search of more amenable company. It was whilst scattering corn for the chickens that she was suddenly startled by the sound of tyres screaming on Tarmac and a sickening thud from the direction of the road. Running to the gate she observed a young man climbing out of an old Cortina that had a distinctly crumpled nearside wing and a shattered headlight. Sarah's shocked gaze absorbed all of this in an instant, as well as the prone body of Gertrude lying dead as a stone in front of the car.

"Ah'm terribly sorry, missus," the driver began to apologise, somewhat distressed, "Ah just didn't see her. Sh' seemed t'appear out o' nowhere."

Sarah looked at him, then at Gertrude and then at the damage to the vehicle and shook her head in bewilderment. "Please don't worry," she said at last, "we'll obviously pay for the damage to your car......"

"No, no," he interrupted hastily, "it's me what should be payin' you f'r your sheep, Ah think."

Having no wish to prolong the discussion any longer than she felt was necessary she compromised, "Well, alright," she said, "we'll just call it quits, shall we?"

Gratefully the young man agreed and drove off as fast as decency would allow.

"And now, Gertrude, what do we do with you?" said Sarah, addressing the dead sheep and hoping for some inspiration. Ignoring the sudden sense of loss at her untimely passing and with her countrywoman's pragmatism taking hold she went indoors and phoned Joe Fletcher. "I've a dead sheep here, Joe, that needs butchering. It's been hit on the head by a passing car so it seems a pity to waste it."

Joe scratched his head. He hated to disappoint good customers. "Well, Ah'll see what Ah can do, Sarah," he said, "but Ah'm runnin' short handed at th' other shop, Ah was just on me way over there now. Ah can't see me gettin' up t'you until after one."

"Oh," said Sarah, "what do I do now?"

"Well," Joe said again, "y'can either call th' hunt kennels or y'can clean her y'sel."

Sarah knew what that meant. If any animal didn't have its innards removed within two hours of its death it became unfit for human consumption. She sat down slowly as she replaced the receiver, "Oh, Gertrude," was all she could think to say. It was one thing sending her stock off to mart but it was a different matter entirely having to butcher an animal, no matter how much she told herself to the contrary, she regarded as a pet. But, steeling herself to the task, her heart heavy and full of foreboding, she tied a rope around Gertrude's hind legs and hauled her to the small shed.

"Where are you now when I need you, Bill Stobbard?" she grunted as, throwing one end of the rope over a beam, she heaved and strained to pull Gertrude skyward. Eventually, after much effort, the poor sheep hung suspended by its hind legs, head dangling and with staring, sightless eyes.

"I wish you wouldn't look at me like that," Sarah cried defensively, "it's your own fault."

Having achieved this much she went to her kitchen in search of her largest and sharpest carving knife. Joe Fletcher had given her specific instructions as to what to do, none of which was remotely pleasant. Returning to the suspended sheep she stuck a bucket under the dangling head, as she had been instructed. "I don't know that I can go through with this," she told herself, gazing helplessly at Gertrude and then at the large knife clutched in her hand.

For several minutes she argued with herself over the advantages of vegetarianism but, eventually, her less than affluent upbringing and her detestation of waste, instilled in her from an early age by a

146

thrifty mother, carried the day. Once she had started she knew that she would see it through to the end, no matter how bad it became; she wasn't going to leave a job half done, it just wasn't her way. But she very nearly turned tail and fled as Gertrude's wet and slippery viscera almost cascaded onto the floor as she slit the belly with her knife.

Bill returned home late in the afternoon to find Sarah packing parcels of meat into plastic bags ready for the freezer. "By, that'll look grand on my plate on Sunday," he crowed, eyeing a fat, succulent haunch. "Where did that come from, my love?"

"Gertrude," Sarah replied shortly.

"Eh?"

"Gertrude," replied his wife again, "she was killed by a car this morning," and she related the whole sad tale, from beginning to end.

Bill was dumbstruck, "Well, Ah'll be damned," he said eventually, his admiration obvious, "an' you're th' one that gets upset when they go t'mart."

His wife gazed at him, her lips tight, "I might have butchered her but I won't cook her and I certainly won't eat her," she cried and, her resolute spirit finally dissolving into a storm of weeping, she fled the kitchen, tears streaming down her face.

19
Thespian Nights

"Quiet everyone please. Okay, Martin, from the top again, and, one and two and three."

Jayne McFadden's voice focused everyone's attention. It, like her presence, was commanding for she was a large lady, to say the least; rather unusual for someone who was so light on her feet. She stood centre stage whilst Martin and the rest of the cast went through, for the umpteenth time, the dance steps she had choreographed for them.

For Jayne was the actor/manager of the Low Cornhill Thespian Society and they were very nearly at final dress rehearsal stage of the musical she had co-written, directed and produced as their latest offering to a deserving public. It was based upon a play by Noel Coward and as such was rather spectacular, not to say ambitious, for such a small company of actors. But what they lacked in professionalism they more than made up for in enthusiasm and led as they were by Jayne, a retired actress and dancer herself, their confidence was boundless.

They had over the years produced a great many plays and musicals, costume dramas, comedies and farces and were regarded by the folk of both villages as not only highly entertaining but a very necessary and essential part of village life, particularly during the long winter nights. For the most part they were an unqualified success but occasionally, just occasionally, they had had their disasters. Such as the night they were performing a noted costume drama set at the time of the civil war.

It was required that one of the cavaliers should faint and a friend, thrusting a taper into the painted fire at the back of the stage, (a hole had been provided in the flat through which the taper being thrust, was then lit by a stage hand) would hastily blow out the flame and then hold the taper under the fainting cavalier's nose in order to revive him. This particular piece of stage- managed sleight of hand worked perfectly well for three nights in succession; until the night the actor concerned didn't actually blow the flame out and set his friend's luxuriant false moustache alight. Needless to say his companion's recovery was both quick and miraculous. The audience loved it.

Rehearsals over for the evening, Jayne stayed behind in the hall to discuss the layout of a scene in the new musical with her leading man and Adam Laidlaw, the carpenter. The reason she needed the carpenter was, as she quite rightly surmised, that the stage was actually too small for the scene, which required a large, spectacular staircase down which she would trip accompanied by an honour guard of top-hatted and tail-coated admirers, to the tune of 'A Pretty Girl is Like a Melody'; all very Fred Astairish.

"All Ah can suggest is that we extend th' stage into th' auditorium," Adam advised on being told of the problem.

"But that will mean, darling," Jayne pouted, "that we will lose perhaps two or three rows of seats, won't it?"

Adam just shrugged. That wasn't his concern. It was finally agreed that they would extend the stage by the diligent use of trestles and boards, even though, as Jayne had rightly pointed out, a number of rows would be lost.

Opening night arrived with all of its concomitant excitement, butterfly stomachs and nerves; for everyone that is except Jayne. She seemed to take it all in her stride for, as she was quick to inform her fellow actors on each and every occasion such as this, she had seen it all before. As first nights go it proved to be reasonably successful, to begin with.

"Have they come?" Jayne whispered to her prompter and stage manager who was peering through a crack in the curtain.

"I can just see them coming in at the back of the hall now," came the hushed response. Why they were whispering was a mystery for very little could be heard out front because of the noise made by the arriving audience.

The party Jayne was interested in was led by Durham's mayor who, accompanied by his wife, the lady mayoress and several civic dignitaries had accepted her invitation to attend opening night and were now taking their reserved seats at the front of the hall, directly below the stage. The first half of the show went smoothly enough and was received with enthusiastic applause from the audience.

During the interval the stage hands sweated and heaved to get the staircase into position, ready for the opening number. The tiny orchestra, two violins, a piano and drums, situated to one side of the hall, it being impossible to station them at the front as well, struck up and the curtain opened to reveal Jayne, in all her sequined and tulle splendour, flanked by her admirers, at the top of the staircase.

As the musicians went through the score and she her routine, she gradually descended, and it must said, most gracefully for such a big woman, to the front of the stage where she was whirled across it from one male dancer to another. This unfortunately proved altogether too much for the temporary structure that was supporting them and, with a sudden creak and a groan, the complete front of the stage collapsed, hurling Jayne and her top-hatted entourage into the lap of the mayor and his entourage.

They disappeared beneath a press of flesh and sequined tulle to emerge several moments later very red in the face and much dishevelled, but unhurt. Needless to say the mayor and his good lady were not amused. The audience, however, were, and they roared out their delight with cries of 'encore' and 'more, more'. It proved to be the shortest show that the Thespians had ever staged for Jayne deemed it too dangerous to continue. The real reason behind her reluctance to retrieve what she could from the wreckage was of course her distinct loss of face, particularly in front of honoured guests. She took several months to live it down and it was a long time before Adam, the company's carpenter, was called upon again.

She did eventually overcome her embarrassment and her fury and, swallowing her pride, she sought Adam's help in the renovation of her bathroom for, as she was fully aware, not only was he an excellent carpenter, he could turn his hand to most things in the building trade, such as plumbing and tiling.

"There y'are then, Jayne, it's all done f'r Christmas, just as y'wanted." Adam was justifiably proud of his handiwork for her new bathroom was indeed most splendid. She had chosen the pale peach suite, matching tiling and carpeting whilst Adam had advised her on the new hardwood door and door furniture. "Y'see how this fancy lock works," he indicated the stainless steel door knob with its integrated security system, "y'just turn this little fancy gubbins in th' middle an' the door's locked from the inside. Y'can turn th' knob, aye, like that, but nowt happens, y'r quite safe an' snug an' can wallow in y'r new bath 'til y're heart's content." It had never occurred to him that to use an adjective such as 'wallow' may have been inappropriate given Jayne's massive eighteen stone or so. As soon as the carpenter had packed up his tools and left, Jayne decided, naturally, to indulge herself, and filling the new bath with steaming hot water and a variety of fragrances so beloved of ladies, she slipped luxuriously below the surface.

Why it was she had locked the door using the 'fancy gubbins' that Adam had so proudly demonstrated not two hours earlier she, on later consideration, never knew, for she was quite alone in the house, her husband being away on business for a few days. It wasn't until she was fully dressed, with a towel around her head, that she realised that she was unable to open the door. Try as she might, the integrated security system resolutely denied her access to the rest of her house, the stainless steel door knob simply turning impotently in her hand.

"Oooh, Adam Laidlaw," she screamed, her rage knowing no bounds, "if I could get my hands on you....." but she knew it was useless; she was trapped, as surely as if she were in a prison cell, and with no one to help her for the window didn't open; it was fitted with an extractor fan. She collapsed onto the loo seat and considered her position; what to do, what on earth could she do? She gazed around her helplessly, at her brand new bath tub, the tiling, the curtains, "What good are you all to me now?" she hurled at them, hysterically. They stared back at her, mute and silent.

She had lost all track of time when she heard the telephone ringing downstairs. It rang and rang for many minutes before finally conceding defeat. "That will be Geoffrey," she thought, "it must be about his time," and for a while her mind was filled with thoughts of her son who, although living only a few miles away, rang her nearly every day, particularly when David, her husband was away. "I wonder if he'll ring again later?" she mused and she brightened her thoughts with the hope that he might even come round if he didn't receive an answer.

It began to get dark and she was reminded of her ever encroaching hunger as her stomach rumbled in protest. It wasn't cold as fortunately she had left the central heating on but she knew that the timer would close the system down around ten thirty that night. She must have dozed, her head falling forward, the low coupled cistern digging uncomfortably into her back, when she was suddenly startled awake by the sound of the telephone ringing again. This time it went on for what seemed an eternity but finally, as before, it eventually gave up.

It was quite dark by now so she rose stiffly to her feet and switched on the light. The bathroom wasn't large but there was sufficient room on the floor for her to lie down so she denuded the airing cupboard of all of the towels and made herself a couch, leaving the largest of the bath towels to cover herself with. She had no idea what time it was but guessed it must be around ten o' clock. The telephone began to ring again. Then it stopped suddenly and just as suddenly, began again. It rang and rang and rang until in the end she felt like screaming, "I'm in here you bloody fool, I'm stuck in here," but she didn't, knowing full well that it must, by now, be Geoffrey. "No one else would let it ring that long," she thought. She wasn't afraid, for she was an extremely resourceful woman, had been all of her life and, apart from starving to death, she knew that there was very little that could happen to her secure as she was in her own little microcosm. "I just wish that someone would come," she moaned, "I'm so bored and hungry." But, as there was very little chance of imminent rescue, she resigned herself to the fact that she would have to stay where she was for at least one night so, laying down on the towels, she slept, albeit fitfully.

It wasn't quite light when once again the silence was shattered by the ringing of the telephone.

"Oh, God," she moaned softly, "tell them to stop. Please just let them know where I am so that they can come and let me out of here." Having nothing else to do she lay back on her improvised couch and waited for daylight proper to make an entrance. She heard the central heating boiler in the kitchen fire up with a dull 'whump', "Isn't it amazing what you can actually hear when the house is quiet," she mused. She lay still for a little while longer until the pressing needs of nature caused her to shift herself. She washed her face and cleaned her teeth and she was just replacing the towels in the airing cupboard with the fervent hope that she wouldn't be needing them again when she heard her son's voice calling from the hallway. He had his own key and had obviously let himself in. "Mum, Mum, are you home?"

"Oh, Geoffrey, darling," she called plaintively, "I'm in here. Please let me out."

"Where the hell's here, Mum?" she heard him call again from halfway up the stairs.

"In the bathroom," she almost screamed, "I'm locked in."

The door swung open and she rushed into his arms like a moonstruck girl, "Oh, darling, darling," she cried delightedly, hugging him to her broad bosom, "I've never been so glad to see anybody, you have no idea."

"Why, what happened?" Geoffrey smiled at her enthusiastic welcome, his eyes twinkling.

"Oh, it's this new lock. It doesn't work properly and...."

"But surely it must, it's brand new," her son responded disbelievingly, "here let me see."

"Oh, no, don't......" his mother, horrorstruck, flung at him. But, too late, he had already swung the door to. "I do not believe this," Jayne shrieked. "You idiot, Geoffrey," she stormed at him. "I've been locked in here for sixteen hours and now you've gone and done it again." And sure enough, the stupid knob simply turned uselessly in his hand, defying him to make it work. But Geoffrey was made of sterner stuff and once he had pacified his hysterical parent he set to to find a way out of the predicament. After all, he had his work to get back to. Seizing the loo brush he told his mother to 'stand back' and in spite of her pleas and entreaties, he smashed the window with the handle, sending a shower of glass and the extractor unit showering into the garden. He cleared the remaining shards from the window frame after which, being young and fit and slim, he escaped groundwards by virtue of the soil stack.

"Sorry about the window, Mum," he apologised as he set his mother free once more, being careful not to let the door close until she was standing safely on the landing.

"Oh, that's the least of my worries, my love," Jayne gushed at him, his earlier faux pas completely erased. "But, as soon as I've had a cup of tea, I know someone who is going to be very worried indeed," she said grimly.

Her thespian activities continued with unabated enthusiasm for a further two years until tragedy entered her otherwise serene existence. David died suddenly; struck down by a sudden and totally unexpected heart attack. His attitude towards life insurance had always been somewhat cavalier and as a result his wife was left with nothing more than a small pension with which to meet her everyday financial needs. True, David had always been fairly successful in his career but he had spent almost everything he had earned, even to the extent of buying himself a new Jaguar about a year before his untimely demise. Apart from the trauma of her sudden bereavement, his widow was extremely perturbed by the precipitate nature of her pecuniary position for, like most of us, she had never believed that such a thing could happen to her. It was quite some time before her forthright nature forced her to shake off the numbness of spirit that had invaded her mind and take stock of her situation. The letter from the bank also helped.

"Well," she sighed, holding the offending missive as though it would burn her, "I've got to raise some money somehow, and quickly."

For the rest of that day she wrestled with the thorny problem of her immediate penury but try as she might no solution reared its head over her dark horizons. Geoffrey rang as usual that evening and, as usual, the topic of conversation was his mother's finances, or lack of them. "The only thing that I can advise, Mum, is to get rid of the car, at any price," he told her dolefully.

"But you've already tried that, darling, and got nowhere."

The second hand car market was pretty flat, to say the least, particularly for large, thirsty saloons.

"Well, I s'pose you could always set fire to it and claim the insurance," her son replied with heavy humour.

"B'lieve me, darling, I'm beginning to get that desperate," was Jayne's parting shot as she hung up the phone.

For the remainder of the evening she watched a TV drama which involved, in part, precisely that which her son had jokingly suggested. "Well, if it's that easy......" she thought, switching off the set and making ready for bed.

All that night she tossed and turned, unable to find sleep, haunted by worry, the theme of the TV play running unbidden though her head until, shortly before dawn, she rose and went into the kitchen to make herself a cup of tea. Sitting at the table, her cup cradled in both hands, the silence and the loneliness threatened to engulf her and, for the first time since the funeral, the tears flowed unheeded down her cheeks.

"Oh, pull yourself together, woman," she scolded herself aloud, fumbling for the handkerchief in her dressing gown and sniffing. She picked up the teapot and freshened her cup before returning to the bedroom.

Sitting on the edge of her bed her eye fell upon the carved walnut deed box which sat atop the Regency chest David had bought for their tenth wedding anniversary and in which he had kept all of his private papers.

She crossed the room and raised the lid. Everything was still there, just as it had always been; the deeds to the house, a bundle of letters tied with ribbon, hers, for she kept every letter that anyone wrote to her, a few documents relating to David's pension, bills that had been paid so long ago she could hardly remember what they had been for, the sad detritus of her life. Idly she leafed through them all, every one of which recalled some memory or other, "Another time, another place," she thought sadly. She picked up a small package of photographs but before she could open them her eye fell upon the long white envelope that had lain hidden beneath them. On it, in David's bold hand was written, 'Car Insurance'.

She slid out the document inside and unfolding it, she laid it on the bed. It was headed with the bank's logo and house style; the very bank who were now pressing her for repayment of the four thousand pounds she owed them. David had insured his Jaguar through his bank.

"That does it," Jayne thought grimly, "they can have their damn' money back but it will be coming out of their own coffers."

She laid her plans carefully, confiding in no one, not even Geoffrey. She knew he would be implacably opposed to her breaking the law anyway; her own conscience wasn't too keen on the idea either but she pressed on with a grim determination that was born out of her desperate need.

Choosing a night that was both moonless and windy, a night when there would be very few of her neighbours out and about, particularly where she was going, she drove the big saloon quietly out of the village and headed south.

The road took her to the top of the fell, where, overlooking the valley below, was a large expanse of scrub. Here she parked the car and retrieved the can of petrol she had earlier secreted in its cavernous boot. She struggled to lift the bonnet as the wind kept buffeting her, causing her hair to fly about wildly but eventually, after much heaving and panting she secured it by its stay.

It continued to rattle above her head as she dived into the engine's innards (the first time in her life she had ever done so) and proceeded to pull off every wire and lead she could find; she felt it would look more convincing if the car appeared to have been deliberately vandalised.

Practically overcome by the enormity of her deed and almost panic stricken at the thought of the fraud she was about to perpetrate she grabbed the can and began to toss petrol everywhere.

Unfortunately, in her panic driven state she had completely forgotten to take into consideration the wind direction. At first she thought that it had begun to rain and it wasn't until the can was half empty, most of which had been blown back on herself, that she realised what she had done.

She very rarely swore but she made an exception this wild night. Running around to the opposite side of the vehicle she quickly emptied the remains of the petrol over the roof and down its broad flanks.

Fumbling in the pocket of her mackintosh she dragged out a box of matches. She struck one, which immediately blew out, she tried again, with the same result. She was about to try a third when she suddenly realised what she was doing. "My God," she thought, horror struck, "I'm covered in petrol. I could go up like a torch." Her hands began to shake and suddenly, completely overcome by panic and the emotion of the moment, her knees gave way under her.

Whilst the wind continued to scream over her head, calmness and sanity, in equal measure, began slowly to return. She pulled herself shakily to her feet by the door handle and surveyed the results of her efforts. "I don't think that I'll be driving you home tonight," she said to herself as she lowered the bonnet. "So, I had better start walking," and following her own advice, she made for the road.

As she trudged along in the wind and the darkness she couldn't help but be wryly amused at the thought her own tragic demise might have had upon the village. "I can just see them all now," she thought, "at the funeral."

'Poor Jayne, couldn't take her husband dying so suddenly like that. But what a terrible way to do away with yourself, setting yourself on fire'.

"Ha, if only they knew," and she actually laughed out loud. She hadn't walked very far when the headlights of a vehicle approaching from behind swept across her path casting her shadow in stark relief at her feet. A large estate car drew alongside and the window wound down.

"Hey, Jayne, lass. Ah thought it was you. Hop in an' Ah'll take y'home." It was Davy.

She smiled gratefully as she climbed in beside him, thankful to be out of the wind.

"What th' hell are y'doin' out on...." he stopped suddenly. "Phwah, y'stink o' petrol. Bin havin' trouble wi' y'motor?"

"You could say that, Davy," she smiled. "I've left it out on the fell."

"Ah, well, never mind," he responded kindly, "we'll get it towed home f'r y'tomorrow. Be th' way," he went on, gazing ahead into the darkness as the big car nosed its way homeward through the night, "Ah had a friend in th' Double Duck' t'night. Told me he's lookin' f'r an assistant an' Ah mentioned your name, thought it would be right up y'r alley."

"Oh," Jayne responded curiously, "who might that be?"

"Peter Benson," Davy grinned. "Y'might have heard o' him, he's director o' th' Civic Theatre in Newcastle."

"Oh, I've certainly heard of him, Davy. That was very kind of you, thank you." She smiled, her heart lightening, "I'll ring him first thing tomorrow."

20
The Wine Merchant

"Yes, yes, that will be fine, Doctor Jamieson. A table for you and your wife for eight tomorrow evening. I Look forward to seeing you then, goodbye."

Davy wrote the booking down in the diary and pulled a long face. He looked up just as Andy entered the room. "Doctor Jamieson's in t'morrer night, Ah'm afraid," he said, emphasising his displeasure by closing the book with a snap.

His son groaned loudly, "Aw hell," he replied, "another joyous evening spent in the company of the good doctor. If he twitters on at me again about French bloody cuisine Ah swear Ah'll, Ah'll..." he stopped short unable to conjure up anything sufficiently horrendous that he could do to the man that would adequately compensate for having to endure his overbearing, pompous and irascible nature.

Doctor Jamieson wasn't one of their favourite customers. He was inclined to find fault with everything, from the way the table was laid to what he considered inadequate parking; which really meant that he very often couldn't get his vehicle near enough to the door and had to walk from the car park.

Davy sighed heavily, sympathising, "Aye, one o' these days Ah might just be tempted to tell 'im what he can do wi' his custom." But they both knew that he wouldn't for, for all of his irascibility, Doctor Jameison put quite a lot of business their way.

As it happened the evening proceeded without any major upset; until wine was mentioned. Now the only wine that graced the cellar of the 'Double Duck' at this time was a mediocre Spanish plonk of indeterminate parentage, euphemistically termed, 'the house red.'

There wasn't a lot of call for a Chablis Grande Cru or a full-bodied, chateau bottled claret as the local populace were more inclined to take beer with their meals. Andy retreated from the restaurant, a look of restrained horror on his face. "Dad, Dad," he hissed urgently as he approached the bar, "he wants a bottle of wine. What do Ah do?"

"Red or white?" his father imperturbably replied.

"Macon Rouge, 1974, chateau bottled." Andy reeled off the request with the air of someone who hadn't a clue what he was talking about.

"Hell's teeth," Davy ground out. "What th' hell does he think this is, the Savoy Grille? Look, Ah'll tell y'what," he had begun to sound as though his back was against the wall, "go upstairs an' get the carafe, y'know, the one Ah got when Ah left Casey's. Stick a bottle o' red in it an' give it 'im. Hopefully he'll never know th' difference." He crossed his fingers tightly as he said it.

The good doctor was of course well acquainted with the subtle nuances between a superior red of good vintage and a carafe of cheap Spanish plonk. He was not amused. However the incident served to highlight the fact that tastes were changing, even in this remote corner of northwest Durham, and the 'Double Duck' had to change with them.

"Ah dunno, Bill," Davy moaned to his friend one evening, "Ah've looked at hundreds o' wine lists this last month an' Ah still can't tell what would sell an' what wouldn't. Ah couldn't tell y'what's a good wine an' what isn't either," he went on, "Ah just really don't know where t'go from here." He looked decisively out of his depth.

"What you need is some expert advice, someone who knaws a bit more than you do."

"Huh, now that wouldn't be hard t'do, now would it," Davy's reply was scornful. "Why, d'you know somebody?"

"Well, not personally," Bill admitted, "but Ah'm sure our Sarah has a friend whose man is in th' wine business. Sh's mentioned him t'me afore. Ah'll see what Ah can find out," he continued, pushing his glass across the bar for a refill.

A few days after this conversation Sarah telephoned Glennis and informed her that she had arranged for a Mr. George Surtees of Dunelm Fine Wines to call. She was sure he would be able to help.

A big Citroen shooting brake drew into the car park of the 'Double Duck' the following afternoon and an equally large individual emerged from its interior. Davy, who was stacking crates in the yard, stopped what he was doing and went to greet his visitor. "Mr. Surtees?" he enquired brightly, extending his hand.

"I'm very pleased to meet you, Mr. Dobson," the stranger boomed heartily, pumping away at Davy's arm. He was a solid, well-dressed man of middle years with broad shoulders and an impressive stomach. He exuded a natural air of good humoured bonhomie. He was so obviously one of life's bon viveurs but one knew instinctively that here was a man of his word, someone one could trust, a man who would not promise what he couldn't deliver. He stood a little under six feet in height and his abundant iron grey hair swept back in waves from a broad forehead giving him an open, honest appearance. He wore steel rimmed spectacles behind which blue eyes gazed out calmly at a world which held no surprises. His face was round, inclined to floridness and looked constantly well-scrubbed. A trim, grey beard ran around his jaw, complemented by a slim moustache which adorned his upper lip.

Davy liked what he saw instantly. "Come on in an' meet th' rest o' my little team," he invited expansively.

It took less than an hour before George had convinced them all that wine was not only good to drink but that it was good for one's health, good for trade and a well planned wine list, which fully complemented their menu, would enhance and improve their reputation as restaurateurs. They were settled comfortably in the empty dining room, an array of bottles before them; a selection from the cellars of Dunelm Fine Wines.

"That's right, Andy," George said encouragingly, "hold the glass by the stem and tilt it towards the candle flame. Now d'you see," he beamed enthusiastically. "Just look at that colour, glorious, isn't it?"

During the short time he had spent with them George's enthusiasm for his subject had begun to rub off, particularly upon Andy, who was becoming very excited about the prospect of starting their own small cellar.

"Well," said Davy, a beatific smile suffusing his face, which was slowly becoming empurpled, "we've certainly tried some good wines George, but Ah still have no idea what would go in this place an' what wouldn't."

"That's no problem, I can assure you," George smiled confidently. "We'll simply have a tasting and find out from your customers just what it is they like, what their particular preferences are."

"A tasting," Andy enquired, raising his glass to his lips again, "what's that?"

"Precisely what you are doing now," replied George. Turning to Glennis he said, "Would you be prepared to provide cheese and biscuits? Preferably one evening when you aren't so busy."

Her blonde head nodded in agreement. "Yes, of course," she said, "that shouldn't be difficult."

"Good," George's enthusiasm revved a little harder, "then I'll provide the wine. Let's say six, no, make that eight producers of red; French, Italian, South African, Californian, Chilean, Argentinian, Portuguese and Bulgarian, how's that?" he ticked the list of countries off on his fingers as he spoke.

"Ah didn't know so many countries produced wine." Davy said in astonishment.

"And you would be surprised just how good some of these wines are," George replied knowledgeably. "The French no longer enjoy the status they once did, not by any means. Now, what about white?" he continued, gazing intently at his host.

Davy merely shrugged and grinned, content to leave the choice to the expert. So George advised a selection of German, French, Yugoslavian, Californian, Chilean and Australian.

"That seems like an awful lot of wine to be trying," Glennis interrupted, a doubtful note in her voice. "What's all this going to cost us?"

The wine merchant spread his palms, the picture of innocence. "Nothing at all, apart from the cheese and biscuits," he said, "and of course," he concluded, "a little effort on your part." Being aware that he hadn't entirely succeeded in convincing her he expounded further. "Look," he said, "If you expand your wine trade, you also expand mine, providing of course that you retain me as your wine merchant, which I hope you will do."

Davy laughed softly and raised his glass, "You keep givin' us service like this George me lad an' there can be no doubt about it."

The evening of the tasting, which George had had widely publicised, proved to be a great success. The 'Double Duck' hadn't been so full on a Monday evening, usually the quietest night of the week, since Grannie Taylor had died and left two hundred pounds in her will for everyone in the village to have drink after her funeral. Even Doctor Jamison seemed happy.

"This is more like it, landlord," he had to raise his voice above the babble of conversation, a third glass of South African red in his hand. "Reminds me of the wine that was served in the mess, y'know, damn' good," and he very nearly smiled at his host.

Against his better judgement Davy yelled back, "The mess, Doctor Jamieson. Were you in the army then?"

"Damn' right I was," the old man said proudly, his red nose almost glowing. "The Fifth Gurkha Regiment, by God. The Fighting Fifth they called us, fought our way right through the Burma campaign...."

"Ah knew Ah shouldn't have done it," Davy thought to himself, quickly changing the subject back to the wine, "So it's to your liking is it, the wine, Ah mean?" he asked, pointing to the doctor's glass.

"Excellent," Doctor Jamieson's white head nodded vigorously, "better than that damn' Spanish plonk you tried to palm off on me a few weeks ago." It was his attempt at wry humour which Davy diplomatically allowed to slide by him. "If you keep some of this in your cellar I'll come for dinner more often."

"Wonderful," Davy thought, raising his eyes heavenwards.

"Tell you what," the doctor went on, "I'll take a couple of bottles home with me tonight, if I can? No, dammit," he quickly changed his mind, "tell your wine merchant chappie to drop a case off for me the next time he calls here, will you? Oh, and a case of that Chilean white too."

Davy nodded at the old man's retreating back as he staggered back to the bar to replenish his glass with the Cape wine he had suddenly become so fond of.

Two days later the big Citroen rolled quietly into the doctor's driveway. It was long and lined on either side with a mixed planting of fir and deciduous trees which extended almost as far as the imposing house, gleaming whitely in the distance.

George drove slowly, his window down, savouring the tranquillity, when suddenly, from away to his right beyond the trees, there was a loud report. He recognised it immediately as the sound of a twelvebore being discharged, particularly as the shot whistled over the roof of his car, dislodging leaves and a shower of small branches and twigs upon the bonnet.

He braked sharply, swearing softly to himself. His foot was still firmly planted on the brake pedal when, to his astonishment, three young men burst out of the undergrowth further up the drive and without pause, dashed past his car at high speed. They were assisted in this by yet another loud bang, closer this time, which again brought a shower of foliage down upon the roof.

"T'hell with this for a game of soldiers," thought George, slamming the car into the appropriate gear and executing a high reverse into the roadway. He quickly caught up with the three runners and stopping the car in front of them, he got out. "What th' hell was all that about?" he asked of the young chap at the head of the procession as he slowed down.

"Dunno mate," that individual panted, droplets of sweat running from the end of his nose. "Ah think th owld bast'd's flipped me sel'."

George wouldn't be put off so easily. "Oh, c'mon, there must have been a reason. That was a twelvebore he was blasting away with. What were you up to, poaching?"

The young man laughed scornfully, "What, at this time o'day? Do me a favour," his sarcasm caused his words to skip in the air, like stones across water. "Look, mate," he went on, his tone slightly milder, "we'd been sent up t'erect a fence on our boss's land, next door t'that big hoose. Th' next thing we knew that crazy auld bast'd's crept up on us from behind the bushes and starts blastin' away at us. Well, Ah for one am not goin' back there, th' bluidy van can stop f'me." There were grunts of assent from the companions at his back. "H'way, lads, we'd better gi' th' boss a ring t'come an' collect us," he finished, leaving George to climb back into his car, a puzzled expression clouding his features.

"I've no idea what it was about, Davy. I couldn't get to the bottom of it and I certainly don't feel inclined to go back up there, not when the old boy is conducting a one man war." George was finishing his second cup of coffee, having just related the tale of his visit to the doctor's.

Davy rose to his feet, "We'll put th' wine in my car an' Ah'll take it up. You wait here, Ah won't be long."

163

Gratefully George agreed, "Righto," he said, "whatever you say. I just hope the old boy's calmed down by now."

Davy was as good as his word and within a very short space of time he returned, a wide grin crinkling his face. "You aren't goin' t'b'lieve this one, George," he chuckled as he entered the bar.

The wine merchant gazed back at him, his expression one of blank innocence.

"Those three fellers," Davy went on, "how were they dressed?"

The question caught George completely at a loss. Like most people who are asked to describe a person or an incident from memory he had difficulty in recalling the details. "Well, I don't know, Davy," he expostulated, "they were workmen, jeans and things, I s'pose."

"An' what else?" Davy persisted.

George looked blank again, casting his eyes around the room helplessly in a bid for inspiration.

"Camouflage gear, perhaps?" prompted his friend, knowingly.

"Yes, now you come to mention it." George agreed, his brain beginning to function a little more freely. "Those green and brown jackets the army uses....."

"Precisely," Davy crowed triumphantly, cutting his friend short.

"I'm sorry, Davy," George was beginning to lose patience, "I just don't follow."

His exasperation was in no way mollified as Davy threw his head back and laughed aloud. Finally controlling himself, he explained. "Th' silly old beggar thought that he was bein' invaded be terrorists, the IRA perhaps. He couldn't believe that y'can buy camouflage gear from any sports outfitters these days. Took him back to his army days, 'the Fightin' Fifth,' y'know," he finished, giving a fair imitation of the doctor's Colonel Blimp mode of speech. "Anyway, he thanks y'kindly for th' wine an' has sent this cheque for you." Davy waved the scrap of paper under George's nose.

"Well, that's something, at least," he responded, slightly placated at the sight of money. "The silly old goat must be losing his marbles."

As time went on the two of them became firm friends and George became a frequent visitor to the hostelry, both on business and pleasure. It was while they were discussing the latest wine order one day that Davy became aware that George lacked the usual good humour that had become his stock in trade. "What's up, George?" he asked kindly, concerned at his friend's downcast appearance. "You aren't your usual happy self t'day."

The wine merchant smiled quickly, making an obvious effort to dispel the dark cloud that hung around him. "Oh, nothing much," he said, with a dismissive shrug of his shoulders, "just cash flow problems. I just can't seem to get the money in like I used to do. Times are becoming harder it appears."

Davy's nod was sympathetic, "Aye, we're all goin' t'have t'tighten our belts shortly be th' look o' things," he agreed wisely. "So who's owin' ?" he asked, on the basis that a trouble shared is a trouble halved.

"Oh, it's not so much the amount," replied George, "as the time people are taking to pay me now. The worst customer in that respect is Mario, not that I should be telling you exactly but I know it won't go any further."

"Y'mean Mario's Restaurant, the Italian place....."

"The very same," George sighed. Having taken Davy into his confidence thus far he proceeded to pull a sheaf of invoices from his briefcase. "Here, look at this lot," he thrust the small pile of paper across the table. "They go back almost nine months and even though I've threatened court action there's still no sign of any money."

Davy looked at the covering statement. The sum owing wasn't large, it came to precisely two hundred and sixty seven pounds, forty eight pence, excluding VAT. "Any more like this?" he enquired, returning the paperwork.

"Aye, a few," George replied glumly, his chin on his hand, "but I'm gradually working my way through them. He's by far the worst."

"Well, y'll just have t'stop his tap until he coughs up," was the only advice that his friend could think to offer.

"Oh, I have, two months since," George stuffed the papers back into his bag, "but short of going round there and breaking his legs, I just don't know what else I can do."

After the wine merchant had left Davy discovered the covering statement lying on the floor beneath the table where it had fallen. He put it to one side intending to return it on George's next visit.

It transpired that a few days later Davy had occasion to telephone his wine merchant to place an emergency order. During the course of conversation he suggested that they should have dinner together.

"Well, that seems a capital idea to me, Davy. I'd be delighted," and he sounded it. "Just the two of us?"

"No," Davy replied, "I thought Bill Stobbart an' Gerry Dixon might like t'come along as well."

As George knew both proposed guests well by now he agreed without hesitation.

"Good. We'll make it Monday night then. I'll order us a taxi from here an' if your missus doesn't mind y'can stop the night wi' us."

George replaced the receiver feeling his natural bonhomie beginning to return.

"Enjoy yourself, love," Glennis addressed her husband as she straightened his tie and generally fussed over his appearance. "And mind, don't come home too much the worse for wear, any of you," she remonstrated, wagging a warning finger in the direction of the other three would-be carousers standing in her hall.

"No, mum, honest," Gerry Dixon grinned at her, crossing his heart.

George, who had made no enquiries on their journey in the cab as to the venue was slightly startled when they were deposited outside of Mario's Restaurant. He was even more surprised, given the parlous state of their relationship, to be greeted by Mario himself who, dinner jacketed and smelling strongly of Italian cologne, conducted them with his usual Latin effusiveness, through to the bar.

Pre-dinner cocktails were ordered, several of which were readily consumed before they were ushered into a slightly overdone dining room decorated with gold filigree and heavy brocade.

They all very quickly reached that stage of supreme carelessness where presentation, aroma, and taste is everything and cost is totally irrelevant. Bill and George shared a Chateaubriand that reached the epitome of culinary art, the pastry of which didn't so much melt in their mouths as dissipate in a sybaritic frisson, whilst Davy glowed enthusiastically at the first sumptuous mouthful of his Lobster Thermidor. Gerry's Tournedos Rossini was the chef's speciality and as such had been created with all of the tender loving care that only an Italian can bring to such a dish. The blend of pate and succulent prime beef created an almost orgiastic experience upon his palate.

George, naturally, was given the task of choosing the wine, which he did so with consummate care, keeping the waiter hovering whilst he slowly turned the pages of the extensive wine list. He finally recommended a wonderfully complimentary Cote de Beaune, 1986 Premiere Cuvee to Bill and Gerry and for Davy and his lobster he suggested a light, dry, crisp Chablis, Grand Cru of course. With dessert, fresh flambed peaches in brandy and cream prepared at their table, they opened a bottle of vintage Pol Roger and finally conceded defeat over Rochefort, Camembert, a prime Mozzarella and an English Blue Stilton helped on their way by several glasses of a Taylors '84 late bottled port. It was becoming extremely late when coffee was eventually served and by the time they had reached the bottom of the pot, complemented by several large Armagnacs, everyone else had left.

Davy caught the restaurateur's eye. He had been hovering for some minutes, waiting for just this moment. "Mario, the bill, if you please."

"I 'ope you 'ave enjoyed your meal, gentlemen," The little Italian crooned softly, laying the cover in front of Davy.

"Absolutely superb," they all chorused cheerfully. Davy picked up the small leather case and opened it. He studied the bill carefully for some moments, made a rapid calculation and then placed a ten pound note and a folded slip of paper inside before closing it and handing it back, with a smile, to their host. "That should cover everything, Ah think," he beamed at the Italian.

The restaurateur, his expression one of extreme suspicion, looked from one to the other before slowly opening the leather binder. He looked at the ten pound note nestling there innocently and then, his voice quiet, calm and with no hint of the alarm that was beginning to churn in the deepest recesses of his bowel, he said, "What ees thees, Mistair Dobson, a joke, I think, yes?"

Davy's three companions were by this time looking equally puzzled and embarrassed. "What th' hell's goin' on, Davy?" Bill hissed at him. "Let's just pay th' bloody bill an' get out o' here."

The grey eyes that gazed back at him merely twinkled, exuding confidence. "Look Mario," Davy turned to their host, who was by now beginning to feel the strain a little, "we owe you," he casually studied the bill again, "two hundred and seventy four pounds and sixteen pence, excluding tip....."

"Yes, indeed," the Italian interjected, beginning to get excited, "that ees what ees on th' bill. You 'ave th' best of ev'rything, th' best in th' 'ouse, th' best wines, th' best food, th' best champagne......"

Before he could get his Latin temperament into full swing it was Davy's turn to interrupt. "An' you'll see from that statement there," and for the first time during their conversation he indicated the folded slip of paper he had placed under the ten pound note, "that you owe my friend George here two hundred and sixty seven pounds, forty seven pence, excluding VAT an' what's more, y've owed it for more than nine months." George opened his mouth to protest but Davy silenced him by raising his hand, "So," he continued mildly, "that tenner should nicely cover th' balance 'cos Ah'm sure George'll write off the VAT as a favour to a valued customer. Reet," he went on rising to his feet, "Ah see our taxi's waitin' so we won't keep you any longer. Thanks again f'r a lovely meal. We'll definitely call again."

They trooped outside without further comment leaving Mario staring after them, too dumbfounded to utter a word.

They were still laughing when their taxi dropped them outside of the 'Double Duck'.

21
Christmas Cheer

It could never be said of Davy Dobson that he suffered from that butt of all stand-up comedians, the mother-in-law; far from it. He was devoted to Glennis's mother, just as long as she stayed in York and he continued to reside at the 'Double Duck'. So it was he heard the news with a certain resignation in his heart that the old lady had announced her intention to stay with them during the Christmas holiday.

"It will be lovely to have her for a few days," Glennis reiterated for the umpteenth time although her husband couldn't help but wonder who it was she was trying to convince. She was standing on the bar pinning coloured fairy lights to the oak beams overhead.

"Yes, of course, my love, whatever you say," Davy replied, casting a look at his son which was reminiscent of a Christian about to be thrown to the lions. He hadn't forgotten the last time she stayed with them and the mayhem it had caused then. She had persuaded him to take her shopping in the nearby village of East Langley. Convincing him, much against his better judgement, that, 'she could manage quite well by herself,' she had left him in the car and had gone off to do what she had to do.

It wasn't until about an hour later that Davy missed her, having snatched the opportunity to 'rest his eyes' for a moment. He searched the village from top to bottom becoming gradually more and more panic-stricken as he asked everyone he met if they had seen her. It was Elsie, Big Jack Lawson's wife who provided a clue; she had seen her boarding the Durham bus. Three hours later she returned, by which time the hue and cry was practically county-wide, having completely forgotten who she was with in the first place.

"Now, now," she remonstrated mildly with her daughter and son-in-law on her return, being completely oblivious of the consternation she had caused, "there's no need to make a fuss over a little old body like me, I can take care of myself."

As it hadn't done Davy's standing in his wife's eyes any good at all, having had to return home and admit that he had lost her mother, however temporarily, he had great difficulty in restraining a violent urge to do her physical harm.

She was a tiny, bird-like woman of some eighty years, with twinkling blue eyes and a personality that everyone immediately warmed to. Unfortunately, as the years passed, she grew increasingly absent-minded, as the elderly are apt to do. As a consequence she could leave a trail of devastation behind her and be completely unaware of the havoc that she so unwittingly caused. However, she was incapable of any unkindness, in either thought or deed. It was this compensatory trait that successfully precluded any ideas of retribution that may have lurked in the dark recesses of her son-in-law's mind. He viewed her temporary lapses with a passive humour born of long practice.

The clock on the mantleshelf chimed four as Glennis, looking up from her task at the dining table, said, "Would you put the kettle on, Mother, please? I'm sure we could both do with a cup of tea."

After what seemed rather a long time the old lady returned from the kitchen looking slightly flustered. "Oh, Glennis," she exclaimed, somewhat exasperated, "I can't seem to light that new cooker of yours. I really don't know how it works."

"I'm sorry, Mother," replied her daughter apologetically, "I should have thought. C'mon, I'll show you," and she led the way back into the kitchen where she explained the vagaries of modern gas appliances whilst her mother looked on.

"That's all there is to it," she said. "You simply select the hob you want, push the knob and turn until it lights up."

"H'mph," the old lady's doubt would not be denied, "I still don't think it's as easy as my old cooker at home. You just have to switch that on."

"Yes, I know, Mother," Glennis sighed patiently, "but that's an electric cooker. This is gas."

"Well, whatever," her mother waved a dismissive hand, obviously determined to remain unimpressed, "let's have that cup of tea, shall we?"

As the festive season began to gather its customary momentum the 'Double Duck' began to get busier and busier until Davy and

Andy couldn't be guaranteed to be able to slide their exhausted bodies beneath their covers much before two o' clock each morning. Then they would sleep like corpses until the dray arrived, usually around eight thirty when it would all start again.

It seemed to Andy that his head had barely touched the pillow when he was dragged awake by the weirdest kind of high pitched shrieking, as though someone were torturing a cat.

"What th' bloody hell's that?" he groaned, refusing to allow his weary brain to comprehend anything other than a swift and immediate return to blessed unconsciousness. But the sound proved stronger than his will, even with the pillow dragged over his head, as it knifed through his effete senses with barbarous ferocity. Gradually he succumbed and relinquishing all thoughts of remaining in bed, he staggered to the door.

Stepping into the hallway, eyes still half closed, he became aware that the sound appeared to be emanating from the kitchen. More curious than alarmed he turned the handle. Immediately, he was engulfed in a suffocating, billowing cloud of thick, heavy smoke. The sound that had awakened him, he now realised, was the smoke alarm.

Quickly slamming the door shut behind him he raced along the corridor to his parents' room. Too panic stricken for ceremony he shook Davy roughly by the shoulder. "Dad, Dad," he shouted, "gerrup quick, th' bloody place's on fire."

At the word FIRE his father was suddenly fully conscious and groping for his glasses. He followed Andy back along the corridor to the kitchen, the moaning of the smoke alarm lending a sense of urgency, if he needed it. Diving into the airing cupboard Andy grabbed a towel and before his father could prevent him, he wrapped it around his mouth and plunged into the kitchen, slamming the door behind him. A few moments later he was back with his father, who had had enough sense not to open the door, eyes streaming and coughing mightily. He leant weakly against the wall trying to force air into his straining lungs. When he had finally gained some of his composure, he croaked, "Someone had lit the gas but left the cover on the cooker."

The new cooker was fitted with a laminated wooden cover that was placed over the hobs when not in use; the manufacturers evidently thought that as a feature it was aesthetically acceptable.

"It hadn't quite caught, thank God," Andy wheezed, still mopping at his watering eyes, "but it was smouldering badly. I've opened the main window and thrown it into the yard."

As he finished his explanation a voice behind them chirruped brightly, "Anyone like a cup of tea? I've put the kettle on. I couldn't sleep either."

They both half turned as Glennis's mother, adorned in nightie, scarlet dressing gown and curlers stepped between them. Davy, who had barely opened his mouth during the whole episode began, chameleon-like, to turn a delicate shade of puce. His jaw clenched and he looked like he was about to burst.

Andy, whose breathing was almost normal again, placed a restraining hand upon his father's arm and shook his head resignedly, "Don't," was all he said.

The Christmas party had traditionally been held on Christmas Eve and as that date drew ever closer the scale of activity reached new heights of frantic urgency as they all struggled to ensure that everything would be ready on time. Davy had just finished bringing in the last of the prizes for the grand draw and sitting in his favourite armchair, a cup of tea at his elbow, he watched as Glennis and her mother stuck the appropriate number to each prize. They had held a party each year for the village and this year, by popular request, it was to be fancy dress.

"I wonder what I should go as?" Glennis's mother asked of her daughter.

Davy, who had picked up his paper, muttered from behind it, "Bloody Guy Fawkes."

"What was that dear?" his mother-in-law asked innocently.

"The talks, the talks, goin' well," replied Davy hastily, indicating an article he was reading.

Glennis stood in the middle of the restaurant and gazed around her happily. "It looks really lovely," she said to herself. And indeed it did. Overhead the beams were festoooned with gaily coloured streamers, tinsel and fairy lights. The Christmas tree, its aromatic boughs weighed down beneath a multitude of blue, red, gold and silver baubles, stood tall in one corner, its topmost branches almost brushing the ceiling. The tables, which had been placed around the walls and covered with crisp, white linen, were laden with platters of cold meats, sandwiches, salads, pies, both sweet and savoury, cakes and trifles.

Standing there alone, surrounded by the evidence of what was for them so much hard work, she reflected upon the people of the village for whom it had been created. She remembered especially those, like Sam Kilpatrick, who were no longer part of village life but who had so enriched all of their lives. Her thoughts encompassed the year and the many funny, and sometimes sad, incidents that had marked the passage of the days. Her reverie was suddenly interrupted by her husband who, unnoticed by her, had entered the room behind her.

"Well, lass," he grinned, eyes twinkling behind his glasses, as he gazed around him "y've done us proud again, eh?"

"Oh, not just me, Davy," she returned his smile fondly. "I just hope they all appreciate it."

"Oh. O'course they will, y'know that. Now, c'mon," he took her arm, "let's get dressed or we'll be last at our own party."

By the stroke of nine the pub was at bursting point with almost everyone present dressed in a costume of one sort or another. Big Jack Lawson and his diminutive wife had been the first to arrive, shortly after seven. He was dressed in an enormous pair of pyjamas that made even his bulk appear small. Upon his head he wore an equally large chamber pot. Davy, without a word, spread his hands, the gesture eloquent. His guest, grinning broadly, turned round. There, pinned to his back, was a scrawled notice which read, 'King of Poland'.

"That's a bit subtle for you, in't it?" laughed Davy. "Ah doubt Miss Jennin's'll see th' funny side."

Jack merely shrugged his shoulders, "Who gie's a toss," he growled, "it's Chris'mas," and he made his way to the bar, his wife, dressed as Minnie Mouse, following obediently in his wake, like a tugboat fussing after an ocean liner.

"Ladies and Gentlemen," Davy raised his voice above the babble of laughter and light hearted conversation, "can Ah have your attention please?"

It was time to begin the grand draw. There were some fifty prizes, which had been purchased through the sale of tickets over the previous two months, all magnificently displayed on a groaning table near the fireplace. The main prize, two hundred pounds in cash, was always drawn last so it was a foregone conclusion that no one's attention was going to lag.

Glennis, dressed as Boadicea, her ample bosom struggling to break free from a leather sleeveless jerkin borrowed from her son, drew the first ticket. There were howls of laughter as Tom Dandridge was called to receive a beautifully gift wrapped box of toiletries. As he had come dressed as Wurzel Gummidge, in an old smock and battered hat with straw sticking out of it, the incongruity of the prize was not lost on him. He graciously presented it to Sarah Stobbard.

Georgina Reynolds, the other half of Hinge and Bracket, resplendent in a late Victorian evening gown that had once belonged to her mother, was the next prize winner and with consummate grace rose to receive a large bottle of gin, donated by George Surtees.

"That will help replenish the bar," her partner was heard to remark on her return.

And so the prize giving continued until the table was completely bare. Then Davy, dipping his hand into the ice bucket that did service as the receptacle for the tickets, produced with a flourish the winning number for the evening's main prize, two hundred pounds in cash.

Sarah Stobbard leapt from her seat as if stung, "It's us, it's us," she cried excitedly, jumping up and down, her eyes sparkling. Beside her the tall, willowy blonde that had accompanied her that evening uncoiled sinuously from behind the table where she had been sitting.

She was outstanding in as much as she wasn't in fancy dress, adorned as she was in a figure hugging, shear evening gown slashed to the thigh, of which many got more than a glimpse as she glided, as smooth as oil on water, through the crowd to where Davy, his mouth half open, stood at the end of the bar.

As the vision drew near he was aware of an expensive French perfume that lingered in the air around her and her full red lips, shining wetly under the lights, pouted invitingly. As he placed the envelope in her gloved hand she leant forward, as though to kiss his cheek. Instead he was startled to hear a deep male voice growl softly in his ear, "Me an' th' lads had a book goin' on how long it would take you to twig on. An' Ah've just won that an' all." It was Bill, his moustache shaved, his make up carefully applied by his wife.

"You, you....." Davy stuttered, his mouth opening and closing as he watched Bill glide back to his seat, the cash stowed safely in the warm recesses of a generous cleavage. There was a sudden roar of laughter, mainly from the cricket team, as he winked lasciviously, his tongue caressing his red lips, at his friend.

As the laughter subsided he called, "It'll cost y' more than two hundred quid for a night wi' me, Davy Dobson, so y'd better take this an' put it behind the bar," and to a roar of approval he tossed the envelope back in his host's direction.

Midnight came and with it Christmas day. Those that desired left for their various churches to celebrate midnight mass leaving behind a large number who were intent on celebrating Christmas in a more secular manner. Helped along by Bill's generosity the atmosphere was becoming ever more high spirited, the drink flowing freely. In one corner of the bar sat Big Jack Lawson, Tom Dandridge, Joe Fletcher, (minus spouse), Bob Dixon, Billy Freeman and Bill, along with their various wives.

"Go on, man," urged Big Jack as Gerry Dixon, swaying slightly, stood in their midst, his eyes gleaming, "show th' lasses, they won't mind, it's Christmas."

Finally convinced, Gerry reached into the pocket of his costume and produced a small packet. "Now, ladies," he grinned mischievously, tearing open the paper envelope and revealing its contents which he held in his open palm, "you all know what this is." It was a condom, which he proceeded to warm in his hand. The women giggled dutifully. "But what y'won't know," he went on, rather in the manner of a conjuror about to perform a trick that would defy all logic, "is what can be done wi' one o' these properly handled."

"Oh, I think we all have a fair idea," Sarah chimed in.

Gerry shook his head, "Knaw, y'haven't, not really," he said. "Watch this."

And as they watched he began to work the base ring of the contraceptive over his head, carefully stretching it with his fingers. Gradually, as they all stared in amazement, by cautious manipulation of the thin latex he enlarged it until he was able to work it down over his face. By now the women were shrieking with laughter and the more Gerry worked the rubber, pulling it lower and lower until his face assumed the squashed, distorted features of a bank robber in a stocking mask, the more they became convulsed.

But this was not all; he pulled the restraining rubber down as far as his mouth where he suddenly stopped. Taking a deep breath, by the simple expedient of raising the base ring from his chin, he blew as hard as he could. Immediately the rubber, stretched as thinly as it was, began to inflate. The harder Gerry blew the larger became the condom and the more the women laughed until shrieks of unbridled merriment cut through the overriding clamour coming from the rest of the pub.

What was even funnier than Gerry's inflatable condom, and completely unbeknownst to him, was Glennis. She stood behind him, not a flicker of amusement on her face, arms akimbo, contrasting darkly, it seemed, with his light hearted entertainment.

Everyone by now was laughing so hard at what appeared to be Gerry's inevitable doom, of which he was totally unaware, that they were practically hysterical.

Suddenly the realisation dawned that his small audience wasn't exactly with him any longer and he whipped round, coming face to face with retribution; retribution in the shape of Boadicea in a leather jerkin. So startled was he that he took an immediate and deep breath, which of course caused the sudden and dramatic deflation of the latex, which collapsed upon his face.

Being, as he was, totally unprepared for this event, unable to see, his eyelids being forced shut, and suffering from severe shock he struggled for a brief moment to peel the rubbery restriction from his face. No one else was in any fit state to help him, having by this time given themselves up to absolute hysteria. He was in grave danger of suffocating before he finally was able to free himself.

"Bloody hell, Glennis," he croaked, his face bright red and his hair on end as he staggered across to the bar to lean on for support, "Ah very nearly suffocated under that thing."

His hostess allowed herself a thin smile, "Serves you right, Gerry Dixon," she said, "I haven't forgotten the last time you tried to take advantage of a defenceless Yorkshirewoman."

It had gone three o' clock when the last of the revellers finally left the 'Double Duck'.

Davy stood on his doorstep, breathing in deep draughts of cold air, and gazed out across the village green, which was a frosted, spangled carpet palely reflecting the soft luminescence from a myriad flickering stars. As he closed the door he smiled quietly to himself as the faint, last calls of 'Merry Christmas' echoed around the village.